ASTROLOGY POND

ASTROLOGY POND

REBECCA ROSSI

This is a work of fiction. All of the characters, names, incidents, organizations and dialogue in this novel are either the products of the author's imagination or are used fictitiously.

Inner Light Publishing books may be ordered through booksellers or by contacting:

Inner Light Publishing
www.innerlightpublish.com
innerlightpublishing@gmail.com

Because of the dynamic nature of the Internet, any web addresses or links contained in this book may have changed since publication and may no longer be valid. The views expressed in this work are solely those of the author and do not necessarily reflect the views of the publisher and the publisher hereby disclaims any responsibility for them.

The author of this book does not dispense medical advice or prescribe the use of any technique as a form of treatment for physical, emotional, or medical problems without the advice of a physician, either directly or indirectly. The intent of the author is only to offer information of a general nature. In the event you use any of the information in this book for yourself, which is your constitutional right, the author and the publisher assume no responsibility for your actions.

ISBN: 978-0-9923940-0-4 (sc)
ISBN: 978-0-9923940-5-9 (e)

Printed in Australia

'Omnia scriptum est in stellis'
'Everything is written in the stars'

DEDICATION

To my two guardian angels, Nonno Oli and Angel

Aunt Eve, may you rest in peace and feel my love through

my writing. I dedicate this book to you both.

ACKNOWLEDGEMENTS

I wish to thank, first off, the three most important and influential females in my life – The Rossi Women. Without their love, support and guidance on a daily basis, I wouldn't have had the drive and energy to finish something I started when I was 17. I love you three for helping me through the darkest and lightest moments of my life and sharing in my success…which is indeed your success.

I would like to acknowledge my amazing support network that is my immediate and extended family, my loving other half, my closest friends, the Inkspotters Group and colleagues that pushed me to keep writing even when I encountered the 'voice of doom' as my late mentor Eve would call it.

A special mention to my ultimate best friend Christine (Graham) who is the only person to have a character dedicated to her in my story. I want to thank you for loving me and staying by my side since I was an awkward eleven-year-old. Without you I would have no way of being able to express the importance of friendship in this story. I'll never forget hiking in Lederderg Gorge for hours bouncing this book's ideas off one another.

I wrote this book because I've been an avid reader and writer since I was physically and mentally able and my dream was to give back to the literary world. I hope I inspire and intrigue whoever picks up a copy and that their dreams begin with the turning of a page, as mine did.

Lastly, my immense gratitude to Inner Light Publishing for making my dreams come true and for sharing the same love of spirituality and the mystical. I cannot thank you enough.

PREFACE

Dear Readers,

The idea for Astrology Pond originated when I was 17 years old and discovered my love of the zodiac. I realised that each of the twelve signs were unique and special in their own way but mixing them all together was bound to cause conflict and tension. My novel introduces an almost 'Big Brother', social experiment concept of putting twelve very different teenagers together and watching them struggle to get along and understand one another.

Set in a fictional town in New South Wales, Danni Hamilton and her two best friends Reilly and Drew form an astrological group that works together to develop personally and discover the secrets behind the stars. In a teenage world filled with hormones and hearts racing, Danni and her friends soon realise that their goal to unite the group is going to be a lot more difficult than expected. Betrayal, lust and tension builds as each member of the group reveals their tragic pasts and secrets. Who is the mysterious figure cloaked in black? What do Danni's vivid dreams mean and who are her true friends and enemies? With conflicting decisions and rifts forming in the group, Danni is forced to be a leader and keep the friendships she has formed closely together before they slip through her fingers.

I've written this story for teenagers who are having trouble finding themselves and feeling like they don't belong. This book encourages young girls and boys to embrace their individuality and the power that stems from their sign. My hope is that they can relate to the character that is matched to their sign and get excited about the personality traits they are able to identify with.

If you ever feel sad, lost or insecure, look up at the stars and know that you are not alone. The answers are written there, you just have to look hard enough…

Rebecca Rossi

CONTENTS

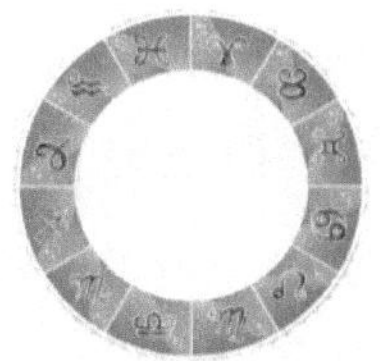

Chapter 1
ONE TROUBLED GIRL

It was midnight and one mysterious looking character stepped out of the darkness and wandered through Bouquet Reserve, the deserted park. Following the shadowed person came eleven other people all whispering incoherent things. The Reserve was filled with swirling leaves and an icy chill, so the person leading the group drew its coat around itself tighter. The leader finally came to sit at the edge of a neon glowing pond and the eleven other members sat down around the figure. They stared at their guide in admiration.

The leader stood suddenly and whispered: 'The stars are calling you.' In an instant the figures were gone and the pond continued to glow eerily.

***

Danni Hamilton sat on her bed and studied her blanket. She traced her finger over the outline of the symbol of the Roman numeral for two, also known as the star sign of Gemini. There were all the other eleven signs on her blanket but Gemini, her star sign, intrigued her the most. Danni lay conscious most nights pondering the twelve symbols in the stars. What were they? Was there a mystery behind them? Did they mean more than just 'you will have good luck in your garden if you're a Leo?' To say she knew them inside out was an understatement. To propose she was interested in them was just insulting. She had an obsession and an overwhelming one at that!

She was a scrawny seventeen year old with a pale but pretty face, shoulder length brown hair and blue eyes, who felt there was more to life than what she was living. And to say she had problems sleeping was just laughable.

Around her tiny room her obsession was plastered. Incense, candles, Ouija boards, stones, statues and hundreds and hundreds of posters with the Wheel of the Zodiac were scattered everywhere. Try as they might, Danni's parents could not get her out of her mystical world. She would drive her family insane by excusing their actions as just part of their sign's characteristics. When they were younger, she and her little brother Colin would race up the stairs for fun. Now she just laughed, ruffled his hair and said 'typical competitive Aries.' She no longer wanted to play and that made him sad.

Apart from that she was a perfectly normal seventeen year old girl who lived in Juggler's Corner which was a small town near Bondi and attended J-Corner High. Her two best friends Reilly and Drew had accepted her "ways" long ago and were actually really interested in the zodiac too. Everything seemed balanced in Danni's world but she couldn't shake off that recurring feeling that very soon her life was about to get really exciting!

Her dreams had made Danni incredibly drawn and tired, so she lay on her favourite blanket for an afternoon nap when there was a loud knock on her door. Still stuck in a daze, she trudged over and opened it, revealing Reilly looking at Danni with her usual expression.

'Oh my God Dan! Are you seriously thinking about them again?'

Reilly barged past Danni and sat on her bed, crossing her legs. Her bossy but honest Sagittarian nature was what Danni loved most about her.

'You know lately I have thought about them more than ever,' Danni said, looking around her room.

'Dan, seriously, maybe you should get a new obsession. Like I don't know Miley Cyrus or something?'

Danni raised her eyebrows at Reilly.

'Well it is better than things that probably don't exist,' Reilly added.

Danni stared at her best friend with an angry expression.

'You know how I feel about this, they're real or else why would they be around?'

Reilly got to her feet and walked over to Danni, putting her hands firmly on her shoulders.

'Danni, I am not saying they're fake, I am just

saying no one can prove these things and I really don't want my best friend losing sleep over something like this.'

Danni softened and hugged Reilly tightly.

'I'm sorry, it's just that lately I have been having more and more of those dreams, like I should be getting out there and figuring out the mystery behind these star signs.'

'Fair enough, well I was wondering if you wanted to come to the Funky Fries with me for a snack?'

'Yeah ok, why not?'

Danni grabbed her black coat and walked down the stairs to the front door with Reilly close behind.

Danni's parents were both at work and Colin was staying with a friend from school. Her mother was a pharmacist and her father worked at the bank next door. They always waited for the other to finish work and drive home together. The rest of her relatives lived in Cairns and only visited on odd occasions like birthdays and promotions. She liked it that way; Danni wasn't exactly the social type and her movie nights with Reilly and Drew was her version of 'going out.'

Danni and Reilly walked and talked all the way to the Funky Fries which was their favourite place to hang out and gossip about normal teenage life, boys, clothes and school. They sat down in a bright yellow booth and talked more about cute guys. As fun as it was, Danni just wanted to spend her time thinking about her premonitions and what they meant for her future. What step was she supposed to take next? Was she the leader in her dreams or just one of the shadowy followers?

'It's just really weird you know?' Reilly flicked her glossy, black locks.

'What is?' Danni asked, trying to move out of her head for a second.

Reilly sighed and got out of the booth.

'Okay, let's go! You are clearly tired and consumed with all things astrological...as usual...'

Danni rose out of her seat and walked briskly out of the diner with Reilly struggling to keep up close behind.

'Danni, you know I didn't mean that?'

Danni stopped in the middle of the path and turned to look at Reilly.

'Yeah, I know...look I really just need to go home and get some sleep. My head is aching and I'm obviously being a crappy friend right now.'

'I understand Dan and I hope you sort out whatever is going through your mind.'

Danni gave Reilly a quick hug to indicate everything was cool between them and walked home alone.

She didn't notice the cloaked figure watching from the distance and rubbing his hands with glee...

***

That night, as Danni slept in her bedroom

surrounded by her astrological objects, she dreamt her recurring dream. There she was, or who she believed was her, walking through Bouquet Reserve with her brown hair flowing over a long black coat and as she peered over her shoulder she noticed the same eleven shadows trailing behind her, whispering to each other. The cold wind encircled her as she led this mysterious group to the pond illuminated by green light and when they reached it, they sat around it in a circle. The neon light that lit up the pond also brightened up the faces of two figures sitting beside Danni and she seized the first opportunity to get a closer look at them. Their faces were bent close together, deep in conversation, but they seemed to sense Danni's eyes peering at them and looked up, revealing themselves. Danni stared back into the faces of Reilly and Drew, her two best friends. They grinned and winked at her, pointing in the opposite direction. Before she could say anything a boy from across the pond let the pool show his face to her. He was gorgeous with brown curly hair and hazel eyes. He winked at her and stretched his hand across the pond to grasp hers. She was startled but let her fingers unfurl from her pocket and leant over the water. Just as they were about to connect he looked at her and said, 'Dreaming again, Dan?' She withdrew her hand and stared at him with a puzzled expression.

'What did you just say?'

He glared at her and screamed from across the

water, *'wake up*!'

All of a sudden reality came racing back and Colin was shaking her while she lay sprawled in her bed.

'Colin! I am getting up! Can you go away now?' Danni yelled at her eight year old brother.

His blue eyes sparkled mischievously.

'Danni, you're talking in your sleep again, you're crazy.'

According to Colin and her parents, whenever Danni dreamt that dream she would either yell loudly in her sleep or thrash about until she wound up on the floor. Danni didn't really realise the extent of it until one day she noticed a bruise on her leg from falling off and hitting the edge of the bed. Danni leapt out of bed and chased him all the way downstairs into the kitchen were her parents were sleepily drinking coffee.

'Morning Danni, early mornings exercise?' laughed her father.

Danni threw him a withering look and opened the cupboard to get some cereal.

'Daddy, Danni was talking in her sleep again,' Colin whined.

'Shut up you little creep!' Danni snarled.

'Danni! Don't talk to your brother that way,' warned her mother.

'Sorry mum, but Colin isn't leaving me alone, just because I have trouble sleeping.'

Danni's parents exchanged concerned glances.

'Honey, can you please sit down, we need to talk,' Danni's mother said.

Danni looked at both of them strangely but sat down across from them at the dining table. Her father leaned over, patted his daughter's hand and cleared his throat.

'Danni, I know you won't like this but Colin is right. You are talking in your sleep nearly every night and quite loudly too. We weren't going to say anything because we thought it might stop but it keeps happening and your mother and I think you should see the local psychologist, Doctor Yates.'

Danni looked from her father to her mother with her mouth hanging open.

'You think I need to see a psych?'

Her mother shifted uncomfortably in her seat.

'Honey, it's obvious something is on your mind; I mean remember the bruise from falling off the bed? We think it's for the best that you get professional help to sort out what it is that makes you talk in your sleep.'

Danni sat and thought about her mother's words. Her family and friends could see that she was disturbed by these dreams and maybe seeing someone experienced might help her figure it all out.

'Ok then, I will see Doctor Yates but only for a bit; I am not permanently insane.'

Her parents grinned and rose out of their seats to hug her.

'Thank you sweetie,' Mrs Hamilton said. 'We will make an appointment tonight. Now get ready for school.'

Danni ran upstairs so as not to be late. Then, when she was ready, she sprinted out the door into the cold and frosty morning, ready for another day.

Chapter 2
BOUQUET RESERVE

As Danni walked through the crisp autumn morning to J-Corner High with Drew and Reilly, she described their presence in her dream and how that had to mean something. She also told them of the gorgeous boy who tried to hold her hand and kept darting her eyes around the streets looking for him.

Drew tilted his head.

'Yo Danni, do you honestly believe that you're going to find a boy you dreamt of?'

Drew was a dark skinned, soulful boy who was very funny at times but mainly kept to himself playing his guitar and writing songs about the love yet to come to him. Danni had been best friends with Reilly and Drew since they were five years old. They had all met at pre-school and fought over the building blocks only to crack up laughing a minute later. Ever since then a firm friendship developed. They knew it was fate because they were all born on the 12th, just different months. Despite their beliefs in destiny, they both found it extremely difficult to indulge in Danni's 'hobby' and that made

Danni's willingness to share all her knowledge quite limited.

'No I don't honestly believe he exists but part of me wants to prove to my parents I'm not insane,' Danni answered.

She was willing to see Doctor Yates but couldn't help feeling resentful towards her parents for suggesting it all the same.

J-Corner High was a vast school which Danni and her friends had attended for four years now under the watchful eye of Principal Mason whose idea of a good time was giving students detention for looking at him funnily. His daughter Parry was in several of Danni's classes and was one of the most beautiful girls Danni had ever seen. Boys trailed after her and while she had dated a few, she was so confident that she felt she didn't need anyone but herself. She was actually quite nice but judged wrongly because her title was 'Rich Principal's daughter.'

At breaks Danni, Reilly and Drew sat on the library stairs and talked or listened to wistful Drew strum his guitar. A flash of beautiful red flowed by the three and Parry's curvy figure strutted past while Drew's eyes followed. Danni and Reilly rolled their eyes at each other because of the usual display the J-Corner boys presented when she came by. When the 'goddess' disappeared, Drew returned to earth, picked up his guitar and sang 'flash of red, touch of green, she makes me wanna scream!'

Reilly laughed at Drew's passion and turned to Danni still grinning.

'So Dan, are you still coming to the Funky Fries after school?'

Every Monday when school was out, the three walked to the Funky Fries, pigged out on its greasy food and then chilled at a different house each week. Danni blushed slightly and turned away from Reilly.

'Actually, I was thinking I might check out Bouquet Reserve just to see how much my dream was real.'

Drew was too entranced in his playing to care but Reilly's eyes narrowed.

'Well ok, but please don't make this every week, you're breaking tradition.'

'Thanks Reilly, I promise we will hang out twice as much at my place next week,' Danni vowed.

'We better!'

When the home bell rang, Danni hugged her friends and ran to Bouquet Reserve, her brown hair streaming back in the cold wind. As she entered the green park, a chill fell around her shoulders. The reason most people never entered the Reserve was because of how spooky and abandoned it was. She had only walked past it before but in her dreams she had explored it in depth. Now to find out how similar it was in reality was astounding! It didn't really surprise her to find the walkway was exactly the same in her dreams. Her premonitions had gotten stronger since the dreaming began. What she was actually searching for was the pond where the twelve members sat around to conduct some sort of meetings she hadn't figured out yet. Danni racked her brain to remember the path she took with the shadowy figures trailing behind her and after scoping the place out she found it. There was the pond where she had stretched her fingers over and nearly touched that gorgeous boy's hand. She sat down on the damp grass just at the pond's edge and allowed the tips of her fingers to create ripples in the water. Danni couldn't believe that this place actually existed but she was used to her freaky premonitions so she shrugged it off and enjoyed her cosmic moment. It seemed to Danni as if she should just give up this charade and continue to focus on more important things like grades and friends.

As she turned to leave she noticed a boy standing behind a tree peering at her. All she could see was a hint of brown curls but that was enough to have her heart leap out of her chest as she knew exactly who he was. Without thinking it through, she ran over to him. Looking at him up close, Danni could see he really was the boy from her dreams and he was just as heavenly in the flesh. He had masses of curly brown hair and sparkly hazel eyes that searched Danni's and wore a lopsided smile.

'Do I know you?' he asked, still smiling.

It then occurred to Danni that just because she

dreamt of him didn't mean he dreamt of her. He had no idea who she was!

'Umm, you just looked familiar, that's all,' Danni replied.

His grin grew wider and he outstretched his hand to take hers. Danni couldn't believe they were really going to touch hands this time. She felt her face burn but took his hand all the same.

'I'm Crawford and you are?' he asked, still holding her hand.

'Danni,' she said quickly, her heart beating faster.

There were so many things she wanted to say to him but she knew she would look crazy if she did.

'Tell me Crawford, what's your sign?'

It was not unusual for Danni to ask this question when meeting a new person. Crawford looked at her strangely.

'Leo, why do you ask?'

Quickly doing the math, Danni realized that Leo and Gemini were extremely compatible and that excited her. A perfect match!

'Oh it's just a crazy obsession of mine,' said Danni smiling.

'If only you knew...'

'Well Danni, I better be off but I'm sure I'll see you around.'

He turned and walked away leaving Danni staring

after him and it only occurred to her when she got home that she never asked *why* he was there in the first place.

Chapter 3
AN UNEXPECTED FRIEND

The night before her appointment with Doctor Yates, Danni lay on her zodiac blanket tracing the symbols with her fingers while talking to Reilly on the phone.

She told her everything that had happened at Bouquet Reserve with Crawford and his mysterious hiding behind trees.

'So Dan, describe him one more time please,' Reilly drawled.

'Gorgeous curly brown hair, hazel eyes, perfect build and just a bit taller than me and cute all over....well what I've seen anyway,' she flushed.

Danni had never had a crush on anyone before. Briefly, in primary school, Reilly and Danni had both liked Drew. Now they were over it and made sure he never found out. They talked about Crawford's godlike physique a little longer until Danni realized they were avoiding the most obvious thing.

'Reilly, don't you think the weirdest thing about all

this is that I dreamt somebody into my life?'

There was an awkward silence on the phone and Danni knew Reilly was carefully picking her words so as not to upset her.

'Well,' Reilly finally answered, 'it's pretty cool, but how do you know you didn't see him in town or something and it stuck in your subconscious?'

'It's a possibility, but I'm sure my psychic stuff has kicked in again and now I just have to find out who the other people in my dream were.'

They both gossiped a bit more about school and its dramas and finally Danni admitted to being really tired, so they hung up.

As she slept, her dream occurred once again and this time she could clearly see herself, Reilly, Drew, Crawford and to her utter amazement, Parry Mason the principal's daughter!

***

The next day at school, Reilly and Drew couldn't help noticing that the dopey boys weren't the only people staring at Parry. Danni was fixated on her, deep in thought.

Drew leaned close to Danni and whispered, 'I know she is hot, but Danni, I never thought you were the type.'

Danni spun around to Drew with her eyes wide.

'Drew, I'm not in love with Parry! It's just that she was in my dream last night and I can't help but wonder why.'

'Dude, most guys dream about Parry and when they wake up...' Drew blushed.

'Too much information,' Reilly grinned.

Danni dismissed her friends as she was debating whether she should talk to Parry, although she didn't know what that would achieve. Still, it was worth a try.

'Be back soon, guys.'

Danni walked across to Parry's circle under the oak tree where she was surrounded by boy slaves drooling and being engrossed in everything she said.

'Umm, Parry?'

Danni ignored the boys' angry stares because she had interrupted their mating ritual.

Parry's head jerked up and stared at Danni with her big green eyes.

'Can I help you?'

'Yeah, umm, would it be alright if we talked in private?'

'Yeah, sure,' Parry looked relieved.

They strode over towards the fence near the back oval and Danni grinned to see the boys' leering after her because a friend of Parry's is a friend of theirs!

Parry leaned against the fence, examining her nails and looking everywhere but at Danni.

'So,' Danni started, 'I was wondering what your views on astrology are.'

Parry looked at Danni in surprise, as if she expected makeup tips.

'Well, umm I guess it's alright.'

'Yeah, well I know this is weird but I am a huge believer in the zodiac and I had a dream, well sort of premonition, about you the other night...I would really like to start a zodiac club.'

Danni felt extremely nervous because this was the first time she had revealed aloud her desire for a zodiac group.

Parry let out a loud laugh and shook her head.

'You know it's normal to dream of me, most people do.'

Danni rolled her eyes.

'What is your star sign?'

'Perfect perfectionist Virgo.'

Parry flicked her red hair back and looking haughtily at her admirers.

That didn't surprise Danni in the slightest. Parry was immaculately detailed like a Rolls Royce.

Danni had been feeling for a while that she wanted to start a zodiac club. After all, in the dreams, she was leading some sort of group.

'I won't explain the whole thing to you but I am a little psychic and this isn't any ordinary dream. It keeps recurring, so when I saw you in it, I thought maybe you were into the same stuff as me.'

Parry seemed almost touched at the thought.

'Well, I like astrology but it doesn't wind me up the way it does you.'

Danni thought that summed it up beautifully. The zodiac wound her up until she felt bound to its mystery.

'Listen, here's my number, call me if you want to talk about this craze,' Parry handed her what looked like a business card.

'It's my mobile number. Dad gets a little wild at how many people ring me at home. Well, you would know that anyway.'

She looked in the direction of her fan club and winked.

'Thanks, I will do that,' Danni took the card.

She watched as Parry walked back to her followers and then she turned to go back to her friends.

Reilly and Drew were staring at her as she came back, almost as if she had turned into a Parry clone.

'Well, what did she say?' Reilly asked excitedly.

'She gave me her number so I could call her if I needed to talk about anything,' Danni shrugged.

Drew jumped to his feet and bowled Danni over.

'Can I see it?'

Reilly got up, brushed herself off and offered Danni a hand to help her up. 'Slow down, Romeo. Parry has probably had enough of guys leeching off her.'

It was a bit strange that Parry would be willing to

give up her boy slaves so easily for an astrology group. Danni wondered if this was related to the fact that she didn't get enough attention at home. Despite her admirers, she always appeared bored and lonely. She smiled at the thought. She was sure Parry would be closer to the three of them in no time...

Chapter 4

THE MYSTERY OF HUNTER

After another eventful day of talking to Reilly and Drew about her obsession, Danni trudged home, her cheerful mood dissipating as the looming psychology session was only half an hour away. She stomped all the way up the stairs, pushed Colin (whose favourite song was now *Crazy Danni*) and changed into her jeans and black jumper. Her dad drove up the driveway and beeped outside. They were silent on the way there and Danni stared at Bouquet Reserve intently as they passed it, hoping for a glimpse of Crawford. When the car pulled up outside the grey building of Juggler's Health Care Centre ('we juggle all your problems') Danni wished she hadn't been born the way she was.

'Honey?'

Danni snapped out of her thoughts and turned to her concerned father.

'Well, I'm going to go now,' she said with a twinge of resentment in her voice.

'Your mother and I don't think you're crazy but this might help the yelling at night,' he leaned over and stroked her cheek.

'Thanks Dad, I know, and I'll give it a try.'

She walked inside and seated herself in the waiting room, thumbing through the magazines and gazing at all the patients, guessing what star sign they were.

Suddenly, she heard a deep yell from inside one of the counselling rooms.

'I'm not crazy!' the voice bellowed.

All the patients looked up as the door flew open and a boy about Danni's age with wild black hair stormed out. Danni stared at the furious boy who turned and saw her.

'What are you looking at?' he snarled.

He stomped out of the centre, practically leaving a trail of smoke behind. A flustered old woman walked out of the room and inquired shrilly, 'Danielle Hamilton?'

Danni stood up and followed the stout lady into a green room with pictures of kittens and sunny beaches. She sat in a chair opposite Dr Yates and noticed that the health centre's pamphlets were scattered all over the floor. She leaned down to pick them up and Dr Yates gave her a kind smile.

'Thank you, dear.'

'No problem. That boy seems like a handful,' Danni said.

Dr Yates positioned the pamphlets perfectly and sighed, sitting down. 'Hunter...well he just needs...' then she trailed off.

She gestured for Danni to sit down and looked around at her pictures. Danni said nothing, watching Dr Yates stare into space.

Suddenly she jerked up, looking at Danni as though she was dressed as a penguin.

'Oh sorry dear, yes, your session can begin now.'

Dr Yates grabbed a pen and clipboard, ready to scribble down notes.

'So tell me Danielle...or do you prefer Danni? Why exactly are you here?'

Danni straightened up in her chair, preparing to be laughed at despite that being unprofessional.

'Danni is fine...well, I keep having these recurring dreams and they're very visual. In fact my parents hear me every night talking in my sleep and sometimes falling out of bed. They are pretty concerned and sent me here to get help.'

She took a deep breath after her unusual introduction.

Dr Yates looked up at the ceiling for several seconds and then returned her gaze to Danni.

'Well dear, the problem you're facing is very common. Stress can bring on a series of recurring dreams and until the issue is sorted and the stress is relieved, those dreams will continue.'

'Dr Yates, I don't feel stressed in any area of my life. Maybe I should explain my dream to you.'

Dr Yates nodded and gestured for her to continue.

Danni started telling her psychologist all about her obsession and how she felt it was her duty to start finding out the mystery behind the zodiac.

'So I feel, until all twelve figures show up in my dream, and we start the zodiac club, I won't be dreaming of Ed Westwick again,' she blushed.

Her counsellor clasped her hands together.

'Well, clearly your parents sent you here because they were concerned about your sleeping habits and that is what we need to tackle. We will discuss these dreams at length and perhaps in the meantime you will find the remaining members which will cause your dreams to cease.'

Danni appeared startled at the solution and Dr Yates smiled.

'Trust me; I'm a vivid dreamer too. If you want to experience a good night's sleep again then try to resolve these underlying issues. Listen to what the dreams are telling you and perhaps that will lead you to the rest of them.'

'Makes sense to me,' Danni said. 'I guess I will be back in a week's time.'

'Certainly, here let me give you a card for your next

appointment.'

Dr Yates pulled out a card, wrote down the appointment date and time and handed it to Danni. Danni took it and noticed an extra number written on the back. There, in scrawled scribble next to it, was Hunter's name. Dr. Yates must have mixed up the cards. Although Danni knew it was wrong, her gut was telling her to keep it and try to persuade Hunter to join her group.

'Ok. Thanks for your help, see you soon.'

'Bye dear.'

Danni ran out feeling more hopeful about stopping the dreams. She saw her Dad's blue Honda and jumped in.

'Well, how was it, honey?'

'It was really good; we sorted out a few techniques to help my dreams.'

'Well that's fantastic; not a waste of time for you then.'

Danni felt guilty that her sessions would be spent discussing a potential astrology group. She knew her parents would think *that* a waste of time.

After talking to Reilly and Drew on the phone that evening, Danni retired to bed and hoped to dream of new additions to the group.

Slipping into sleep again, she was pleased to see the usual people lounging around the pond wearing black robes lined with different colours. The other people were still hidden in the shadows. To her delight, Crawford was holding Danni's hand and talking to her excitedly when a huge rock was thrown into the pond. Danni looked up and saw a familiar shaggy, dark haired boy snarling at her.

Hunter!

Chapter 5

ASTROLOGY…AND A SPRAY TAN

When Danni woke up the next morning, her stomach was tied up in knots. She wasn't looking forward to calling Hunter after he'd given her such a menacing stare the previous day.

Danni slowly changed into her school uniform, examining the Wheel of the Zodiac poster that took up her whole left wall. *The stars are calling you…*what did that mean? She decided that when she had her appointment next week, she would go earlier and speak to Hunter so that there was no chance of him hanging up on her when she called.

Her mother was waiting in the kitchen when Danni finally came downstairs. She handed her a steaming coffee mug.

'So, how was your appointment yesterday Dan?'

'It was helpful; going back next week.'

Her mother went over to her, gave her a hug and then walked out of the room. Danni stared after her sadly.

Needing to see a counsellor because of her erratic sleeping habits made her feel like a freak.

Grabbing her school bag and walking outside, she saw Reilly and Drew waiting for her at their usual corner spot and the three walked to school chatting about their problems.

'So, this Hunter guy?' Reilly enquired. 'Was he hot?'

Her two best friends were now aware that Danni planned to begin an astrological group.

Danni raised her eyebrows. 'I don't know. I was too busy wiping spit off my face after he screamed at me.'

Drew was holding his guitar case in one hand and a colour coded timetable in the other.

'You know Danni, we have a lot of assignments coming up soon and if you keep going with this astrology thing you'll be so distracted. Then bam! Fail all the way.'

Danni smiled at Drew, hitting him playfully.

'Thanks for being concerned but I'll be fine loser.'

'So, how many more numbers do you need?' Reilly kicked a stone along the path.

'Well, so far there is me – Gemini, you – Sagittarius, Drew – Pisces, Parry – Virgo, Crawford – Leo and Hunter who hopefully wants to join and isn't one of the already taken star signs. So I would say about six more.'

Reilly shuffled her feet awkwardly.

'What?' Danni said, narrowing her eyes.

'Well...you know my cousin Hannah?'

Danni vaguely remembered a pretty blonde girl who cried at everything and literally had an exclusive handkerchief set.

'I told her about your club and she might be interested in joining.'

'What sign?'

'Cancer the crab.'

Danni chuckled. She knew Cancerians to be highly emotional. That explained Reilly's story about Hannah sobbing last summer over a wilting flower.

'Well, I'm sort of leaving it up to fate. Now, whoever I dream of around the pond is meant to be in the group but I would like her to join. We need a Cancerian.'

'Thanks Danni,' Reilly said warmly.

Danni had pondered all night about this group and how there must be twelve members, one of each star sign. She would lead it and through astrology, teach them all about themselves and each other. It sounded strange but exciting.

When they arrived at J-Corner High, Danni was surprised to see Parry sauntering over to her wearing a tight white dress. Drew went bright red and Reilly pulled him off to class.

'Hey, Danni is it?' Parry asked.

Danni nodded. She was surprised at the connection she felt towards the Virgo.

'I've thought about this group thing and I am going to join on one condition,' Parry grinned.

'Ok...sure.'

'Has anyone ever told you, you're so pale?' Parry unzipped her handbag.

'Yeah, all the time,' Danni replied feeling self-conscious. Her mother always said she never got enough fresh air.

'Well, here is a voucher for Maltin's Tanning Salon and if you say Parry sent you, you can get a gorgeous, half-price spray tan for face and body.'

She handed her the business card. Danni felt uncomfortable. She had never really been the glamour type but Parry had to be in the group. She was in her visions.

'What the hell? I'll go tonight,' Danni said, surprising herself.

Who knew her passion for the zodiac would lead to her looking like an orange?

After Parry had walked away, Reilly and Drew inevitably wanted to know what the conversation was all about.

'Oh my God Danni!' Reilly exclaimed. 'You have never gotten a tan before! I have always thought you should but I never...' she stopped short, seeing Danni's glare.

'I am only doing this so that she can be in the

group.'

'Does that business card have her number on it?' Drew asked.

Danni hit him over the head.

***

After another day at school, Danni strode nervously over to Maltin's Tanning Salon and walked into the bright pink and white studio. Loud colours struck Danni as the walls were filled with different portraits of nails and hair styles. Women in white coats who smelled of acetone were rushing all over the place, attending to their clients. Danni had never felt more out of place in her life. She walked up to the elaborately decorated counter where a flamboyant boy about Danni's age was filing his nails.

'Hi I'm here for a….'

'Nail file, Leg, Underarm, Bikini Wax, Peppermint Facial, Spray Tan, come on come on, I don't have all day!' the boy ushered frantically.

Danni stared at him in disbelief.

'Umm...I have a voucher for a spray tan and Parry sent me.'

His eyes widened in excitement as he snatched the voucher out of her hand.

'Ah, Parry...our best customer, how does her hair stay so fresh?' He dreamily looked at the ceiling for answers.

'Well can I umm… do it now please?' Danni said

impatiently.

The boy snapped out of his daydream and frowned at her.

'Yes, if you must. Follow the hallway to the first room on your right, Leanne will be there waiting.'

Danni strode down the whitewashed halls to the first door on her right and saw a big shower with changing cubicles and tanning beds at the far end of the room. She sat down and waited, debating whether to run away or not but before she could decide, a woman with long red hair stepped in and smiled at her.

'So Parry sent you, did she?' Leanne asked.

'Yeah, I'm here for a spray tan.'

Leanne studied Danni up and down and frowned at her pale skin.

'Yes, Parry always makes the best beauty choices. Ok, please go into the cubicle and strip down to your underwear.'

Danni walked into the small cubicle and slowly took off her school uniform.

I have to do this for the club.

Realising how ridiculous that thought was, she walked into the shower.

Leanne peeked in and studied Danni's pale figure with pursed lips.

'Well, we might have to spray you twice for longer lasting impact.'

Handing Danni a shower cap and goggles she signalled for her to turn her back to the nozzle first. She turned the showers on and Danni felt the hot spray gush onto her skin. She squinted under the pressure of the goggles, allowing the liquid to change her into someone more confident. She was instructed to turn around several times and face the nozzle at different angles, ensuring that her hair and eyes were unaffected.

After twenty minutes or so, the shower was turned off and Leanne stood there admiring her work of art.

'Gorgeous! Never fails.'

Danni stepped out, removing the goggles and caught a look at her new skin in the mirror. She was startled at how brown her legs were and how much she liked it. She caught herself wishing Crawford could see her.

'Wow, I'm not pale anymore,' she whispered.

'That's right!'

Leanne walked over to her and took off her shower cap.

'Maltin's is the best tanning salon in Juggler's Corner and believe me; there are heaps in this town!'

Danni couldn't recall ever seeing a single one but then again, she was never looking out for one.

She put her clothes back on, thanked Leanne and walked over to the counter to tip. The boy was now holding a hand mirror and adjusting his blonde waves. He turned to Danni who was waiting patiently.

'Well, we do clean up nicely now, don't we?' he said, examining her.

She smiled and handed over the voucher with a tip. She noticed his name tag read *Graham Maltin*.

'Your family owns this place?' she wondered aloud.

'Yes we do, and let me say we do a fantastic job, don't you think?' he said smiling at the mirror.

'Well just look at me,' Danni said excitedly. 'I walked in here an albino and now I'm European!'

Graham laughed and winked at his reflection.

Danni turned to go and saw a girl walk up to him.

'Here's your chocolate milkshake. I can't believe you've never tried one before!'

She handed him the polystyrene cup.

'I told you, they're too fattening.'

Graham took a sip and screwed up his face in disgust.

'Ugh! This is gross! Oh well, my star sign said don't rush into any changes today.'

Danni whirled around and without thinking ran back up to the counter.

'Sorry Graham, what's you star sign?'

He frowned at her. 'Scorpio.'

Danni's heart leapt. She briefly explained her ideas for the zodiac group she was forming and asked if he wanted to join. Graham was reluctant at first but agreed when he heard Parry was joining too.

'I can get more beauty secrets!'

Danni walked out of the salon with a new look and a thumping heart.

Chapter 6

THE PERFECT MEETING PLACE

When Danni awoke on the weekend (dreaming of Graham braiding Parry's hair) she had one plan. Visit Bouquet Reserve with the intention of seeing Crawford (if he was there) and to scope out the area she planned to hold her meetings in. She hadn't really thought how this was going to go or how these meetings would be conducted but she knew it was her destiny to find out. Colin kept getting on Danni's nerves. He had now made a decorative, colourful poster of 'Crazy Danni.'

Danni knew she wasn't insane; she just had a strong love for something no one else did. It took a lot of willpower to push herself onto the morning bus and visit a place that could eventually become a big part of her life. She couldn't stop fidgeting on the bus, nervous that she might see Crawford and that this wild idea might not even work out for her.

As she stepped off the bus and walked over the road, she noticed the dilapidated sign beckoning to her desires. The grounds were no bigger than their school gymnasium with green benches scattered everywhere and autumn leaves covering the floor. Down the path with shady willows, rippled the beautiful pond she treasured in her nightly mind adventures. Danni pulled her black coat around her tighter and set off towards the mysterious body of water. She already knew this was where she would lead the meetings but if only they could be run here without the fear that outsiders would disrupt them! Why had Crawford been here in the first place? She bit back a smile and leaned down to trail her fingers in the clear water. What would await her here? There were just so many questions that were begging to be answered. As she continued to daydream and plan the meetings mentally, she felt a gust of cold wind around her shoulders and sensed a presence behind her. Danni slowly turned to see Crawford standing there and smiling, holding a rake.

'I wasn't going to bother you yet; you looked so peaceful,' he said softly.

Danni immediately stood up, flushed and jittery.

'Sorry! I swear I'm not stalking you!

He walked forward and sat beside her, resting his rake against a tree.

'You don't have to be sorry Danni...I'm actually on my break.'

She wrinkled up her nose. 'Break?'

'Yeah, my father works for the local council and I help out when I can. Believe it or not, some couples still enjoy having their wedding pictures taken here and I clean the area twice a week.'

Danni's heart leapt up in excitement. The fact that Crawford was paid to clean Bouquet Reserve meant she had a valuable connection. She definitely wanted him in the group so perhaps they could trade.

Bravely, she leaned in closer to him.

'Listen Crawford...I have this crazy idea or passion about forming a group.'

As she explained the details and what she wanted from Crawford in return for him joining, she noticed an unmistakable pleasure in his face.

'I would love to join! We can hold these meetings once a week. My dad won't question anything because I usually clean the park at the hours I choose.'

Danni was overjoyed that Bouquet Reserve was now the official meeting place for her group and she couldn't wait to get started.

'Ok, so when will our first meeting be?' Crawford asked, picking up some rubbish and frowning at it.

'Well...I'm looking for the last four members to join...plus one tentative...' Danni said, thinking of Hunter.

Crawford walked around her, placing the litter in the bin, then raking some leftover autumn leaves into a pile. Danni enjoyed watching his muscular arms as he worked hard to preserve her meeting place and blushed when he caught her staring. She wished it were warmer so he could see her tan. Even her parents hadn't seen it properly yet.

'I'm just glad that this is working to my favour,' Danni said hurriedly, hoping he didn't notice.

'I'll give you my mobile number and you let me know when you're ready. Which day or night will suit best?'

Crawford wrote his number on a piece of paper and handed it to her.

'Friday night, so that everyone is alert and they don't have to go to school the next day.'

She took the paper, their hands touching momentarily just like in her dream. Electric shocks ran up her arm.

'Well, I have to go but I will let you know when this is happening okay?'

Crawford grinned and started to walk off.

'Can't wait,' he called after her.

Danni did an unexpected jump in the air and then ran to the bus stop. It was amazing how one dream was leading her to all these new people. It was time to find the remaining members and fulfil her destiny!

***

After an uncomfortable evening of watching television with her parents staring at her, Danni trudged up to her room and decided to give Hunter a call. As she dialled his number, her nerves were racing. Their last interaction had resulted in him screaming at her. It rang a number of times and just as Danni was going to give up, she heard a click and a familiar raspy voice on the other end.

'What?'

Danni took a breath and spoke. 'Hi, is this Hunter?'

The phone was silent for a few moments.

'Yeah?' Hunter replied.

'This is Danni, from Juggler's Health Centre. I wanted to talk to you about something,' she was now shaking slightly.

'I don't know who you are. Do you work there or something coz all I know is Dr. Yates,' Hunter was starting to sound impatient.

'Actually, I don't know if you remember but at your last session you came out and yelled at me,' Danni trembled, sounding braver than she felt.

More silence.

'Oh yeah, you're the girl who stares,' Hunter sneered. 'How did you get my number?'

Danni swallowed quickly. 'Umm...Well you kind of dropped your session card.'

'Hmm and you thought it was cool to just ring me? What the hell is wrong with you freak!'

His tone was past the point of anger.

'I...I just wanted to ask you something,' Danni stuttered, ready to hang up and never to go back to the health centre again.

'What?'

'When is your birthday?'

'What so you can stalk me? What is it with your need to know about everyone else's private life?'

Danni decided to just explain it all to him.

'Please, just hear me out Hunter.'

Once again she explained her idea, knowing with full certainty that he would find it ridiculous and her insane.

After a deafening amount of silence he spoke.

'Hmm, it sounds weird. I dunno if I wanna come. What's in it for me?'

Danni hesitated, trying to think of what to offer.

'Well, all I can say is it will be fun and you can get lots of new friends.'

Hunter snorted.

'Friends? I don't need or want any friends and in answer to your question...I'm an Aries.'

And with that, he hung up on Danni. Danni stared at the phone in shock. Nobody had ever hung up on her. She felt excited that he was an Aries because she didn't have one yet but she still didn't know how to get him to join.

That night, as she dreamt of the group she had accumulated thus far, she was not surprised to see Hunter throwing rocks at her from across the water.

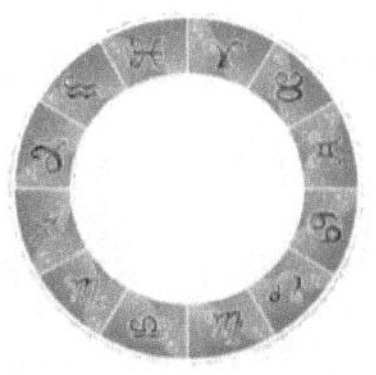

Chapter 7

A COUNSELLING SESSION

Time flew for Danni that week as she planned more and more meetings in her head and actually started putting them on paper, excited at what was coming.

She knew she could make this work if she just stayed dedicated and ignored the voice in her head that kept telling her it was a ridiculous idea. Reilly had confirmed that her cousin Hannah was happy to join as she didn't have many friends and normally kept to herself. It filled Danni with such happiness to know this group wasn't just about star signs but also meeting people and learning to come out of your shell which she really needed to do more. The only downside to all this was Hunter's stubbornness not to join. Three more times after the last phone call, Danni had asked him again, and each time he hung up yelling and scoffing at her. She was becoming restless. She knew this group would help him if he just gave things a chance but she had no idea how to get him to join.

After school, Reilly and Drew walked Danni to the health centre for her second session with Dr. Yates.

'So, seeing that you have forty minutes of to discuss crazy dreams, what else do you actually plan to do? Talk about kittens? Maybe help her with the knitting?' chuckled Drew.

The three of them crossed the street laughing.

'Actually Drew,' Danni smiled. 'I'm going to use these sessions, however many I need, to get advice on how to get Hunter to accept my offer without telling her how I got his number. I mean, she knows him better than I do and is a psychologist, so how hard can it be?'

Reilly looked up from the magazine she bought, frowning.

'Dan, you can't possibly expect your psych to give out confidential details about her patient; that's illegal.'

'I know and I don't expect her to. If Hunter becomes our friend then he can tell us why he is so angry when he's ready but at the moment I just need some tips on how to calm an angry ram.'

The three walked on in silence and finally reached the building. Danni turned around and hugged her friends.

'Wish me luck guys.'

'Good luck,' they said grinning and made phone signals with their hands, suggesting she should call them afterwards.

Danni walked in and sat down again, looking at everybody and waiting. It didn't surprise her that a second later, Hunter came storming out and gave Danni as well as all the others watching an extra glare. He stopped in front of her, fuming.

'If you even knew why my mum sent me here, you would know I don't need this!'

Danni grinned. 'Actually, my parents sent me here for no reason either. I hate it but what can I do?'

This wasn't entirely true but she was trying to relate to him.

Hunter nodded, shook his wild black hair and walked out. Danni sighed. This was harder than she thought. She almost didn't care about him joining. She just wanted to help him and be a shoulder to lean on. Then Dr. Yates bustled out of her quaint office and beckoned.

They walked to her office in silence and Danni was pleased to note the room wasn't in such disarray this time.

'Well Danni, how have things been since I last saw you? Are you still having restless dreams or have they eased up a bit?'

Danni started informing her of everything that had happened since their last session. How Crawford had allowed Danni to use Bouquet Reserve and how Hunter refused to join the club. Danni made it sound as though they had spoken after her first session and not on the phone. However, she couldn't help but wonder if Dr. Yates had purposely given her the wrong card. It felt really nice to just talk and be listened to. Her parents were always too busy to make time for her and when you have two best friends, you constantly have to share the spotlight. Dr. Yates frowned when Danni had finished talking and studied the wall for a few minutes.

'Well,' she finally spoke. 'You know I can't divulge any confidential information on Hunter.'

Danni nodded.

'All I can say is that I'm glad you haven't given up on him just yet. Even those who seem angry or annoyed need love and friendship too.'

Danni looked doubtful and Dr. Yates smiled.

'The thing everyone should learn in this world is to find the good in everybody because there is always a little bit there. If everybody was given a chance, the world would be a much better place.'

Danni stared at her psychologist in admiration. She hoped this club would make her grow but at that moment all she wanted to do was help everyone else.

'I hope he will be a big part of your life soon.'

'I hope so too...'

They continued to talk about various other issues and Danni even mentioned how annoying her little brother could be at times.

Looking up at the pink flowery clock, she realized they had gone ten minutes over their session.

'I have to go Dr. Yates, thank you for today. I won't stop trying.'

Dr. Yates opened the door and walked Danni to the front.

'I look forward to seeing you next week dear.'

Danni waved goodbye and jumped in the car next to her mother.

'Good session sweetie?'

Danni stared at her hopeful mother's face.

'I'm fine; we're really making a breakthrough.'

Her mother looked sad.

'I don't think you're crazy darling. I just feel that discussing these dreams with a professional may help you sleep a lot easier. Once we can see that you're not so tired you won't have to see her anymore.'

'Ok mum, you know best,' Danni rolled her eyes and then cracked a smile to show her mother she was joking.

At home, she found on her bed a red card with scribbled writing and two stick figures of a boy and girl made by Colin. On it was written *Sorry Danni* and lots of hearts circled around it. Danni smiled warmly. It seemed her family was finally starting to realize she wasn't a nutcase. This was the first time she felt she was doing something meaningful with her life. This group was her ticket to a whole heart.

Chapter 8

THE NEIGHBOURS MOVE IN

Danni had finally given up on trying to convince Hunter to join over the phone. She wasn't sure why he even bothered answering anymore...it was always her! It was time to set the angry Aries aside and focus on finding the four remaining members. Nobody knew, but Danni had stored in her cupboard, a diary of all the meetings she was planning when they finally began. They spoke of all her knowledge of the topic. This included: the Elements, Chinese astrology, tarot cards, celestial charts and basically every detail about the twelve signs. Danni always tried to ignore that a Gemini had an evil side because its symbol was the twins. She liked to believe there was no nasty part in her but sometimes she felt any day now it would present itself. She was so frustrated trying to make this happen and her dreams had her thrashing around in bed. Only the eight usual people roamed around the pond while the other four were mere shadows murmuring secrets. Danni worked out that it was probably like Graham's situation. She met him and then he appeared in her dream confirming his membership. However, she didn't want to wander around the town looking desperate and there was that shaking suspicion she might never find her remaining four. If that was the case then everybody would feel as if she had wasted their time.

Reilly and Drew kept encouraging her to try with Hunter.

'Maybe you should go to his place?' Drew suggested.

'Drew,' she sighed. 'I don't know where he lives. When he does answer the phone he hangs up instantly. That guy won't let anybody get close to him!'

Apart from this dilemma, Danni also had her role as a high school teenager to fulfil. Mr. Tenesson, her grumpy history teacher kept bugging her for her overdue Greek Mythology poster and Reilly and Drew constantly wanted to hang out. This wasn't a bad thing but she would have loved more time to plan the lessons she would present to the group when it started. She had spent weeks researching her knowledge on the topic. From ancient runes to the planetary alignments, she knew it would all be useful once things got running.

One sunny Sunday morning she shuffled downstairs to get some cereal and was surprised to find her parents peering out the window, their heads close together.

She raised her eyebrows and walked up behind them.

'You know, I never picked Librans to be the inquisitive type.'

She had always looked at her parents' relationship with admiration. It was a well-known fact to astrologers that a partnership of the same sign signified extra compatibility.

The two of them jumped and turned around.

'Oh sweetie, we didn't know you were there!' Her mother said, walking over to the kitchen table.

Danni rolled her eyes, walked to the window and stood next to her father to see what was happening. She peered at her next door neighbours and noticed they had finally sold their house and a new family was waving to the leaving vans.

'I have to go greet them!'

Danni groaned. It was just like her father to greet anything that moved. His over the top friendliness was almost humiliating. Once, he had invited Danni's enemy in primary school to dinner thinking it was her friend. Needless to say, that was the most awkward night of her life.

She watched her father race out the door with Colin whose new craze was running around in circles barking. Her mother sighed and followed them, almost obligated to appear nice. Danni sat down and ate her cereal. It wasn't that she was anti-social but Drew and Reilly were the only two who she could really be herself with. That was why she was surprised every time she thought about the astrology group. It was not in her nature to lead anything but she realized it was time for a change. As she was about to put her bowl away she heard her father calling her name to come out. Danni ran upstairs, discarding her pyjamas and throwing on a shirt and some jeans, and then raced outside to where her father was chatting animatedly with a man and woman.

'Ah Danni, I would like you to meet Mr. and Mrs. Drayman, our new American neighbours.'

Danni shook hands with both of them. She wanted to go back inside.

'So Paul, do you have any children?'

Danni noticed her mother frown at Mrs. Drayman's tight dress which left little to the imagination.

Paul laughed heartily.

'Sure do! But those little scamps are checking out their new rooms. Marcia, get them out please honey.'

Mrs. Drayman yelled into the house beckoning for her children.

'We have a boy and girl who are about your age Danni, and will be attending your school. Is it nice there sweetheart?' Mrs. Drayman asked.

Danni found her tone to be sickly sweet.

'Umm, yeah, it's alright I suppose.' *One more time with enthusiasm Dan!*

'What's up mum?' A girl's voice said.

Danni looked up and noticed two stunning teenagers coming out of the door. They both had striking, white blonde hair and sapphire eyes. Danni immediately felt uncomfortable. She wasn't used to associating with the popular types but the boy and girl were smiling quite harmlessly. Despite their designer clothes and honour roll impressions, she didn't mind the look of them.

'Brodie and Slade, I would like you to meet the Hamiltons and their daughter Danni and son Colin.'

Paul looked delighted to show off his beautiful offspring.

The pair shook hands with Danni and her family. Colin yelped like a dog as Brodie ruffled his hair as a friendly gesture.

'Well Paul, I think you should come round some time and we can have some beers and watch the game. What do you think?'

Danni stared at her father strangely. He had never drunk a drop of beer in his life!

'Sure thing Terry, maybe we can have an all family… Barbie is it?' Paul grinned, holding his wife's hand.

Danni watched the Draymans retreat into their new home and noticed her father walking with an extra spring in his step while her mother appeared silent and brooding. Colin was now barking in circles and Danni hit him on the head.

'What a nice family, hey honey? Marcia seems pretty friendly.'

'Yeah...only to you,' muttered Danni's mother and walked back inside.

'Slade said he would teach me to skate!' squealed Colin.

Danni's father beamed and patted Colin on the back.

As they were about to watch television her father turned around to Danni. 'Oh sweetie, could you go get Friday's mail please? I always forget.'

Danni sighed and walked out into the cold, the fading sun barely keeping her warm. She didn't know what it was but being outside always made her feel better. As she walked over to the letter box she noticed Slade coming outside with a board in his hand. Before he skated off she decided to talk to him. She wanted to step out of her comfort zone and make some more friends.

'Hey, Slade is it?' she asked, walking over to him.

He turned and saw her, dropping his board on the ground and mounting it.

'Sure is. And you're Danni, I'm pretty sure.'

Danni crossed her arms.

'Correct. So how do you like Juggler's Corner?'

Slade skated once around his driveway and then came back to her.

'Oh it's awesome. Yeah the whole family needed a

change and it's so quiet compared to L.A.'

'Wow L.A? Were you constantly star struck?'

Slade laughed, pushing his wavy hair out of his face. Danni noticed in that moment how cute he really was.

'It's amazing how many people ask that. Nah, it wasn't like that. We lived mostly in the suburban areas where not much happened. Enough about me though, what do you do for fun? You look like the shopping type. I know Brodie is. What a shopping machine my sister can be!'

Danni laughed out loud.

'Shopping? That would be the last thing. I'm actually into astrology.'

She felt pretty comfortable with her new neighbour and told him about her idea. He didn't snort like Hunter had but nodded quite casually.

'I don't mind a bit of fortune telling myself now and then.'

'Well, to me it is so much more than fortune telling but don't get me started! I desperately want to get it going but I can't exactly ask everybody at school without looking a little freaky.'

Slade winked at her and began flipping his board with talent.

'What?'

'Well, how would you feel about an Aquarian

joining?'

Danni's heart leapt a mile high. 'Serious? That would be awesome!'

Slade seemed pleased. 'Also Brodie is a Libra; you don't have one of those yet, do you?'

Danni couldn't believe her luck.

'No! Slade, you're the best and I don't even know you yet!'

'Glad to be of assistance madam,' he said, feigning a British accent.

Danni giggled. 'I will give you all the details once my last three members join...hopefully.'

Slade grinned and set off on his board down the street.

'Seeya Danni! Who knew J-Corner could be so fun?'

Danni stared after him and then ran inside as excited as Colin. She nearly started barking herself!

Chapter 9

THE PROBLEM WITH THE CAPRICORN

Danni now looked forward to going to bed and dreaming. They were so magical yet so real at the same time. To her delight, Brodie and Slade now sat around the pond talking excitedly and even Hannah wasn't crying as much as she did in reality. The odd thing was that even though there were two shadows remaining, one of them was only half covered in black mist. From what Danni could see, it was a male with sandy coloured hair and his expression showed disgust when he looked at the female members of the group.

When Danni awoke the next morning, ready to go to school, she realized she didn't really want a sexist male in her group but she had dreamed of him, so it was meant to be. As she ambled into the school grounds, she noticed everybody staring at her tanned limbs. Danni couldn't help but smile. Today was slightly warmer so she could wear her school skirt and shirt. It was a nice change from having a pale complexion. Parry skipped over in a green mini skirt with matching top which looked gorgeous against her emerald eyes. She didn't seem to care for school uniform rules. She gasped at Danni's skin, looking her up and down.

'Oh my goodness! You look hotter than me! Well, maybe that's going too far but you still look awesome.'

Danni blushed, clearly uncomfortable at compliments which she hardly ever received.

'Thanks. So what do you think? Will you join?'

Parry nodded. 'Of course I will. Graham rang me and said he is joining too. Let me tell you, that guy does the best highlights...but enough of that. Just give me details and I'm there.'

Danni explained that everybody would get a letter when she was ready and watched Parry walk off to her boy toys.

Drew whistled. 'Danni you look good but Parry cannot be competed with!'

She snorted. 'Do you honestly believe this is a beauty pageant? I just want her to join.'

'Me too,' growled Drew.

Reilly laughed and pushed him. 'So you coming to Funky Fries this time Dan? Come on, say yes.'

'I wouldn't miss it Reilly,' Danni answered and walked to her home room.

***

'So wait, this doesn't make any sense. Explain it again,' Drew said, with a mouthful of Funky Burgerino.

The three sat around their favourite yellow booth in

the 50's themed restaurant. Famous jazz and soul musicians' memorabilia covered the walls and a giant jukebox stood in the centre.

'I don't get it either Drew; it's never happened before but this shadow was only half covered and it was clearly a guy who hates girls.'

Reilly smothered ketchup all over her fries and Danni made a face of disgust. The Sagittarius laughed playfully, smearing it on more just to tease her.

'How do you know he hates women?'

'I'm telling you Reilly, he looked at all the girls with a look of pure hatred.'

Drew seemed thoughtful.

'Well, then why do you want *him* to join?'

Danni sighed. 'Because of fate and I don't really want a grenade in the group too but I *am* trying to get Hunter.'

Reilly pointed to the billboard at the new Funky Fries special: *double chocolate groove sundae.*

'I'm so gonna get that!'

She called for a waitress and they couldn't help but stare at the girl who came over. She had jet black hair with shaved sides and three piercings on her ears as well as on her tongue and chin. Her name tag read *Hi I'm Amber* but her attitude proved different. The gothic girl was chewing gum and looking as though she would rather live in the jukebox than work in such a bright atmosphere.

'Can I help you?' she huffed.

Reilly looked terrified.

'Umm...I would like the double chocolate groove sundae please?'

The strange girl stared at the ceiling and then sighed loudly.

'When will you people learn that stuff is just made from animal exploitation?'

She stormed off to get the order.

Reilly looked taken aback.

'What was her problem? Just because she is a gothic vegan chick she can't force her beliefs on me!'

Drew and Danni chuckled into their French fries. They knew it was just like Reilly to get huffy when it came to people insulting her food. She basically went to parties just for the food!

'Her attitude is likely to get complaints from other customers here,' Drew sucked the salt off his fingers.

Reilly crossed her arms and glared at the gothic waitress.

'Trust me, I will complain.'

But as soon as her elaborate sundae hit the table she looked too much in love to care.

'What am I supposed to do now guys? Search for the sexist guy?' Danni asked, getting out her backpack.

Drew picked up a spoon and poked at the sundae, receiving a frown from Reilly. 'Well, it seems this group is going to change the lot of us and hopefully in a good way.'

Danni smiled at him. She was so lucky to have such supportive friends.

'So, if we allow this guy to join then maybe we can show him that girls aren't all bad.'

'Yeah, but they aren't all good either,' joked Drew.

Danni and Reilly ran out and left Drew to pay for them.

*

Before going home, Danni decided to pay a visit to Juggler's Corner Library to check out some books on astrology. Reilly and Drew were going to join her but felt this should be done her way.

'If you find anything interesting, call us, ok?' Reilly said.

She watched them stroll around the corner and then entered the grey building which looked rather creepy on a dreary day. Inside, she noticed two teenagers from Danni's school cramming for a test. They looked up at her but didn't bother to say hello. This wasn't a surprise to Danni as most kids, apart from Reilly and Drew, found her strange and brooding. Lines and lines of book shelves filled the room and colourful posters saying *Book Week* were put up on the stone walls. Danni rarely visited the library but she knew the people who worked there because Juggler's Corner was a close-knit community. She strode up to the desk smiling at Mrs. Pearce, the desk clerk.

'Hi Mrs. Pearce, how are you?'

Danni didn't really like her but thought it best to be polite.

The rotund woman peered over her glasses and beamed.

'Hello Danni, I'm well sweetheart. The other day I bought some perfume your mother recommended from the pharmacy.'

'Oh umm cool,' Danni mumbled. 'I was wondering where the astrology section was?'

Mrs. Pearce wrinkled her nose.

'Astrology? Don't tell me you believe in that trash?'

Danni's face turned red and she found it difficult not to yell at the large woman staring cynically at her.

'Yeah, I do.'

'Well, in that case follow me.'

Mrs. Pearce led her down the very last aisle and pointed at some dusty books at the bottom of the shelf.

'There you go…enjoy,' she sniffed haughtily.

Danni reached down and picked up a few titles that read: *Modern Astrology and the World around Us, The Zodiac Knows* and *Star Signs: A Beginner's Guide.* Danni was no beginner but she felt it would ease her group slowly into the process. She got up to go and walked right into a tall, sneering boy.

'Watch where you're going!'

'Sorry, I didn't see you...' She gulped nervously.

The boy flicked his golden hair back. Danni couldn't help notice he was oddly familiar.

'Hmm, just like a girl!' he scoffed.

Her heart jumped. It was the sexist boy from her dreams!

'Hey! That wasn't called for.'

The boy shrugged and walked off. Already Danni disliked him but he was obviously meant to be in the group.

'Hey, what's your view on astrology?'

The boy looked at her as if she needed a straightjacket.

'Hmm, yeah like I just go up to people and say stuff like that.'

Danni fumed inside.

'Well, it's just that I'm starting a zodiac group and we are short on members.'

'Are you leading it?' the boy asked.

'Yes. Problem?'

He looked taken aback at her determined attitude.

'There's seriously nothing to do in this town. Can you believe that I am actually borrowing books?'

Danni smiled. 'Well, I'm Danni and if you give me your address I can drop the details over once I am ready.'

She pulled out a scrap of paper from her pocket and held it out to him.

He hesitated but then snatched the piece of paper from Danni's hand, making sure they didn't come in physical contact. Danni sighed. She knew the group was going to hate her for bringing in a loser.

'So what is your sign by the way?'

The boy walked outside and down the path. Danni just stood there in astonishment. He turned around and looked at her rolling his eyes impatiently, signalling for her to catch up.

She ran after him amused.

'Capricorn, yeah I know I'm a boring old goat!'

Danni laughed and immediately stopped when he gave her a disapproving look.

'Well actually a Capricorn is one of the wisest signs and they are also said to be quite…'

Yeah, save it for the lesson Galileo,' he cut her off.

Frowning, he scribbled his details on the paper and handed it to her rather roughly.

'Look, I'm going to go now, so just come by when you need me.'

Danni stared at him. She couldn't understand why he was so bitter towards females but she was determined to find out. As she turned to leave she took a look at the paper with the messy address and read the name: 'Ronan.'

Chapter 10

THE REMAINING MEMBER JOINS

That night, Danni wrote out the names of all the members she had so far with their allocated sign underneath. Then she added a question mark next to Hunter's name. All that she needed now was the Taurus but that was easier said than done. Basically luck had been on her side getting her as far as she had come but now Danni knew that her final member was going to be tough. She also knew that Ronan was going to need some work as his attitude wasn't exactly pleasant. Already Reilly and Drew had expressed their concerns.

'Danni, I am not going to hang around with a sexist pig!'

'Yeah I love girls and I'm not taking that crap,' Drew agreed.

As she sat on her blanket, she didn't realize how many personality clashes there would be when the group began. Danni sighed heavily. She hated the fact that she was actually reconsidering the whole idea. What if she just made things worse and everybody fought? She shook her head. No, she had come so far and wasn't going to quit now just because of some possibilities. Her thoughts were interrupted as she heard a knock at her door. She stared in surprise as both her parents walked in and sat beside her on the blanket.

'Hey honey, you're not busy, are you?' Her mother asked.

'No,' she mumbled.

Her father put his hand on her shoulder smiling.

'Sweetheart, your mother and I have noticed a big improvement in your sleeping and decided to stop your sessions with Dr. Yates.'

Danni wasn't shocked. She had nearly found all her members, so the yelling in her dreams had stopped. Yet she wasn't entirely finished.

'Thanks but would it be alright if I continued? Dr. Yates has really helped me and I just need a few more sessions,' Danni grinned at their faces.

Her mother looked speechless.

'Umm sure honey, whatever you need.'

'Yes, whatever you need,' Her father looked confused.

'We're really glad she has helped you; knew she would.'

They both walked out of the room rigidly. She laughed and highlighted Taurus in a red marker.

***

The next day after another painful time at school

with Parry's boys leaching after Danni now, she walked once more to the health centre for another session. This time, she decided to give Hunter his letter with the details on it. Seeing that she only had one more member to find, she had printed all the letters with the Wheel of the Zodiac on it and the meeting time and place. She was so excited that it was almost there. After so much work and a change of her character she had finally taken a chance into the unknown.

Entering the usual health centre with its air conditioned rooms and clusters of depressed people, Danni noticed that although she had protested at first, coming here was a work of fate and a really good thing for her. As usual a loud noise erupted from Dr. Yates's room and Hunter stormed out nearly bumping into Danni.

'Get outta my way!' snarled Hunter.

Danni stood her ground, shaking in her usual response to Hunter's fierce manner.

'No, just wait a minute,' Danni pleaded. 'Here are all the details for the first astrology meeting.'

She handed him his letter. He didn't even look at it but crushed it into his pockets.

'Hopefully by next week when it begins, I will have my final member and it would be great if you joined. Just think about it Hunter.'

He glared at her and walked out. Danni turned around and noticed that Dr. Yates was there looking at her.

They both shook their heads.

*

Not only did Danni doubt Hunter's appearance at the opening night which she had planned thoroughly but time was running out for the final member. Reilly and Drew were constantly suggesting idiotic ways to track the person.

'Why don't you announce on the loud speaker at school for all Taureans to assemble in the gym and then you use your mystical senses to choose?' Drew proposed.

Danni stared at him. 'So Reilly, any good ideas?'

Drew stalked off grumpily while the girls laughed.

Her dreams now showed Ronan fully visible but the final shadow wavered now and then. Danni fought for some clues but they were all too difficult to comprehend. There was one where a pig jumped in the pond and the shadow leapt in after it but that just meant nothing to Danni except the final member liked pigs! Drew of course told Danni to check the butchers' but nobody worked there except crusty old Mr. Peterson who wasn't joking when he threatened to use his meat cleaver on nosy kids. Danni spent hours in her room using her intuitive senses to locate the individual but all that came to her was a cloud of darkness. It infuriated her and she was constantly irritated with all those who came in close contact with her. Her parents and Colin were steering clear of her and she heard them whispering 'must be the hormones.' No it wasn't the hormones. It was the fact that she had gotten so close and now one person was making her goals unattainable, apart from Hunter.

One afternoon, Danni was so annoyed at the world that she asked Drew and Reilly to be left alone and went to the Funky Fries for a comforting thick shake. She got the feeling that as considerate as her friends were, they were glad to have some time away from her grumpy, brooding self. She was so angry that it took the gothic waitress who yelled at Reilly to get her attention.

'Miss! Please let me take your order!'

Danni glared upwards. The last thing she needed was a feminist punk.

'Can I get a vanilla milkshake?'

The gothic girl played with her tongue stud and frowned.

'Where is the please? God what happened to manners?'

Danni slammed her menu down.

'Look I don't' have time for this...Ambrite?'

Danni stared at the girl's name tag. The 'Amber' had been scribbled out in fury.

'So please just get me my order and let me drink it in a personal rage!'

Ambrite opened her mouth in surprise and to Danni's amazement sat next to her in the yellow booth.

'You know…my parents named me Amber but I thought it sounded too cheerleader-like, so I asked everybody to call me Ambrite.'

Danni softened her expression and grinned.

'Sorry about before; I'm just annoyed at a stupid problem.'

Ambrite set her pad and notebook down and turned to Danni.

'I totally get you; I mean I am so sick of people forcing me to eat pork and I love black so what? I just want….'

'Hang on, what did you just say?' Danni said excitedly, an idea forming in her head.

Ambrite narrowed her eyebrows. 'I said I like black.'

'No! About not eating pork!'

'Oh well, I'm a vegan as you can probably tell and everybody else, including my parents and friends, think it's a big joke. I am so tired of people not allowing me to be me.'

She sighed unhappily and Danni took her hand.

'I don't mean to change the subject but what star sign are you? Trust me, this is important!'

Ambrite pulled up her long yellow dress and on her ankle sat the symbol for Taurus. Danni leapt from her seat and hugged Ambrite. Ambrite looked at her strangely but hugged her back.

'I have been looking for you! Let me tell you about a place and group where you won't be judged for being a little different.'

And Danni sat there explaining her beautiful plan to the last member of the group.

Chapter 11

I FINALLY FEEL LIKE I BELONG

When Danni arrived home from talking to Ambrite, she practically skipped up the stairs singing and laughing. Colin stared at her on the landing, sticking his tongue out and making crazy faces.

'Mum, Dad, Danni needs to go back to the psycho lady!'

Danni just stuck her tongue back at him and ran into her room, cuddling her astrology blanket. Then she opened her closet and pulled out the letters she was going to give out to all the members before next Friday night where Crawford had promised the first meeting would be held. They indicated the symbol, the person's name and address and the time. She knew her parents wouldn't care because she usually went out late with Reilly and Drew anyway but she was hoping the other parents wouldn't mind. It was crucial that she fulfilled fate's wishes and her own. She picked up her phone and rang Reilly to tell Drew to get over to her place and help her give out the letters. Twenty minutes later they both burst through the doors talking quite animatedly at the same time.

'So who was it Dan?' 'Is she hot? It's a she right?' 'How did you get her?' 'Oh my God Danni now we can start!' 'We are starting now right?'

Danni picked up her blanket and covered them both with it receiving shouts of protest from the pair.

'Ok you both need to shut up! Her name is Ambrite and she is the gothic waitress from the Funky Fries.'

Reilly pulled the blanket off, keeping Drew covered and struggling to break free. Her face was masked with disgust.

'Her? I hate her! She was trying to force her punk beliefs on me!'

Danni sighed. She knew this would be the case but what could she do? These were the chosen eleven.

'Reilly I have spoken to her and she is actually quite nice. Just a bit misunderstood.'

Reilly's mouth dropped.

'Misunderstood? That is an understatement! She needs something like a manual to figure her out!'

Drew finally fought his way out of the attacking blanket and put his arm around Reilly.

'Girl, she just needs some loving and I am the man for the job.'

Danni threw the blanket on him again much to his despair.

'She doesn't need loving, she just wants to belong to a group of people who won't judge her for being an individual. Trust me Reilly; she won't be the worst one in the club,' Danni stated, thinking of Hunter and Ronan.

Reilly's expression softened a little but Danni could tell she was still worried about the clashes in the group.

'Ok Dan, I know how important this is to you, so I'll do my best.'

Danni hugged Reilly. 'Thanks.'

Drew emerged out of the blanket again and put his arms around their shoulders. 'Awww. How cute is this?'

They both hit him over the head playfully. Danni picked up her blanket, then set it on the ground and got out her list of all the members, sitting cross-legged.

'Ok now I will give the letters to Parry, Slade, Brodie, Ronan, Ambrite and Crawford; Hunter already has his. Now can you Reilly give one to Hannah? Parry can give one to Graham and that will be that!'

She couldn't help but beam from ear to ear.

Reilly grabbed Danni's hand.

'You know Danni, in all the years we have known you, you have never looked so happy. I am so glad you found your true passion. You're so much more confident now.'

Danni nodded gratefully. It felt so nice to have friends who understood how difficult this was for her to speak up and do something out of the ordinary. She was looking forward to giving out all the letters, especially

Crawford's, but she couldn't mention that to her friends. They would plug her with never-ending questions of how she felt about him. Danni wasn't quite sure what she felt for him but she knew there was a connection that only two compatible signs could feel. This was probably the only flaw Danni held in her astrological beliefs. If the signs weren't compatible then they shouldn't be together. Reilly and Drew had attempted many times to tell her that it was the feelings and not zodiac matching that kept two people in a steady relationship but Danni would not listen. That's what comes of an obsession. She couldn't believe that two days from then, they would be sitting around the mysterious pond and beginning their quest to discover why they were all brought together. To all the others this seemed like a fun outside-of-school activity but Danni knew that somewhere, someone was trying to connect with her spiritually. This undefined figure was showing her the exact members for the twelve signs and encouraging her to reunite them and teach them about astrology. But why? Why did she have to do this? She was determined to use these meetings to find out! Sometimes in her dreams with the members in Bouquet Reserve, she could hear somebody whispering her name but when she turned around, nobody was there. She believed that as soon as the meetings commenced, the mystery figure would emerge and explain to her the reasons behind everything.

After Drew and Reilly left, Danni went downstairs grinning like a chimp finding her parents sitting around the kitchen drinking coffee. They stopped talking as soon as they saw Danni beaming at them. Her father got up and walked over to Danni, peering at her closely as though she was a rare specimen.

'Are you ok sweetheart? You seem...happier than normal.'

Danni hugged him unexpectedly.

'More than ever Dad. It's so awesome!'

Her mother walked to the sink, rinsing out her mug.

'What is awesome honey?'

'Well it's a secret but I finally feel I belong.'

Danni went to walk outside to catch the last minutes of sunlight before it was dark and she had to go to bed.

She heard her father turn to his wife.

'Honey, I think we owe Dr. Yates a giant tip!'

Danni chuckled and walked to the front of the house, seating herself on the letter box and swinging her legs. After a few minutes, she noticed Brodie and Slade walk up the drive with a girl Danni didn't know. Brodie waved and walked inside with the girl but Slade ambled over to her and slumped against the letter box.

'Evening neighbour,' he grinned.

He looked extra dreamy in stonewashed jeans and a

white shirt. Danni smiled warmly, still in a good mood.

'Evening, I trust you got my letter?'

Slade wiggled his eyebrows.

'Hmmm, I don't know how long it will be before I get it, you just can't rely on mailmen these days.'

Danni giggled. She liked Slade. Not as much as Crawford but he still managed to make her weak in the knees. Slade stood up and walked in front of her, making sure he didn't get kicked by her swinging legs.

'I got it and will be there, Brodie too. It's gonna be rad!'

He then went silent and studied her face. Danni's stomach did a back flip but she maintained eye contact. Slade smiled at her again.

'So it looks like our families are getting along nicely.'

Danni jumped off the letter box and felt her face turn red as she noticed how close they were.

'Yeah well, my Dad jumps at the chance for new friends.'

She looked nervously away as if she felt in that moment that temptation would take them over. Sensing her discomfort Slade edged away and started to walk to his house.

'I'll be seeing you Hamilton. You better make these meetings awesome or I'll be forced to take the lead.'

Seeing his joking grin, she smiled and walked back

into the house, unsure of why her heart was thumping so fast.

Chapter 12

DANNI'S EVIL TWIN

Danni paced up and down her room, breathing heavily and full of nerves. Friday had finally arrived and in one hour she would be at Bouquet Reserve, starting something she was sure would change all their lives. In her hand were cue cards, which would prompt her in case she forgot how to conduct the meeting. She was wearing her midnight blue dress and more makeup than usual. It seemed like a strange idea to get so dolled up for a park at night but this was really important to Danni. She was also ashamed to admit it was to impress Crawford. Normally, guys never made her this self-conscious, but Crawford was something different. The element of Air and Fire combined, excited her.

Exhaling deeply, she checked her hair and walked downstairs. Danni watched her parents sipping coffee and chatting in the lounge room. She descended the stairs slowly and stood in front of them.

'Honey,' her mother gasped, 'where are you going?'

Danni smiled. She was nearly eighteen and her parents were used to her going out on the odd occasion but never looking like this.

'Just out with Reilly and Drew.'

Her father grabbed her hand.

'Make sure no boys look at you. And if they do, they get ten seconds tops.'

Danni laughed and squeezed her father's hand. She kissed them both and ran out to catch the evening bus to meet her two best friends.

Reilly and Drew were dressed up too, clearly trying to get into the spirit of the evening. Eyes wide, they both whistled at her dress.

'Danni, you haven't worn that since my brother's wedding,' Reilly gaped.

The bus drove up at that point and they quickly stepped in.

'Times are a changing Reilly,' Danni grinned. *Especially tonight…*

The bus rattled to Bouquet Reserve and Danni had to keep swallowing her nerves. She really was hoping for success. Dr. Yates was positive Hunter would show but Danni wasn't so sure. She just hoped she was right. Drew and Reilly were singing along with the top chart songs on the radio but Danni couldn't join in. She couldn't understand why they were so calm, but then again, they hadn't gone through what she had to in order to get here. What if they entered the Reserve and it was just the three of them? She pushed the negative thoughts out of her mind as the bus stopped just outside the Bouquet Reserve shelter. They hopped out and walked into the cold park. The weathered sign was still swinging and creaking but to Danni; it was the most beautiful thing she had ever seen.

They ventured into the dark place looking for the illuminated green pond. Danni knew the place better than the back of her hand and practically ran to it. Drew and Reilly fought to catch up.

Danni stopped to let them catch up and led them to the pond which shone brighter than usual. She positioned herself at the centre, identical to its image in her dreams, and made sure Reilly and Drew were on either side of her. She looked at her watch. It read 9:30. The later it began the less chance of being discovered by outsiders. She knew the rest of the members would arrive soon. Again, her nerves caught up with her. What if they couldn't find Bouquet Reserve? What if their parents were against it? Reilly rubbed her back, noticing her troubled face. Her heart leapt as she noticed Crawford walking towards her, wearing navy jeans and a black jumper. She walked shakily over to him, noticing Reilly and Drew nudging one another.

They know. They know how I feel about him.

Crawford hugged Danni and she nearly melted in his warm embrace. He released her and stepped back, studying her.

'You look amazing Gemini.'

Danni blushed. 'Thank you and thanks for coming, please sit.'

She led him over to the pond and introduced him to Reilly and Drew, all the while ignoring Reilly's looks of *he's cute!*

Soon after came Parry and Graham, arms linked and gabbing about the best hair products. Drew flushed and leapt up to offer Parry a spot next to him but she sat on the opposite side, telling Graham about her conditioner. Reilly's cousin Hannah ran in and sat near her. She seemed nervous but Reilly patted her arm and they began to chat about family dramas. Danni noticed that Crawford kept sneaking glances at her and she couldn't contain her excitement. It would be wonderful if he felt the same way about her but how could she be sure? It was nearing ten and still five members were missing. After another ten minutes of darting her eyes at the entrance, she noticed Ronan walk in with Ambrite slowly following, glaring after him.

Great. He's already insulted her with his weird female-hating thing.

She knew there would be clashes in the group but this might get disastrous. There were just so many different personalities being brought together. Reilly stopped talking to Hannah and glared at Ambrite. Ambrite noticed and glared right back, acknowledging their unspoken hatred. Danni sighed inwardly, hoping they wouldn't fight. Ronan barely noticed Danni or anybody and sat by himself near the pond.

Ok, this is going to take some time.

She walked to the centre, nearly ready to begin, and then saw Brodie and Slade walk in with the same girl she saw at their place days before, wearing a silky silver dress and pouting. She didn't understand why this girl was here. There were only to be twelve members but she decided to deal with her later if Hunter didn't show. Meanwhile everybody was eyeing Brodie and Slade. They looked even more angelic at night and she noticed even Ronan couldn't keep his eyes off the gorgeous Libran.

Parry turned to Graham. 'I'm prettier right?'

Graham nodded, patting her arm.

The siblings waved to Danni and she couldn't help but notice Slade's eyes on her dress. She felt hot and turned around to notice the silvery girl walking over to her.

'Hi!' the girl called. 'I'm Charlotte Orion and I was wondering if I could join your group? Brodie made it sound so interesting. I'm her friend from cheerleading practice.'

Danni stared at her in disbelief.

'Well… Charlotte, it's nice to meet you but there can only be one member of each sign in our group, what sign are you? You might replace the guy missing tonight.'

Charlotte smirked. 'I'm a Gemini and I reckon I can

replace you perfectly.'

Danni nearly smiled until she noticed, from the fact that Charlotte was grinning, that she was also serious. She was nervous but also more concerned about her group than some spoilt girl, so she hardened her gaze.

'Well, nobody will be replacing me Charlotte, so please leave and find another group to join.'

Danni blinked in surprise at her unexpected assertiveness. She had never had this much courage to stand up to someone before. In an instant Charlotte's sweet face turned into a snarling scowl. Her lips were pursed in fury and her eyes flashed with contempt.

'Listen!' she spat angrily. 'Do you know who I am? The Orion family are incredibly important to this town and nobody, not even loser brats like you, says no to me.'

Danni took a step back to prevent a saliva shower and suddenly realized who Charlotte really was. She was the dark side of the Gemini that Danni had never possessed. She was the other half of Danni – the cold, double-faced one. Danni couldn't allow her 'evil twin' to ruin everything she worked so hard for. She took a step forward so that they were almost touching faces and could see Charlotte's foundation dripping off her face from angry sweat.

'Well Charlotte, I would like you to meet the first person to say no to you! Now please leave, I'm busy.'

A look of surprise swept across Charlotte's face and

then in an instant it vanished in defeat.

'Ok freak! But this isn't over; you'll get what's coming to you...'

With that, she turned on her heels and stormed out of Bouquet Reserve.

Despite not having heard their private disagreement, all the other members stared after the huffing fireball and Danni inhaled deeply with a quick shiver.

This was far from over...

Chapter 13

THE FIRST MEETING

Danni finally felt ready to start, so she made her way over to the pond. Brodie leapt up and cornered her with a genuine look of concern.

'Sorry about Charlotte; she had nothing to do on a Friday night and insisted on joining me. She can be a bit….'

'Bitchy?'

Brodie smiled. 'I was going to say 'loud' but yeah, that just about covers it.'

Danni frowned and looked behind her.

'She said this wasn't the end for tormenting me but I can handle her.'

'Good. I hope she leaves you alone, she is just angry because she hates the fact you're in the spotlight and not her. If anyone can handle her, it's you Danni. I mean you got this whole thing started… so let's get started.'

Danni giggled. 'Finally someone is making sense.'

She walked over to the centre of the pond and nearly jumped at how accurate the whole setting looked compared to her dreams. There sat the ten members, not shadows anymore but visible figures, assisting her in the mysterious quest of astrology. She cleared her throat and they all stopped talking and looked up at her.

'Well…' Danni began, her voice shaky. 'Well tonight we commence the first of many meetings concerning the Zodiac. It has always been a passion of…..' Danni trailed off as she noticed a familiar figure skulking up the path. The group turned their heads, following her gaze. When the light caught his face, Danni's heart leapt. Hunter. She didn't have to say anything and neither did he. He simply nodded at her and sat next to Graham and Ronan. She smiled at him, but then quickly turned to the group again.

'As I was saying, it has always been a passion of mine to explore the depths of astrology.'

Danni felt better now that Hunter had arrived and realised she didn't need her cue cards. Her legs stopped shaking and adrenaline took over.

'But this group isn't just for me. It is for all of us to discover more about ourselves and each other, so let's first go around the circle and say our name with our sign. I will start. I'm Danni and a Gemini.'

She nodded at Reilly on her right.

'I'm Reilly and a Sagittarius.'

Hannah stood shyly, her voice squeaking. 'I'm Hannah and a Cancer.'

'I'm Slade and an Aquarius.'

'I'm Brodie and a Libra.'

Danni smiled as each of the members were acknowledging one another. She felt just like a teacher with a host of ready pupils.

Parry leapt up and struck a very dramatic pose.

'Parry Angelica Mason and a cute Virgo!'

The others laughed while Danni and Reilly rolled their eyes. Drew was salivating.

Graham performed the same kind of introduction, flipping his wavy hair back. 'Graham and a Scorpio.'

Ronan and Hunter looked speechless.

Hunter barely stood and mumbled. 'Hunter, Aries.'

Ronan stood confidently, looking as if he had better places to be.

'I'm Ronan and a Capricorn.'

Ambrite glared at him. 'I'm Ambrite. Not Amber! I'm a Taurus, don't forget that!'

The group looked intimidated, even Hunter.

Crawford jumped up happily. 'I'm Crawford and a Leo.'

Danni felt her mouth dry up at the smile he cast her way.

Finally Drew stood up and pulled a sexy face which was reserved for Parry only. 'Drew...I'm Drew Jaxter and I am a Pisces. Very romantic,' he added.

Danni and Reilly pulled faces. Parry didn't appear to take any notice while Graham began braiding her hair.

Danni took the lead once more.

'First of all I would like to thank Crawford over here.' She pointed to him and felt her cheeks redden.

'His father is caretaker of Bouquet Reserve, so Crawford helps out part time and has been generous enough to allow us to use this place every week.'

Crawford smiled around at the group. Danni stepped closer to the pond so that her face was illuminated once more.

'Basically, this meeting is to introduce everyone to one another and the idea of the group. I would like you all to give a solemn promise that you won't tell anybody about this group. It is our secret to be kept at all cost. I have quite a risky idea that will keep us bound together but I want to run it by you all first.'

Danni glanced at Ambrite's tattoo showing on her ankle and grinned.

'If you will all look at Ambrite's ankle, I think you will see what I mean.'

The group turned to her leg and noticed the Taurus symbol shaped like a circle with horns, small but permanent. Hannah shrieked, understanding Danni's idea first and slowly the others followed, all talking at once.

'So what do you say guys? You up for it?' Danni asked.

Reilly and Drew stood up on either side of her.

'We're in Dan!' Reilly declared.

'Yeah, if you guys want to commit to something then get the tattoo.' Drew added fiercely.

Danni smiled at them. 'I can understand there will be reservations but I really want you guys to know how serious this is and how powerful we can all be if we are marked as the twelve signs of the zodiac.'

Graham stood up and boasted. 'At Maltin's tanning salon there is a guy named Steve who does tattoos for only fifty bucks! I can get you guys a discount if you're willing.'

Danni beamed at him. 'Thanks Graham, that sounds awesome. If you want to show your devotion to the group I suggest you go there before next Friday.'

Most of the group, Danni was happy to note, didn't seem too fussed about getting a tattoo but Hannah looked pale. Danni was sure Reilly could talk her into it!

'Ok well, that's that guys! Be here next week and hopefully you will be marked by your sign. Don't worry, there is no time limit, but I would like it done.'

The group started to leave when Danni was startled to see Hunter put up his hand.

'Yes Hunter?'

He stood up and the group turned to look at this strange, dark figure.

'Umm' he muttered. 'Shouldn't we have like a…code name?'

Danni looked at him in disbelief. Hunter was actually contributing to her group? Suddenly, Danni was really glad she never gave up on him.

'I guess you're right. I never thought of that. Okay, you all have heard Hunter, you can make it up and tell us next week.'

Danni couldn't wait to tell Dr. Yates. She knew she would be proud of him for getting involved. Hunter grunted in response but she could tell he was already brain-storming away. The group walked off waving goodbye except Reilly, Drew, Crawford and Slade.

'We'll wait by the bus stop for you Dan,' Reilly said and dragged Drew off with her.

Slade walked up to her and Crawford did the same. Danni didn't know what to think. No boys had ever paid attention to her and now two of the most attractive ones were standing next to her.

'Good meeting Dan,' Slade mumbled clearly, not wanting Crawford there.

'Yeah, it's going to be awesome,' Crawford added uncomfortably.

Danni felt the most awkward of all. Sure Slade was funny and sweet, not to mention gorgeous, but he just wasn't Crawford. Nobody could be Crawford. From the moment she dreamt of him holding her hand, she was smitten.

'Thanks guys... I should go...my parents will be worried.'

She walked away before they could say anything

but she could feel their eyes on her back. It sent a shiver down her spine in the best way possible.

That night, as Danni slept soundly, she dreamt of Bouquet Reserve's pond and there stood all her members around her, waiting for their destiny!

Chapter 14
PAIN FOR LOYALTY

The next morning, Danni received calls from Reilly and Drew telling her how awesome the group was going to be. They also asked if she wanted to come down to Maltin's and get the tattoos together.

'Ok we will meet you there in five,' Reilly squealed.

Danni threw on her faded jeans and grey sweatshirt, knowing full well that her parents would never allow her to get an extra ear piercing let alone a tattoo.

Suddenly, she found herself cornered by them in the kitchen.

'So honey, where did you go last night?' her father asked suspiciously.

Danni knew she couldn't hide this from them forever but it was too soon for her dream to be stopped now. How was she going to get out of this one?

'We just hung out at Reilly's watching movies and stuff, you know, the usual?' Her father beamed but her mother didn't seem convinced.

'In that fancy dress you wore? Was there anyone else there dear?'

Danni knew her mother thought there was so much more going on than what she was telling her.

'No…it was just us three. We still hadn't seen *American Pie* so we were catching up on our teen flicks.'

'Alright well I hope that's all…'

'It is,' Danni murmured and walked out of the house.

***

As they walked to Maltin's, Drew was speaking really quickly, Reilly was swallowing hard and Danni repeatedly inhaled and exhaled. They had never been fond of needles, especially in Primary School when they got their shots and cried for a good hour. Now they were struggling not to hold hands the way they did when they were young.

'You know Danni, I never thought I would hate you but I do,' cried Drew.

Danni smiled weakly and patted his arm.

'Think of the group Drew.'

Drew hugged himself tight.

'I will not think of the group! I will think of my poor ankle!'

Reilly just whimpered and walked faster.

Finally Maltin's loomed in sight and they took one deep breath, before stepping into the building. Reilly and Drew, who had never been in Maltin's, stared at the whitewashed walls and bright colours. Danni marched up to the counter where Graham was sipping a chocolate milkshake and wearing a bright yellow top. She stared at him and then at the drink, remembering how he hated it when they first met.

Graham caught her eye and frowned.

'What? They get addictive!'

She grinned and then the smile quickly disappeared as she remembered why they were there.

'Umm…we're here for our tattoo.'

She wasn't quite eighteen yet although most of the members were, some a bit older, but Graham had promised, due to it being a family business, that nobody would know or care.

Graham flipped through the orange appointment book and pressed his finger on a page.

'Ok Reilly, Drew and you Danni babe are ready to go down the hall. It is the last door on the right.'

She turned to go but Graham ran around the counter and stood in her way.

'Almost forgot, check mine out.'

He pulled the leg of his skinny jeans up and revealed the curvy mark of the Scorpio with the arrow on the end, representing the sting on his left ankle.

'Parry got hers done with me too.'

Danni swallowed loudly. 'Does it…umm…hurt?'

Graham put his arm around her and she could swear he was wearing the exact same perfume her mother wore.

'It only hurts if you let it hurt. Now go!'

He pushed her towards Reilly and Drew.

Danni was not comforted by that at all.

'Ok guys, we're in now and apparently it's the last door on the right.'

Not caring anymore, they held hands and shook as they walked down the long hallway. When they entered the room, they gasped simultaneously at the man with the tattoo gun. He was literally covered in tattoos of all different snakes. They slithered and squirmed around his biceps and down to his legs, almost hissing in life-likeness. He stood up and walked behind them, shutting the door while ignoring their shocked faces. Clearly he was used to this.

Finally, after setting up his table, he looked up at them with wide eyes.

'Ready to have your skin destroyed?'

Reilly looked as though she was about to scream and Danni could swear she saw a single tear slide down Drew's cheek. The man named Steve stared at them seriously for a moment and then burst out laughing.

'God gets them every time!'

Reilly and Danni stared, still frightened and Drew went bright red. Steve heartily slapped Drew on the back.

'Just kidding guys. Ok who is first and what do we want?'

'We would all like our star sign on our ankles,' Danni said bravely.

Steve frowned at them.

'My God, you are like the sixth person to ask for exactly the same thing. What is going on here?'

Danni ignored his question.

'I would like to go first please. I'll take the Gemini symbol.'

Although terrified, she wanted to prove to her friends how much group dedication meant to her. Reilly and Drew opened their eyes wide at her and Steve raised his eyebrows.

'What, are you the leader of the group? Ok girlie, hop up on this chair and take the squishy ball to squeeze if it hurts too much.'

Danni gulped at this and her two friends looked ready to bolt. He gave her a squishy ball with a smiley face. *This is supposed to be comforting?*

Reilly finally spoke with a squeaky voice.

'Do you mind if we wait outside Dan? We're about to faint.'

Danni nodded and Steve laughed.

'Go on guys, you're next though.'

They hurried out of the room and he pulled out a plastic folder. He flipped through the pages and then showed her a picture of the Roman numeral for two, also known as the Gemini symbol. She nodded again, unable to speak. He then pulled up the leg of her pants and turned on the gun which buzzed loudly. She squeezed the ball instantly and he pressed the print on her leg, then lowered the gun on it and began tracing. The pain was excruciating and Danni nearly screamed for him to stop but then after a while she relaxed and allowed it to numb her skin. Every now and then she would glance down and marvel at the beautiful symbol appearing on her ankle. Steve kept whistling, humming ACDC tunes and laughing at her facial expressions. After another fifteen minutes he turned the gun off and applied some soothing moisturizing cream. Danni unclenched her joints and enjoyed the cool substance on her stinging leg.

'So what do you think girlie?' Steve asked, pulling her leg up and inspecting it.

Danni stared at it and truly felt like a Gemini. She laughed inwardly at how so many people got their lovers' names marked on their skin and then broke up. At least her star sign would never change.

'It rocks Steve; thanks heaps. I'll call in the others.'

Steve chuckled. 'I better call emergency services because one of them will pass out…'

Walking home was difficult as all three friends' ankles were sore. Reilly admitted that she cried and Drew didn't speak. He was clearly ashamed of his reactions to it. Still, every now and then they would pull up their pants and check it out.

'It looks so cool…' Danni clapped.

She also loved Reilly's arrow of wisdom and Drew's fishy lines of serenity.

'Yeah it does Dan, but you better hope this group lasts or I will kill you…' Reilly warned.

'Great. Drew hates me and you might kill me. What did I do to deserve my two wonderful friends?'

*

Feeling brighter, Danni passed Bouquet Reserve on her way home, hoping to spot Crawford there but to her dismay it was empty. She sat in her usual spot, in front of the pond, and allowed the crisp wind to encircle her arms. Danni closed her eyes and felt so peaceful that she drifted off to sleep for a while and when she awoke, she was lying on the ground and a dark man wearing a top hat was bent over and staring at her.

'Nice sleep?' he chuckled.

She blushed, scrambled up and brushed the dirt from her clothes.

'I really shouldn't talk to strangers. '

Danni began to walk away in a hurry.

'Hmmm, like how you shouldn't talk to people you've only dreamt of?' he called after her.

Danni spun around suddenly.

'How do you know about that?'

He grinned and adjusted his top hat. The dark man was wearing a full-length leather coat and looked remarkably like Morpheus from *The Matrix*. He stood there, just staring at her, boring into every thought and idea she had ever imagined. Danni couldn't explain what she felt but it seemed this man had the astrological answers she had been seeking.

'Oh, you'll find out in due course. In the meantime, you should continue your group and teach them all they need to know. I'll return when the time is right.'

He bowed and removed his hat and then turned to walk away.

'Wait!'

He faced her, still grinning.

'What is your name?' How do you know about my group and why will you return?'

The man looked thoughtful, as if trying to figure out the same things she wanted to know.

'I can only answer one of those questions. My name is Garth.'

Then without letting her interrogate further he swept off, out of the Reserve, his leather jacket flailing in the wind. Danni ran after him but when she emerged out of the park, he was gone.

Chapter 15

THREATS FROM A GEMINI

When Danni awoke the next morning with a throbbing headache, she found herself on the floor as usual. She had a sudden urge to remember her dream the night before. After all the members were gathered she had just gone back to dreaming about Crawford and other crazy things but now that she thought about it, it was another psychic one. The team were standing around the pond, chattering and laughing while showing off their fresh tattoos and Danni was staring at an animated figure jumping around quite strangely. She stepped forward to take a closer look and noticed it was Garth, the mysterious dark man who told her he would return when the time was right. He would not take his eyes off Danni, trying to ensure he had her full attention. Garth ran over to the pond and pointed to it several times with an urgent look on his face and then nodded his head furiously at Danni. She nodded back just to calm him down and then watched as he jumped in the air pointing at the sky. He kept repeating the pattern. First point at the pond, then point at the sky. Danni now understood why she had a headache when she woke up. He had made her insanely dizzy with his manic message. What was he trying to tell her? What was it about the pond in Bouquet Reserve that coincided with the sky?

She rubbed her sore head and checked the time. It was 10:30. She was late for her early session with Dr. Yates! Danni tore down the stairs, ignoring Colin's taunts of 'Crazy Danni, Crazy Danni' and ran into the kitchen, opening the cupboard to get some cereal.

Her dad walked into the room and just chuckled.

'Late again sweetheart?'

Danni munched furiously and glared at him, her cheeks bulging with muesli and milk.

'Ok, ok,' her dad said putting his hands up. 'I'll wait in the car for you.'

After throwing on some track pants and a hooded jumper she ran outside off for another therapy session. Danni had made her appointment early so that she could enjoy the rest of the day checking out Bouquet Reserve to decode her dream about Garth.

Dr. Yates seemed thrilled to see her.

'Ah Danni, good to see you again dear! Come, tell me all about your group!'

Danni sat in her usual chair and noticed Dr. Yates wasn't using her clipboard this time. It was almost as if this was a casual conversation between friends. Danni liked the idea of that.

'Well, it finally had its first meeting and was so successful. You were right, it all worked out in the end. And guess who came along? Hunter! It was amazing but he seemed to really enjoy it and I think he'll come back!'

Danni spoke so excitedly and Dr. Yates beamed at her.

'Well dear, I would be surprised about Hunter but he came to see me yesterday and told me all about it. He wants to come back and apparently you've let him decide a name for the group?'

Danni opened her eyes wide in disbelief. She couldn't believe Hunter had told Dr. Yates about the group and wanted to join permanently.

'Umm…yeah I let him pick the name, so when we get together again on Friday he is going to present it. I hope it's a good one because I would hate to say no to him.'

Dr. Yates chuckled. 'Best to give Hunter more confidence by praising the name he gives you.'

Danni nodded. 'I will, but I really want to help him with his past; until he gets more confidence and opens up he'll be known as the grump of the group!'

Dr. Yates bit her lip, frowning.

'Give it time dear and eventually he'll tell you why he is the way he is. I can't tell you and don't want to anyway because if Hunter does it himself it will be an enormous breakthrough for him.'

Danni's heart filled with determination. She wanted to be the one to help Hunter with his breakthrough and she would be the one to achieve it!

***

After walking around Bouquet Reserve one last time to see if Garth was around, she decided to give up and let him come back to her. Also she was hoping Crawford was working but the Reserve stayed empty. Danni truly loved this place now. She loved what it meant to her. She loved its peaceful scenery and its mystery most of all. Danni sat down at the pond where she led the meetings and stared into the water. Its weeds and litter made it look trashy but to her it was a thing of beauty. It was her pond. There was nothing in the water that made it look inconspicuous but then again it only glowed at night. Danni was determined to find out why it only lit up as soon as the sun fell. She stood up and walked out of the pond, almost certain that it glittered green for a second as she walked away.

That night, as Danni tackled her history assignment on Greek philosophers, her phone started beeping and she noticed a message from an unknown number.

It read; *'you won't get away with this, your little fan club is going down.'*

Danni growled in frustration. Charlotte!

'How did she get my number?'

She closed her folders and textbooks, raced past her

brother who was making mud pies in the kitchen and ran to her neighbour's house, banging loudly on the Draymans' door. Mrs. Drayman answered, wearing a short apron and apparently nothing else. She looked at Danni as though she was a filthy rat.

'Hey Danni, is there a reason why my door has to be knocked over?'

Danni glared impatiently. 'Is Brodie here?'

Mrs. Drayman sighed and turned to the hallway.

'Brodie! Danni's here.'

Mrs. Drayman turned back to Danni smiling.

'Well I'm outta here but when you see your father tell him I say hi, won't you?'

Danni stared after her fuming. Seconds later, Brodie appeared at the door in her full cheerleading outfit and her hair in pigtails.

'Wow' Danni said. 'You really are the stereotype of American teenage girls.'

Brodie giggled and stepped outside.

'So what's up Dan?'

Danni pulled out her mobile and showed her. Immediately Brodie's face darkened and she looked deep in thought.

After a few moments of silence she spoke.

'You know I remember her going through my phone at cheerleading practice this morning but I thought nothing of it. I'm so sorry Danni; I hope she leaves you alone.'

'Well so do I! I have worked too hard on this and I really want it to succeed. Charlotte will just have to learn that she can't always have her way.'

Brodie frowned. 'If only it were that easy! But she is used to having her way all the time. She reminds me of some of my friends in L.A. Now that you've rejected her, she may try to make your life a living hell.'

Danni grinned. 'I know it's not over with Charlotte, but I am not giving up now.'

'Cool, I can't wait until the next meeting. Slade just won't stop talking about it.'

Danni blushed as she recalled their last awkward moment together.

'Well I'm gonna go back indoors. Seeya Brodie, oh and sorry about your door!'

Chapter 16

A MYSTICAL WORLD MORE POWERFUL THAN REALITY

Danni could barely sit still. The week had passed slowly and tonight, being Friday, meant that another meeting was in order.

'Calm down girl!' Reilly urged.

Danni grinned stupidly at her.

'You do realise that tonight there is another meeting? A meeting that *I* organised, me! Since when have I started organising anything?'

Drew laughed. 'The last thing you organised was that trip to the Astronomy Museum and we all know how much fun that was!'

Danni turned to Drew with a sad look on her face.

'I thought you enjoyed it.'

Drew's smile faded and he cuddled Danni.

'Oh Dan….no.'

Reilly cracked up and shoved them both, causing Danni to wobble and Drew to fall out of his chair. The three of them burst out laughing.

Hearing their teacher clear his throat quite loudly,

they looked up.

'Ah if you three are done socialising can we get back to the Great Depression? No one got to socialise like you monkeys back in that time!'

'Yes sir,' the three chorused in unison. Drew humbly sat back in his chair.

Mr. Tenesson, the History teacher, always got very animated about his topics. He believed that if the people during a certain era missed out on fun, so should his students. Everybody was equal but not in a positive way.

Danni picked up her pencil and chewed on the end, dreaming about that night when the whole group would be reunited once more and she would lead them into a mystical world more powerful than reality. She was also looking forward to hearing Hunter's suggestion about the group name and of course to be in the presence of Crawford. What adventures would come Danni's way that night? She was hoping all of them didn't involve Charlotte and her rejection issues.

After Danni had walked Reilly and Drew home, she nearly skipped all the way to the front door, not being able to silence the excitement in her heart. She opened the door and left her shoes in the hall, something her mother hated, but Danni was too thrilled to care. As Danni entered the kitchen to grab a snack, she noticed her mother sitting at the table with her head in her hands. Danni sidled over to her and touched her arm.

'Mum, are you okay?'

Mrs. Hamilton nearly jumped out of her chair and put her hand on her chest, panting heavily.

'Oh it's you; how are you sweetie? I didn't hear you come in.'

She got up, opened the fridge, stared at the ice box and then closed it, appearing confused. Danni narrowed her eyebrows and sat in the chair her mother was sitting in. It was still warm.

'She must have been here for ages,' Danni thought.

'Mum, what is going on? Are you alright?'

Danni's mother peered out the window, made an angry face and then turned back to her daughter.

'I'm fine honey; I don't know what you're talking about.'

Danni looked at the window and then it hit her.

'Mum, this wouldn't have anything to do with Mrs. Drayman from next door, would it?'

As soon as Danni spoke, her mother's face went black and before Danni could recite the alphabet, she was being screamed at.

'You know, that woman thinks she can move next door and take my husband? I won't have it! No, no, she will not get anything from him! Wearing her short dresses and low cut tops! What a filthy, little….'

Danni stared at her mother, as she called Mrs. Drayman every name under the sun. She had never seen her this angry before.

When Mrs. Hamilton had finished pouring her anger out, Danni stood up and hugged her.

'Mum, Dad loves you, don't worry about Mrs. Flirt-A-Lot; he won't give her anything and you are the one that he wants.'

Her mother's facial expression softened and she hugged her daughter tightly.

'I know sweetie; where would I be without you? But at the moment I would advise you not to speak to those two children of hers; it will only fuel her fire.'

Danni stared at her in shock.

'But Slade and Brodie are part of the group!'

As soon as Danni said that she regretted it. Her mother looked at her suspiciously.

'What group?'

'Umm…the study group I wanted to start next week! We are all learning the same thing so it would be good to have them there.'

Her mother still didn't look convinced but gave in.

'Well, a study group is fine, but that is it! As long as it's just for now, okay sweetie?'

'Sure mum,' Danni complied.

Her mother walked to the fridge and opened it again. This time she took out some minced meat and set in on the cutting board.

'So are you going out with Reilly and Drew again

tonight?'

Danni looked up at her mother and could swear she saw a hint of disbelief in her face.

'Umm yeah, we are just going to chill, maybe see a movie.'

Danni's mother smiled.

'Honey, have there been any boys, other than Drew in your life lately?' Danni blushed and saw her mother's grin grow wider.

'Umm well, there is one guy I like but I don't think anything will come of it.'

Even as Danni said this, she felt a tug at her heart and a longing for Crawford she never knew she possessed.

Mrs. Hamilton rubbed Danni's shoulders.

'Any boy who can't see how perfect you are isn't worth longing for.'

Danni hugged her mum tightly. She then left the kitchen and walked up the stairs into her astrological bedroom. She stared at her favourite poster. The Wheel of the Zodiac. Each symbol gleamed but the one that shone the most was the twins. Gemini. What would happen to her that night? She shook her head. It was time to find out!

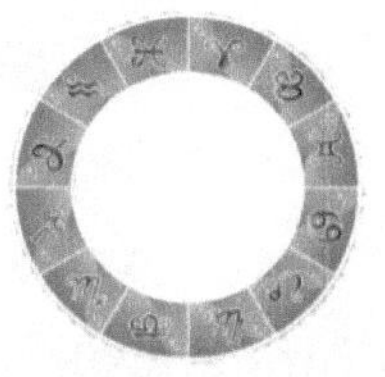

Chapter 17

THE ASTRO A TEAM

Danni shivered with excitement as she watched the usual eleven members circle around her and sit cross-legged by the pond. Their eyes gleamed as the water began to shine with neon brightness, eerie yet enchanting.

She noticed that Ronan, Hannah and Parry were glaring at her in a way that made her want to run for the hills. It was then that she realised they were cradling their ankles.

Danni smiled. 'So how did the tattoos go guys?'

Hannah rubbed her leg furiously. 'Not funny Danni, this killed!'

Reilly stood up and walked over to her cousin, rubbing her shoulders.

'Dan explained what it would take to be serious about this group; you just have to show your commitment.'

Danni winked at Reilly and stood up, ready to begin the meeting.

'So everyone, firstly, I want to thank you for making it to the second meeting of the zodiac group and also for getting the tattoos. I realise it was a bit of a big favour to ask.'

'You got that right,' muttered Ronan.

Danni threw him a look. 'It was a bit of a big favour to ask but it proved your commitment like Reilly said. So again, thank you. Now before we go on I must ask Hunter if he could present us with the name he thought of for the group.'

Danni felt her insides drop as Hunter stood up and brushed his shaggy mane off his face. She was hoping he chose a good enough name for the group so that she wouldn't have to say it was bad and make him want to leave. She could hear Dr. Yates's voice in her head telling her to praise it no matter what it was.

He walked over to where Danni stood nervously and cleared his throat.

'Umm…yeah I got asked to think up of a name of the group and at first I couldn't think of anything but then one night I was lying in bed and it kinda came to me.'

Danni swallowed repeatedly, trying to moisten her dry throat.

'The Astro A Team!' Hunter said proudly and he smiled for the first time.

Drew and Reilly burst out laughing and Danni's heart sank. It sounded like a basketball team but she remembered Dr. Yates's words and smiled weakly back at Hunter.

'Well done Hunter! That is an awesome name you thought of so…Astro A Team it is!'

Hunter nodded and actually looked quite happy. Danni sighed inwardly and turned back to the rest of the group.

'Well, that's our group name guys, so use it if you need to refer to it. Keep in mind this group is confidential.'

The rest of the group nodded except Drew and Reilly who were chuckling into each other. Hunter's face grew black and he looked ready to kill.

'Umm guys…what are you both laughing at?' Danni enquired.

The pair straightened up and stopped grinning as they caught Hunter's expression. Reilly wiped a tear from her eye and looked at Danni.

'Well, it's just that if you shorten the name it sounds like A.A. and Drew and I were laughing because that stands for…'

'Yes we all know what that stands for Reilly!' Danni cut her off quickly, fearing for Hunter herself, who was now actually turning red.

"Hmmm? The Astro A Team? Well I suppose you're all going to end up as sad, sorry alcoholic losers anyway," said a voice from behind a tree.

Danni spun around and to her extreme irritation saw Charlotte step out of the darkness and walk right over to them. Her silvery blonde hair was blowing back in the wind and she threw Danni a wicked grin.

'What do you want now Charlotte? Clearly the word no doesn't exist in your dictionary.'

She walked over to her while the rest of the group stared fascinated. Charlotte appeared startled but continued to place her hands on her hips and maintain her domineering manner.

'I told you before Hamilton! I don't get said no to and until you realise that, I'm not leaving! I don't care what your snotty friends think!'

She turned quickly to glare at the pack, leering at her, and smirked when she saw them look away in fright. Even Hunter didn't want to face this demon!

But Danni remained stable. She had worked too hard on this. This wasn't even about astrology anymore to her. It was about friendship and working together. For the first time in her life, she was actually determined to put away her fears and attempt to create a new world for herself and nobody, not even the 'teen queen', would stop her!

'So what's it going to take then Charlotte? Should I get down on my hands and knees and beg you to join even though that would mean there is an uneven number in the group?'

Charlotte turned her nose up in disgust, as though she was just asked to join the circus.

'Join?' she laughed bitterly. 'I may have wanted to

join at first, just to see what all the fuss was about, but then you made it something much more! Now I'm going to show you what happens when you deny an Orion!'

Danni laughed, even though she was miserable inside. Why couldn't she just have this one? Why couldn't her plans ever go right?

'So what is this infamous plan Charlie? I can call you that right?'

Reilly and Drew stood up and edged closer to Danni until they were by her side. She felt their warmth and relaxed a bit more.

Charlotte appeared bored, examining her fingernails and smoothing down her dress. Finally she looked up at Danni and just laughed. Danni shivered.

'You will just have to wait and see what I have in store for you and your little group. As if they are going to stick around for you anyway. They are just here out of curiosity and once they see what a pathetic leader you are…they're outta here!'

Danni kept her gaze level and tried to stay calm. She knew Charlotte was just trying to wear her down but she was also scared that her group might leave after they got a taste of the group. Charlotte, seeing that she struck a nerve, giggled.

'Awww poor baby, frightened that she may be ditched by her new friends? This is probably the most human contact you've ever had. I bet you've never even had a boyfriend!'

Danni, hurt by that comment, glanced quickly at Crawford who shrugged. Charlotte, noticing Danni's rapid look, widened her eyes. She strutted over to where Crawford was sitting and with fluttering eyelashes, she purred.

'Don't worry, that girl isn't half of what I am. If you want to know all of me here's my number.'

She quickly scribbled out her number and passed it to Crawford. Then she strolled past Danni and whispered in her ear, 'the hurting has already begun.' The group watched her saunter off, her pale dress swishing in the wind. Danni shivered in contempt and fear.

Reilly and Drew immediately hugged Danni.

'Don't worry about that bitch!' Reilly snarled.

Danni pushed them away gently and sat down, head in her hands.

'It doesn't matter anymore. That girl is gonna do whatever it takes to make my life miserable and there is nothing I can do about it.'

Parry jumped up suddenly and the boys focused on Danni swerved to look at her.

'Wrong! There is something you can do about it,' she urged. 'You have all eleven of us to back you up and the moment she tries something, just let us know and we will take her down!'

'She's just threatened by another plastic doll,'

murmured Ambrite.

Danni was shocked to see Hunter chuckle at the comment.

Parry glared at Ambrite and then stood with her hands on her hips, a dominant gaze on her face.

'I'm serious! Who is going to help Danni with me?'

Danni looked up to see Reilly, Drew, Parry, Slade, Brodie, Ambrite and Crawford throw their hands in the air.

Graham shrugged, 'I'm just here for Parry.'

Ronan leaned over to Hunter and exclaimed a little too loudly 'probably for a different reason though.'

Parry nudged Graham hard in the ribs and he cried out with pain, slowly lifting his arm in defeat.

'Well what about the rest of you?'

Hannah looked too scared to do anything, so she quickly put up her hand.

Ronan just snorted. 'I barely know Danni. Why should I give her my word that I'll protect her at any cost? Besides at least the other girl has spunk.'

Ambrite stood up, her face like thunder.

'Listen here girl hater! You're like the opposite of me and it makes me sick! You are so lucky to have a friend like Danni and be a part of this group, so stick that freaking hand in the air or I'll make you!'

Every member in the group cowered beneath her fiery gaze and Ronan just stared at her in shock. With absolutely no self-control, his hand rose in the air.

Hunter's hand shot up along with Ronan's and it was refreshing for Danni to see him scared for once.

Parry nodded at the group with self-assurance.

'Good. Now that we have established loyalty to the group, how about getting to business?'

Chapter 18
CONFLICT BETWEEN PARENTS

Danni walked along the streets of J-Corner on her way to school. She felt that something was different.

She was whistling.

She was actually whistling.

Drew and Reilly were holding each other and pretending to shiver.

'What's going on Drew? I'm scared. So, so scared…'

'It's ok Reilly. It's going to be ok. I'm here for you.'

Danni stopped humming and turned to look at her two idiotic friends, raising her eyebrows.

'Ok, you two die right now.'

They both laughed and ran up to her, grabbing an arm each.

'Don't worry Dan, we're just kidding,' Reilly reassured.

'Yeah' Drew added. 'We're just not used to seeing you this happy. I mean, we have seen you happy but not *this* happy.'

'Get used to it guys! As long as my Alcoholics Anonymous group is up and running then I can't complain.'

She then cracked up at her own joke.

Reilly grabbed Drew again. 'I'm scared!'

Drew laughed and then grew serious. 'We are actually keeping that name?'

Danni smiled. 'Drew… this is the only way Hunter can feel comfortable around us. Besides, it's kinda growing on me.'

Reilly clicked her tongue. 'The guy is a ticking time bomb waiting to explode! How can we trust him?'

Reaching J-Corner High, the pair trudged off to their lockers, stowing their bags in the tiny metal compartments.

Danni picked up her books and out fell the card with Ronan the Capricorn's details on it. Examining it, she turned to her friends.

'We don't know if we can trust any of them but how do we know if we don't give them a chance?'

Drew sighed. 'The future Dr. Yates is in the house…'

Danni laughed. He wasn't wrong.

The bell rang in the distance somewhere and for the first time, Danni was pleasantly surprised to see the Drayman twins amble over to her. The pair looked like perfect dolls, their clothes fitting correctly and showing off the best of their features.

Drew as usual slobbered over Brodie's petite frame

and received the expected clock on the head by Reilly.

Danni blushed as she noticed Slade grinning at her while Brodie chattered animatedly.

'Wasn't that just an awesome session? Oh you did so well standing up to Charlotte. I don't really care for her but yah know, she is one of the team so I gotta practice with her.'

Reilly shrugged. 'I don't care what she is a part of. The girl is a snob and deserves a good kick up the ass.'

'Someone is starting to sound like Ambrite,' Drew chuckled but stopped when he saw Reilly's death glare.

While the group argued, Slade took Danni aside by dragging her by the arm. They stopped outside the library.

'Ok what is it?' Danni asked, rubbing her arm.

Slade shuffled his feet nervously and scratched his nose.

'This is gonna sound stupid but I have to tell you something.'

Danni immediately turned two shades of red and looked away, breathing deeply. *Oh my god he is going to ask me out! Wait, why do I care? I like Crawford.*

Turning back to Slade, she appeared calm, putting her hands on her hips. 'Yeah?'

'Well...I need to tell you that I...umm...err...my mum doesn't want us seeing each other anymore.'

He immediately shook his head in frustration and Danni was surprised to find her heart dropping a little.

A minute later, she cracked up laughing.

Slade stared at her as though she was doing a crazy, tribal dance.

'What's so funny?'

Danni slapped Slade heartily on the back. 'So does *my* mum too!'

'She doesn't want you seeing her?' His eyebrows rose.

'No! She doesn't want me seeing you guys either! I told her that we had a study group and that's it.'

Slade laughed at that and then stopped. His gaze became serious again. 'Wait…that's still not funny. Why is *your* mum against this?'

Danni's eyes widened. 'I think the question is why is your mum against this?'

This was clearly the part Slade didn't want to elaborate on.

'Well…she and my dad have kinda been going through a rough patch at the moment. He doesn't pay her enough attention and so she looks for it elsewhere…and she found it in…'

'My dad' Danni finished. 'Well, that's the same with my mum. She feels threatened by yours and now doesn't want us associating with anything related to her.'

Sighing heavily, Slade leant against the library wall.

'What are we going to do? I don't wanna lie to her but I don't exactly have the guts to tell my mum she's being ridiculous and needs to sort out stuff with dad.'

Danni nodded. 'I don't exactly have the guts to tell mum she is being stupid either. Dad loves her and she has no reason to feel threatened. But I gotta tell you straight Slade; your mum better back off coz she's causing tension in my family.'

'Yeah I know…she just has insecure issues. It's probably a mid-life crisis thing.'

They began walking back to the group who were still debating furiously whether Charlotte should be burnt at the stake or not. Danni turned to Slade before they joined them.

'Slade. This group has to stay united. Don't let your mum's issues affect that, God knows, I will not.'

He flashed his usual lopsided grin and she felt the familiar jelly eat at her knees.

'Nothing can stop me from being near you…'

***

Danni found herself whistling again as she walked to the health clinic for the usual session with Dr. Yates.

As hard as she tried, she couldn't stop thinking about what Slade had said to her: *Nothing can stop me from being near you.*

Shaking her head, she ran into the clinic and was somewhat surprised to find Hunter flipping through a newspaper in the waiting room. She bounded over to him, flopping into the seat near his.

'Hi! Whatchya doing?'

Hunter barely looked up at her, when he mumbled: 'Dr. Yates wanted me to wait while she gets a book for me.'

At this, Dr. Yates walked out in her usual bustle, grinning at the pair of them.

'Ah, Danni dear! Lovely to see you again.'

'Hi Dr. Yates, you too.'

Dr. Yates turned to Hunter and gave him rather a thick book.

'Don't read it all at once love; just what you want…the bits you find most useful.'

Hunter muttered his thanks and as he turned to leave, not saying goodbye to either of them, Danni noticed the book was titled *'How to Deal with Unfit Parents.'*

The mystery of Hunter's past was just starting to unfurl.

***

Back at home, Danni lay on her bed, recalling her session with Dr. Yates.

'I need to ask you just one question dear…' she heard Dr. Yates saying.

'Of course, ask away.'

'Why are you doing this astrology group? I mean, it sounds like a wonderful idea and I'd almost love to join if

I wasn't so old but why astrology and why now?'

Danni turned over on her bed and found herself gazing at the Wheel of the Zodiac, remembering Garth's words: *I'll return when the time is right.*

'I'm doing it because I'm meant to do it; it's my destiny. I don't really know why but I feel it's something I just have to do.'

Thinking over what she said to Dr. Yates, she knew that nothing she had ever said before was more real and truthful than that.

It wasn't enough for her to sit still and be quiet anymore. She had to stand up and speak out about her greatest passion. And for the first time in her life, she was doing just that.

The fact of the matter was that it wasn't just about her anymore either. She thought about Hunter and Ambrite and all the rest who were lost and looking for their way. This group could lead them on a good path to follow.

At that moment, her phone rang and instinctively Danni knew it was Reilly.

'Hey Reilly,' Danni chirped.

'Hey Dan! I wanted to ask you something that has been on my mind lately.'

'Shoot.'

'Well...correct me if I'm wrong but is there anything...erm...going on between you and Slade at all?'

'Slade?' Danni's voice squeaked higher than usual.

'Yeah…while Drew and I were talking to Brodie, you two seemed pretty cosy at the library chatting away like old friends. Aren't you in love with Crawford or something?'

Danni snorted. 'I'm not *in* love with Crawford; I just have a crush on him and Slade and I are just friends. The only reason we were talking in private was because both our mothers are feuding at the moment and we were discussing strategies.'

She slumped down on her bed sighing inwardly. She still couldn't get his words out of her head and how she felt whenever he gave her that lopsided grin. But Crawford was just as beautiful and intriguing. Danni found herself actually amused at the fact that for once in her life she was torn between two guys.

'Oh okay,' Reilly murmured, not sounding convinced. 'That was all I really wanted to know; keep it real dude.'

'Catch!' Danni said, hanging up her phone.

She was a little confused at why Reilly was suddenly so interested in her and Slade.

'Arrgghh!' she yelled, grabbing her pillow and flinging it at the wall. 'What am I feeling?'

Getting up from her bed, Danni strode over to her bookcase and started flipping through the pages of a zodiac guide just to get some ideas for her next meeting.

She didn't seem to realise her mother standing at the doorway with a horrified look on her face.

'Danielle Hamilton!' her mother shrieked.

Danni whipped her head up and threw the book out of her hands. 'What?'

Mrs. Hamilton just pointed at Danni's ankle and she felt her heart drop. Danni hadn't realised her track pants were riding up. Damn it! She had worked so hard to keep it a secret!

'Okay Mum I can explain.'

'You can explain?'

'Please just listen to me!'

'Wait till I tell your father!'

'There is a story if you just listen!'

'Grounded for a month sweetie...no wait...two months!'

'Mum, that is so unfair!'

The conversation streamed back and forth for at least twenty minutes until her mother sat down on her bed and nodded solemnly, waiting for an explanation. Danni sat down next to her and felt her mother's deep inhales and exhales, like a calm before an already raging storm.

'Ok Mum, ' Danni began using a soothing tone to keep things stable. 'There is so much going on in my life right now that you probably won't understand it all. I want to explain them to you but I am afraid that you will just double my sessions with Dr. Yates. You see...well you know…err…how I like…well love astrology, right?'

Her mother just nodded in an eerie, calm fashion.

'Well, I love it so much that my friends encouraged me to start an astrology group. We hold meetings every week and… I am their leader.'

By now Danni's mother was staring at her daughter, dumbstruck. Danni nearly laughed out loud. She sure wasn't known for being the leader of anything.

'The reason I started this group was because of the vivid dreams I've been having for the last couple of months. I know this sounds crazy but the dreams were telling me to start an astrology group and to lead them. They seemed to assure me that eventually all will be explained.'

More concerned staring.

'So one by one I began to recruit members. There can only be 12 members to the group and they all have to have a different zodiac sign. Together we talk about finding the truth and learning more about ourselves through the stars. There are so many conflicting personalities in the group but I believe that together we can unite and become a powerful force…so to speak.' She chuckled nervously.

Danni could notice her mother's hands clenching together, the knuckles turning white.

'So anyway!' Danni hurried her speech along. 'The Taurus in our group, Ambrite, has a tattoo of her sign on her ankle. I thought it would be a positive way of showing devotion to the group by getting all of us to do it. The Scorpio in our group works at Maltin's Tanning Salon…well his family own it and we got discounted tattoos. I know you're angry mum but this is the best time of my life. I am actually coming out of my shell, exploring my passions and making a ton of new friends. Please say you forgive me!'

Danni watched her mother open her mouth, get up and walk out of the room.

Chapter 19

HE WILL BETRAY YOU

The next day Danni found herself daydreaming again in class over two members of the A.A. Team.

The fantasy was quite strange; Slade and Crawford were sparring with daggers and leaping over Bouquet Reserve's pond, shouting 'she is mine!' Danni was, for some reason, floating on the pond beaming from ear to ear, not caring at all that one could perish.

'Yes fight for me!' she squealed, clutching her hands together.

Crawford knocked Slade over and held his dagger against the poor Aquarian's throat.

'Take that!' He boomed.

Danni frowned. Was this fantasy telling her that Crawford was the one she preferred? Slade was equally as charismatic.

'Any last words?' Crawford growled, his hair flowing back like the Leo's mane.

Slade turned to Danni in the pond and whimpered, 'He will betray you.'

The last image Danni saw before snapping back

into reality was Crawford plunging his dagger through Slade's throat and watching his blood shower her and the pond.

'Dan, are you okay?' Drew whispered from the next table.

Danni shook her head fiercely and regained focus.

'Uhh...Yeah sorry...just a weird daydream.'

At that moment, the bell rang and Danni raced to the library steps. Drew and Reilly followed closely behind.

'Okay what was that all about?' Reilly demanded, sitting next to Danni.

Danni opened up her bag and took out a sandwich. It was packed with lettuce, olives, tomato, relish, beetroot and capsicum. She couldn't wait to eat it! Setting it back down, she turned to her friends.

'What if I told you that I just had a prophetic daydream? Not a dream when you fall asleep. A vision of the future?'

Drew whistled. 'Wow, your intuition is growing stronger.'

'What was it about?' Reilly asked.

Danni blushed violently and turned her back to her friends.

'I don't want to tell you...it's very embarrassing.'

'Awww come on Dan!' Drew whined.

'Okay but please don't laugh. I'm begging you!'

'We promise,' Reilly nodded and punched Drew's

arm. He quickly shook his head in agreement.

'Well, as you both have probably figured out, I kind of have a thing for Crawford.'

Drew and Reilly both let out a squeal that sounded like air escaping from a balloon.

'Stop! Just let me finish, then you can both interrogate me.' Danni pleaded.

The pair just grinned rather creepily and clutched one another.

'Well, this vision showed Crawford and Slade fighting over me to the death at Bouquet Reserve. Crawford somehow managed to wind up on top and had his dagger against Slade. He asked him for any last words and Slade looked at me saying 'he will betray you.' Then Slade was murdered by Crawford. It felt so real! Do you think this is a prophecy of the future?'

Reilly frowned and gazed at the sky while Drew cacked himself on the library steps.

'What?' Danni threw up her hands.

Wiping tears from his eyes, Drew rasped, 'Well Dan, I don't really know many guys that fight with daggers nowadays so no, this is not a prophecy for the future.'

'Hang on a minute' Reilly interjected. 'I thought you said there was nothing between you and Slade. Why was he in the vision fighting over you?'

Danni blushed but didn't want to reveal her partial

feelings for Slade.

'I guess Crawford had to fight with someone otherwise he would be duelling alone and the vision wouldn't make sense. Maybe it was Slade because he and Crawford are the best looking guys in the group?'

Drew looked wounded, clutching his heart in jest.

Reilly didn't look convinced. 'Well whatever the case, Crawford doesn't sound very trustworthy. Maybe we should toss him out.'

'Well that kind of defeats the purpose of our group Reilly,' Danni pointed out. 'This whole A.A. Team is supposed to trust and unite together. I can't distrust Crawford over some vision…can I?'

'I guess but just be careful. I trust everything you dream and everything you dream has come to be accurate. We can't just let this one go and not be cautious.'

Danni laughed rather half-heartedly. 'Do you really think Crawford would betray me guys? And how would he do it?'

'Maybe he will stab you in the back with his dagger!' Drew exclaimed, bursting out into laughter again.

'That's the last time I tell him anything,' Danni muttered to Reilly.

***

Waving goodbye to her friends, Danni slung her backpack over her shoulder and strolled to the bus stop. Reilly had dance practice and Drew was playing guitar for the school production of *Footloose*. It was the first time in a long time that she made her way home without her best friends. Reaching the exit gate of J Corner High, she noticed a familiar shaggy figure waiting by it.

'Hunter?'

The troubled boy walked up to her and nodded hello.

'Ummm…what are you doing here?'

She noticed his eyes darting everywhere before resting on her face.

'I need to talk to you…in private.'

Surprised, Danni found herself leading him towards Bouquet Reserve which was only a couple of blocks from her school. They walked in silence the whole way, the only sound being what was made by their shoes along the pavement. Finally they settled in the middle of the grass near the pond and Danni shivered, feeling that familiar tingle associated with the place. Hunter pulled at a blade of grass and twisted it between his fingers, creating a loop. He refused to look at her.

Danni began. 'Look…I think I know what this is about.'

His eyes immediately shot up. 'You do?'

'Of course,' Danni proceeded cautiously. 'I understand that the group name A.A. is not ideal but if you want to change it, I completely understand. After all it does stand for…'

'What?' Hunter interrupted, looking genuinely confused.

Danni widened her eyes. "Ah...so this isn't about the group name?'

'No!' Hunter snorted. 'Why would it be? What's wrong with it?'

'Nothing!' Danni answered quickly, in a very high voice.

Hunter gazed at her with a look that made her feel really small.

'This is actually about Dr. Yates.'

'Oh really?' Danni sat up. Was he about to open up to her?

'Yeah...err...I think I'm ready to tell you why I go to see her.'

Danni smiled warmly. 'You don't have to,' she told him though she was dying to know.

'Nah it's okay. You should know. Just promise me you won't tell the rest of the group?'

'I promise.'

Hunter half-smirked and ran his hands through his shaggy mane. Danni grinned. She had read up on the sign of Aries many a time. Their fiery tempers and issues with expressing emotions were being displayed through Hunter.

'Well, as you know, my mum sent me to see a psychologist. Yates is great though I do tend to yell at her a lot.'

Danni bit her tongue. She was tempted to agree whole-heartedly.

'The reason why she sent me there is because I witnessed something a couple of years ago that scared me pretty badly. It affected me so badly that I began flunking out at school and eventually was expelled. Now my mum is in the process of finding another school for me and in the meantime my principal suggested seeking professional help. It's the only way I can get my life back on track. But I ask myself what the point is? I have no reason to try anymore.'

'You poor thing!' Danni exclaimed. 'What you saw must have been so terrible and life-changing.'

'It was,' Hunter nodded.

Danni noticed he was having trouble continuing. He kept breathing in and looking away. She placed her hand on his arm and was surprised that he didn't pull away.

'Hunter, you honestly don't have to tell me if it is too hard.'

'I want to…but I can't. I hate this! Why did this happen to me?'

Danni felt a tear run down her cheek. He looked so helpless. She hated that he had to witness such a traumatic thing.

Hunter looked up at her in alarm. 'It's okay Danni;

it's my shit to deal with.'

She nodded, a little winded. 'I just hope Dr. Yates can help you with it. You can tell me whenever you want or you don't ever have to tell me.'

'Thanks mate.' Hunter exhaled. He looked more subdued than Danni had ever seen him before. He also called her 'mate' which startled her a bit but made her happy. It was strange how the powers of astrology and fate had brought them together. She stood up and pulled him to his feet. For a second they just gazed at one another, a new understanding blossoming between them. It was the connection Danni had been striving for ever since she first met him. Dr. Yates knew what Hunter had seen but it was illegal for her to tell Danni. Danni knew eventually he would tell her. Hopefully it was something they could get through together.

***

Arriving home, Danni could hear her parents arguing in the kitchen. She edged closer to the door and pressed her ear against the frame.

'It's as if I don't even know you anymore!' Danni heard her mother yell.

'Honey, be reasonable; she is nearly 18,' Mr. Hamilton calmly responded.

Oh so this is about me.

Every time her parents argued, her mum would yell and her dad would remain placid.

'She has a tattoo Terry! A tattoo! When did our little Danielle ever do a crazy thing like that?'

Uh oh, so she is still hung up on the tat.

'I think you can't handle the fact that she is growing up Vic.'

'This is not growing up! This is completely out of character! Remember how we used to force Danni to participate in team sports and school productions? She was so anti-social! All her life it has been just Reilly and Drew. Not even a single boyfriend! That is not normal for a teenager. Now she has strange dreams and yells in her sleep and gets tattoos!'

Danni was fed up at this point. She drew in a deep breath and walked into the kitchen.

'Hey guys, I think we should talk about this.'

Her parents both jumped in surprise.

'How long have you been listening?' her mother asked her.

'Long enough mum. Can we please sit?'

Danni gestured towards the dining table. The three of them sat down, looking nervous.

'I think it's time I tell you a bit about me guys,' Danni began.

It sounded like such a weird thing to say to her parents but the truth was, not many people knew the real Danielle Hamilton. Reilly and Drew knew 75%. Danni knew 80%. The other 20% was still to be discovered.

'I know I can be a strange girl and most of my life I have kept to myself but that isn't exactly a bad thing. I just have a passion that not many people understand.'

'Yes we know honey, your astrology means a lot to you.' Her father smiled warmly.

Danni returned the smile. 'Well, it's a lot more than that. It's like a part of me. I am very connected to the universe which I know sounds crazy but it isn't. I am quite intuitive and can sense certain things. I dream about people I don't know and then meet them the next day, I am…well…special.'

She was happy to see her father nodding in agreement while her mother still appeared reserved but a lot calmer than before.

'The 'crazy' dreams I've been having are about astrology and a group of people that examine the stars and learn more about themselves. I decided it was time to extend my social life outside Reilly and Drew and created this group of 12 people that do exactly what the figures in my dreams do. It's amazing but I actually have a new group of friends! There's Parry, Graham, Hannah, Ronan, Ambrite, Hunter, Crawford and umm…Slade and Brodie. As well as me, Reilly and Drew.'

She noticed her mother tense up at names of the Drayman kids but gave her a look to continue.

'We meet every Friday night at Bouquet Reserve and talk about astrology. It's quite funny actually. Hunter, a guy I met at the clinic and now the Aries in my group, was assigned to give us a name and he called us the Astro A Team. Like A.A.?'

Her father chuckled and her mother grinned reluctantly.

'We all have such diverse personalities but together we are really committed and loyal to one another. I'm finally a lot happier with myself and I'm gaining more friends every day. This is good for me, please see that!'

Mr. Hamilton shifted in his chair.

'We do see that honey, especially more, now that you have explained the group but your mother is not happy with the tattoo. She would like it if you considered laser surgery.'

Mrs. Hamilton looked away, prepared for the outburst.

'No!' Danni yelled. 'Look, I get that you are angry mum, but dad is right. I am nearly 18 and I got this tattoo to symbolise my loyalty to my sign and the group. The leader of the A.A. Team can't get her tattoo removed. Then it will appear that the rest of the group went through pain for nothing!'

'Honey, it's okay. You don't have to remove it,' her mother answered. 'Now that you have explained things better, I feel a lot more rested. But you have to see this from our point of view. As a child, you were always estranged from other children and social activities. It is really odd for us to see you now happy, disappearing all the time and getting a tattoo! Not that we aren't thrilled at your newfound group of friends.'

Danni sighed. 'I guess you're right. I was a bit of a loner. But all that is about to change. I am so sick of myself! I'm ready to get involved with what I love and share it with other people! Dr. Yates has helped me see that.'

'Well, then we are glad we sent you there,' her mother smiled.

'There's just one more thing…'

'What's that honey?'

'Can I talk to mum in private for a second, dad?'

He raised his eyebrows but got up and walked into the living room. As soon as Danni heard the news from the television, she turned to her mother.

'Mum, do I really have to stay away from Brodie and Slade? I'm sorry I lied to you but now you know they are part of the group, I can't exactly stay away. I really like them.'

Her mother let out a loud groan.

'Oh honey. I hated asking that of you. It was just creating so much tension between me and your father but it's still not right. Why should you have to suffer because the bitch next door has self-esteem issues?'

Danni laughed. Her mother got so heated up at times.

'Thanks mum, she really is a bitch but I'm glad you and dad are talking it out.'

'Yeah, well sometimes I forget that your father is just a friendly guy and that he is only interested in me.'

'Of course!' Danni said, banging her fist on the table. 'Mrs. Drayman is just feeling neglected by Paul and is enjoying dad's attention but she should still stay away.'

Mrs. Hamilton squeezed her daughter's hand and stood up.

'You know…I always wanted a tattoo when I was a teenager. Can I see it properly this time?'

Danni stared at her mother in disbelief but stood and pulled up her pants leg. Her mother cooed in admiration.

'It is a beautiful symbol. Is it the roman numeral for two?'

'Yeah it symbolises two of everything. That's why Geminis can multitask and are never really one personality. It also represents the twins Castor and Pollux who rule over the Gemini constellation.'

'Wow you really do love the zodiac, don't you sweetheart?'

Danni looked down at her ankle. 'You have no idea.'

Chapter 20

AN ASTROLOGICAL SONG

'Okay fellow A.A. Team members! I believe I gave you some homework last week that I wanted you to complete? I want you to go around the pond and use three words to describe your star sign and you. In order to feel more connected to your sign you must be able to identify with the personality traits your horoscope is known for.'

Danni was immensely excited. This was the first proper session she was having with her group after the introductory ones. She cast her eyes over the people seated around the pond...so closely resembling the Wheel of the Zodiac.

'I will volunteer to go first and then we will begin clockwise, so after me goes Reilly.'

Although Danni always sat at the head of the pond, she was wondering whether to have an order that began with Hunter because Aries is the first sign of the Zodiac. It could all be sorted out later.

'Alright...Gemini! My three words are: communicative, intelligent and adaptable. I would certainly love to believe I possess all those traits. Geminis

143

are the social chameleons of the Zodiac and can blend into any situation. Because of my newfound confidence, I know I can begin to extend my Gemini wings and behave in the social manner they normally do. Okay Reilly, your turn.'

Standing up, Reilly clutched a piece of paper and cleared her throat. A few chuckled and Ambrite let out a rather obvious snort which caused Reilly to glare in her direction.

'Umm…yeah okay, well, Sagittarians are brutally honest. I can relate to that. I mean, how many times do I tell you and Drew that Goths are lame?'

Ambrite immediately stood up in protest but Danni urged her with a look to sit down and stay quiet. Reilly let out a snigger of satisfaction.

'Yeah, so my three words are: honest, loyal and energetic. I am all of those and proud of it!'

Danni beamed at her best friend and gestured for Hannah to go next.

Standing up shakily, Hannah muttered quietly and looked at her paper with an intense focus.

'Uh Hannah, do you mind speaking up please?' Danni asked gently. Reilly rubbed her leg in encouragement. Hannah nodded meekly.

'Hi…everybody. Umm…I am Cancer…uh I mean I *am* a Cancer and we are shy, loving and empathetic.'

She quickly sat down and clutched Reilly for

support.

'Good, good job guys, you are really connecting with your sign.' Danni smiled. 'Hunter, why don't you go next?'

'I am not standing up.' Hunter grunted and glared at the rest of the group. Although Danni still didn't know the reason for his pain…she knew he was upset today because of it. The others looked at Danni in silent outrage and Hannah actually gave her a little frown but she nodded for him to continue.

'Aries are fiery, competitive and sporty. I know I am all those things.' Hunter read from his page but refused to look at anyone.

Danni quickly pointed to Parry who not only stood up but thrust her chest out and flicked her copper hair back. All the boys including Graham (but for different reasons) paid a lot of attention.

'Hi my lovelies! As you know Virgos are the virgin maidens of the group… although personally I must disagree.'

She let out a shrill laugh that made the girls groan and the boys moan. Walking around the pond as though she was telling a nostalgic story, Parry sighed and continued.

'What can I say about Virgos? They are perfectionists, which is so me. I can't finish any project until it is perfect and doesn't make me sick to look at! A

Virgo is also critical but fair and is always coming from a good place. Thank you for listening to the best sign in the Zodiac!'

Danni grinned and shook her head. Parry was indeed confident but a valuable asset to the team and she certainly did her research.

Graham leapt up and struck a pose with his hand on his hip.

'Well done Parry, that was just fantastic and I know we can all agree on the perfect part!'

Parry beamed at him and nodded as if it was just fact and Ronan murmured 'asskiss' to Brodie who giggled.

'Scorpios are quite deep for want of a better word. I am a complex being! Graham Maltin is more than mysterious!'

Hunter looked ready to punch Graham out and Ambrite was sticking her finger down her throat in mock sick.

'Guys!' Danni interjected. 'Can we all listen to each other please? Every sign is different and we need to learn to get along or else this group won't work. Graham is right. Scorpios are incredibly deep and mysterious. They don't always reveal their feelings to others, so you never quite know what they are thinking.'

Graham nodded appreciatively at Danni and puffed his chest out in importance.

'Scorpios are also quite emotional and are sensitive

to another's feelings.'

Ambrite stood up next and gave Reilly a special sneer just for her.

'Hi, the Goth here! Look, I know all you haters out there look at my views and judge but remember I am just a human being trying to express herself.'

The group nodded in agreement and Danni noticed Hunter eying Ambrite with respect. Reilly kept her head down and avoided eye contact. This was her way of showing guilt.

'I am a Taurus and as a proud Taurean, I am creative, stubborn and comfortable with routine. I have always been able to identify with those traits and I love that my star sign sums me up perfectly in three words.'

Danni nodded in approval. This was going well apart from the obvious personality clashes in the group. She hoped one day they all couldn't get enough of each other.

Ronan was the next to stand and he always gave the arrogant appearance that this group was too good for him. But then why did he keep coming back?

'Alright, so Capricorns, I have just recently found out, are known for their organisational skills, cleanliness and quick humour. I have a bit of a messy room but I still like order in other areas of my life and my humour is certainly quick and original.' The rest of the group raised their eyebrows in agreement that they hadn't seen that side of Ronan at all.

Danni was glad to be getting to know her group a lot better. Even if Ronan declared he was the 'funny one' of the group, she believed it would show when he loosened up.

Brodie followed and she looked absolutely breathtaking in the night, her silver hair flowing down her back and her bright blue eyes scanning her page. The entire group paid plenty of attention when she spoke.

'Hi all! I am a Libran and like the scales we are perfectly balanced. We believe in love not war, and enjoy a good flirt.'

Sitting down again, she shared a secret smile with Danni. The two had become quite close through being neighbours and battling the Charlotte ordeal. Little did Brodie know that Danni was also confused about her feelings for Slade...

She felt her heart do a quick jump as Slade stood up and looked just as overwhelming as his sister. He parted his metallic hair and gave a quick azure wink to his group.

'Hello, my name is Slade as you all already know and I am an Aquarian. We are the humanitarians of the Zodiac and are apparently fascinated by sci-fi and the latest technologies. I would say that not only do I enjoy helping people but I am a big *Star Wars* buff.'

The group laughed and Slade did a mock bow and sat down. She noticed there were only two boys left. One she loved and one she could possibly be in love *with*. Crawford looked absolutely gorgeous in his light denim jeans and white polo shirt. His curly brown hair framed his perfect face and his hazel eyes gave a twinkle as he swept his gaze over her. In that moment she was 90% certain Crawford was the one she wanted to be with. After all, he had been the one she dreamed of at Bouquet Reserve and they had met before Slade had ever entered the picture. Maybe she had a crush on Slade merely for his good looks and American drawl. All Danni knew was, she couldn't get either of them out of her head! Crawford looked at her as if he could read her mind and gave her a sweet smile. She took a deep breath and gestured for him to start.

'Hey I am Crawford and a Leo. Firstly I think we should all give Danni a clap for being an awesome leader and bringing us all together. Before her I never knew anything about my star sign and now that I do, it explains more of my behaviour.'

Danni immediately went red as the entire group (even Ronan and Hunter!) started to clap her efforts. Drew and Reilly were throwing their fists in the air and cheering; Slade was clapping but she was sure he frowned at Crawford. Danni immediately flashed back to the dream she had about the two duelling over her but shook her head. She curtseyed.

Crawford let out a chuckle and then continued.

'Okay thanks guys, so Leos are known for their big egos, their sense of pride and a strong loyalty to their friends. In many ways they do resemble a Lion and the need to feel important in his jungle.'

Danni smiled graciously at him and held up her hand.

'This is a very important point that Crawford made. Most of our personalities are exactly like the symbols we have tattooed on our ankle. The way a Gemini can have dual personalities because her symbol is the Twins or the way a Cancer can retreat into their shells like an introverted Crab. However, every symbol in the Wheel has a story behind how they came to govern each sign. I suggest you look up your individual story and read it out at next week's meeting.'

Taking a breath, Danni cast her eye to the last member, her best friend Drew. She was surprised to see he had brought his guitar with him. She smiled at him and gestured for him to stand.

'Drew, do you want to finish up the meeting?'

Picking up his guitar, Drew cleared his throat in exaggeration which made all the other members laugh and pulled out a piece of paper.

'Yo Astro A Team! How we all doing tonight?"

The group cheered and clapped, while Reilly and Danni rolled their eyes.

'Fantastic! Well, I have actually written a song for

the group tonight but before I do, I would like to tell you what I learned about being a Pisces. Being Danni's best friend since Kindergarten means I already know a lot of my traits because she told me like every day!'

The group chuckled again including Danni.

'A Pisces is the dreamer of the Zodiac. We tend to get lost in our own world and are also creative like the Taurus. My guitar takes me out of my element and it always soothes my soul. A Pisces is also quite placid and always up for a laugh at themselves. I haven't told Danni or Reilly about the song I have been working on for two weeks now but I would like to perform it to the team if that is okay?"

Danni nodded in agreement and Reilly clapped her hands excitedly.

Drew picked up his guitar and began to strum.

'This song is for Danni and our group. I called it 'What Are They All About?'

'Oh I, Oh I, was looking at the stars tonight
The way they shimmer and shine so bright
Oh what, Oh what, are they trying to tell me?
When the stars are out, they whisper quietly

But here we are, all together searching
For the meaning behind our hearts
Oh why, oh why, can't the stars just listen?

So that my best friend can feel more a part…

Of a world that shines the light on her
An explanation of a Leo or a Cancer
What does it mean when you're born in July?
And how does one define the crazy Gemini?
Where do I begin with a Taurus and a Virgo?
They are shrouded in mystery and ergo
I can't understand what happened to definitions
Why does December equal Sagittarius?
Why does the water match an Aquarius?
And how about those pesky little Pisces?
Swimming like fish among the high seas
What are they all about I beg the heavens?
But all they say is begin with an Aries
They start the Wheel of the Zodiac
And by studying them you will crack
The secret behind a Scorpio or
The reason a Capricorn can't let go
Of anything that hurt them in the past
But wait, the Libran will fix them fast
With balance and love and a proper beginning
This group can achieve the first Zodiac winning
To solve the mystery behind those twinkling lights
And forever prove that Danni was right
To believe in herself and shout
What are those damn star signs all about?

Exhaling loudly, Drew put his guitar down and threw up his hands in question.

'So what did you all think?'

Immediately the group began a roaring applause and Reilly and Danni ran up to him and threw their arms around his neck. He wiped fake tears from his eyes and clutched his heart mockingly.

Danni wiped actual tears away and whispered 'thankyou' in his ear with all her heart. As she watched all the members of her group praise Drew, she knew that moment was one she would never forget for the rest of her life!

Chapter 21

DANCING AMONG THE STARS

Skipping down the stairs the next morning, Danni caught herself humming Drew's song, *'Why does December equal Sagittarius? Why does the water match an Aquarius?'*

She was so incredibly happy and fulfilled by the A.A. Team and couldn't remember a time in her life where she ever hummed in the morning. Danni was equally glad to find her parents canoodling in the kitchen, knowing they had worked out their issues with the Drayman situation next door. She made a face as she watched her father nuzzle into her mother's neck but still grinned as she walked out the door.

It was a crisp, autumn morning and Danni had plans to shop around town for next week's meeting. Then at night, she, Reilly and Drew were going to meet at Drew's to plan the following sessions at Bouquet Reserve.

Drawing her coat tighter around her, Danni started a brisk pace along the pavement, enjoying the browning foliage and the fresh air. She tilted her head to one side, remembering the meeting last night and how they had all happily produced their research. Each member of the group had managed to find three personality traits that defined them while corresponding to their star sign. Danni let out a small laugh as she recalled Parry strutting around the pond saying *'they are perfectionists!'* It was heart-warming to feel their commitment and loyalty to the group. Despite Charlotte's threats, Danni knew she had eleven people at her back that would ensure her and the group's protection.

As she walked through the main street of Juggler's Corner, passing Maltin's Tanning Salon and the Library where she had met Ronan for the first time, her phone began to buzz with a text message. For a split second, she almost expected it to be another nasty threat from Charlotte but to her heart's jumpy delight it was Crawford.

The message read: *'Meet me at Bouquet Reserve ASAP…come alone :).'*

Danni took one look at the text and quickly turned on her heels towards the direction of her new sacred space. As she walked (at an even brisker pace) she let Crawford know she was on her way and quickly forwarded Crawford's message to Reilly and Drew who both replied with at least five exclamation points.

Stopping in front of a shop's window, Danni smoothed her long, brown locks off her face and pinched her cheeks to give her usual paleness some colour. Because of the increasingly cold weather, she couldn't wear clothing that could show off her tanned limbs. Danni had never found herself attractive although her friends always assured her she had a cute pixie face. However, she was tired of being seen as 'cute' and wanted to step into a sexier realm where she blossomed as a beautiful woman.

With her heart racing and legs shaking, Danni power-walked into Bouquet Reserve, ready for her 'alone time' with Crawford. To her delight, she saw him raking the leaves near the pond and then gathering them into big piles to be disposed of. He was wearing a short sleeved T-shirt that accentuated his strong arms and a pair of dark, denim shorts. Danni took a deep breath, taking in the gorgeous sight before her and strolled towards him. Crawford turned around before she got to tap him on the shoulder and beamed at her.

'Danni, I am so glad you made it. I wanted to talk to you about an idea I had for the group.'

'Oh okay.' Danni felt her heart sink a little as she realised their meeting was more for business than pleasure.

Crawford put his rake down and walked over to the pond that always looked so normal in the daylight. He patted the ground next to him and Danni sat herself rather close on purpose. He stared into her eyes for a while and she felt the heat rise into her face. Her cheeks reddening, she quickly signalled him to begin.

'Well,' Crawford began. 'I believe these weekly meetings have been a huge success and the location is a huge factor in contributing to that, don't you think?'

'Certainly, Bouquet Reserve couldn't be more perfect for the A.A. Team. But what is your point?'

Crawford took in a deep breath as though he was about to announce a big secret and Danni couldn't help but notice his perfect abs beneath his shirt.

'In a month, my dad is going on a business trip to Adelaide for some Environmental Protection Seminars. He is expecting me to keep watch over Bouquet Reserve all weekend and I figured what if we held a dance? An astrology dance?'

Danni just sat there in shock with her mouth open. Did Crawford just say an astrology dance?

'I realise it is a bit far-fetched,' said Crawford laughing at her surprise. 'But what better time to have an event where we all get dressed up and really get to know each other? I feel we are only learning more about one another through the signs but what about the actual Danni or the actual Crawford. Don't they deserve to know each other more intimately?'

He grinned at this last remark and Danni's heart went haywire.

After a couple of seconds, her face lit up with excitement.

'Wow Crawford, you would really let us use the

Reserve for the weekend?'

'Sure! We could still hold a meeting on the Friday and then have the dance on a Saturday night. That will give me the Sunday to clean up before my dad arrives home on the Monday.'

Danni gave out a little screech that had Crawford laughing.

'Oh this will be an awesome night. I have so many ideas that will fit in astrologically! Thank you so much Crawford!'

Without realising what she was doing, Danni threw her arms around his neck and they fell backwards onto the green. Both of them were laughing and Danni could swear she saw Crawford blush. He hugged her back and stood up, pulling her on her feet. She was wiping grass off her jeans, heart racing like a gazelle when Crawford said: 'Will you be my date?'

Danni's nerves ran amok in that moment 'ddaate?'

'Yeah,' said Crawford grinning. He pushed back his curls and Danni melted on the spot.

'This dance should have partners. After all, there are six girls and guys each, so we can all bring a date. Oh, and they need to bring someone they are astrologically compatible with! Gemini and Leo is a perfect match for sure.'

'That is so true!' Danni squealed.

She couldn't contain her excitement at going to a

dance with Crawford. Better yet, an astrology dance which was so up her alley.

'That is such a great idea; I can't wait to tell the others...'

'Can we announce it together at the next meeting?' Crawford asked shyly.

Danni couldn't keep the smile off her face.

'Of course, I reckon everyone will be so excited! Well, maybe not Hunter or Ronan or Ambrite but the rest will be thrilled!'

Crawford picked up his rake again. 'So glad you love the idea.'

Danni brushed off the last of the grass and walked over to the pond.

'It is amazing Crawford. I really want my entire group to get better acquainted. At the moment there are a few personality clashes which I guess is expected when the whole Zodiac get together but hopefully this dance can ease the tension.'

Nodding, Crawford walked over to her. 'That isn't the only reason I want this dance.'

Danni looked deep into his hazel eyes. 'What is the other?'

'To get you before someone else does...'

***

'Can you please turn that down?' Reilly yelled.

'Hmmm, no!' Drew yelled back.

Danni got up and turned the CD player off (blasting Rise Against) which received a grin from Reilly and a glare from Drew.

The three were seated in Drew's bedroom/music room. Several guitars were lined up on a stand while posters of Bob Marley and Oasis lined his walls. Reilly always complained his room wasn't girl friendly enough and he always responded with 'well what do you expect?'

Danni lounged on Drew's bed and was barely paying attention to their squabbles. She couldn't stop thinking about the upcoming dance and trying to decipher Crawford's last message *'to get you before someone else does.'* Was he talking about Slade? She had sensed some rivalry between them before. All she knew was that she was going to the dance with him and thoughts of Slade were now pushed to the back of her mind. She was almost certain now that she felt more romantically towards Crawford and was just attracted to Slade. The vision of the two fighting came into her mind again and she felt a tinge of guilt as she wondered what Slade would think of Crawford being her date. Danni thought he probably wouldn't care and returned to focus on her friends. She had sworn to Crawford before she left that she wouldn't even tell Reilly and Drew about the dance until the next meeting. Already, they had both begged her to tell them what happened at Bouquet Reserve but she just said 'wait till next meeting' which resulted in her being hit with tons of pillows!

Danni changed the subject by asking her friends to assist with the next meeting. After seeing Crawford, Danni had returned to her original plan of buying supplies for the next meeting. She had told her group the previous night to read up on the back story of their Zodiac symbols and read them out next Friday. Danni had decided that if they got their research correct (which she already knew extensively) she would reward them with gifts that corresponded to their sign in some way. She was already extremely grateful to them for getting tattoos, so they deserved a present. Danni had hidden Reilly and Drew's so her friends pored over the other gifts she had bought. Drew laughed at the stuffed goat toy she had bought for Ronan.

'Can you imagine his face when you give him a fluffy toy? He will hate you even more than he already does!'

'He doesn't hate me!' Danni glared at Drew. 'He just has issues with females and I am sure in time he will warm to us.'

'He is a creep!' Reilly groaned. 'The only female issue he has is wishing he was one!'

Danni and Drew burst out laughing while Reilly snatched the goat out of Drew's hand and threw it at the both of them.

Not all of the gifts were stuffed bulls and rams. They had something to do with the back stories that were to be revealed the following week. Danni was pleased to see Drew had borrowed a few astrology books and they were piled on his desk.

'Drew, it looks like you may get your stuffed fish toy,' Danni joked.

Putting on a serious face, Drew picked up one of his books and imitated being smart. He flipped to a random page and for some reason put on an English accent.

'Well Danni, I believe once I relay this information to our little organisation, I will be receiving the real fish kind of compensation…'

Reilly giggled. 'You think you're going to get an actual fish?'

'With any luck!' Drew raised his eyebrows at Danni in hope.

Winking, Danni patted Drew's head. 'We will see my boy!'

***

In another world, unknown to any mortals, a mysterious figure dressed in black clapped his hands together in joy. This figure was known to Danni as Garth; a *Matrix* type character who told her he would return when the time was right.

In this alternate universe, Garth was ecstatic. He

expressed his happiness to a male presence with a white beard. This bearded man was responsible for the stars and constellations in the sky. No this man was not the almighty God. He was a worker of the Heavens; a powerful ruler determined to set things straight.

'An Astrology Dance! Can you believe it? An Astrology Dance!' Garth sang.

The booming voice of the bearded man replied with a chuckle.

'Ah yes, an excellent idea and what a festive way to unite the twelve signs.'

Garth nodded vigorously. 'You must admit my Lord; she is doing a wonderful job.'

'Hmmm, oh yes, a very fine job indeed Garth. You have done well with your projection dreams; guiding her to form this group that may very well save us once and for all. In fact the vision of the pig jumping into the lake was a nice touch.'

The bearded man lay back in this throne, allowing his sandals to rest in mid-air. 'But they are far from ready. It will be a while yet before they enter our world.'

Garth spun around from his excited pacing and faced the mysterious man with a concerned look.

'Do you think it will take years? I mean, we just don't have that time! The Taurus is very opinionated and the Capricorn fights against happiness and don't get me started on the…'

'Garth!' boomed the sandal wearing figure. 'Relax please! She knows what she is doing. Slowly, slowly I see her lowering all their defences and forming some wonderful friendships. Did you really think the twelve signs of the Zodiac would bond instantly?'

Chuckling, Garth resumed his happy pace. "Of course, you are right. With so many personality clashes, I mustn't expect a miracle!'

'Oh but Garth, that is where you are wrong…'

'My Lord?'

'Danni *is* the miracle…'

***

'Oh my lovely beauty, with your hair so red, I am having trouble getting you outta my head!'

Drew was strumming his guitar and his two best friends were rolling their eyes at him.

'Oh my God, Drew,' Reilly groaned. 'You have got to stop mooning over Parry! She is not interested in anyone other than herself!'

Danni laughed and Drew just muttered 'yeah…Parry.'

The three friends were sitting on the usual stairs at J-Corner High, eating their lunch and enjoying the warm, autumn air. With the next meeting looming, Danni had everything prepared and was excited about the joint announcement she and Crawford were going to make at the end. She felt bad keeping it from her best friends but she had given her word and intended to keep it.

Leaning her head against the steel railing, Danni let her headache from that morning subside. She had dreamt of a strange, bearded man with big sandals and a dark figure who could have been Garth. She still didn't understand who or what Garth was. How did he fit into her astrological plans and what were his motives for returning when the time was right?

'So then I was like…what is your problem bitch?' Reilly growled.

'Huh?' Danni said, snapping out of her reverie.

'Weren't you listening Dan?' Reilly frowned. 'I was telling you about the fight Ambrite and I got into after the last meeting. She was trying to persuade me to become a vegan and I said 'every food should be enjoyed!'

Danni nodded in a daze as usual. 'Oh well, Ambrite has her beliefs and she is a strong, opinionated girl. Just accept her for who she is.'

'Accept her for who she is? What about her getting off her high horse and getting a life!'

Drew patted Reilly on the shoulder and began to sing another song.

'Accept her for who she is! She is a strong, opinionated girl. But I just wanna hold her until I make her hurl!'

'Drew? Does everything have to be about girls?'

Danni asked.

'Sure, what else is it gonna be?' Drew scoffed.

Danni threw up her hands in defeat and turned to Reilly who was still fuming.

'Do you want me to talk to Ambrite? I can let her know that she needs to cool it.'

Reilly snapped out of her rage. She tapped her toes in times to Drew's song.

'Are you sure? It would probably make things easier. Oh but don't mention my name! I don't want her to know she is pissing me off!'

Smiling, Danni patted Reilly's arm. 'I will be happy to. I can walk to her place after school. I still have all the members' addresses and phone numbers in my bag.'

'Stalker,' murmured Drew.

Danni stood up in a huff. 'Well, now guess who isn't getting a fish?'

Reilly cracked up laughing as she watched Drew run after Danni, a string of apologies running down his lips.

***

Danni held her jacket close as she walked past J-Corner Library and into the winding street where Ambrite lived. The wind was cold but Danni could hardly care. All she kept thinking about was the Astrological Dance that would be held in two weeks' time. She had decided that each member could only take a partner to whom they were astrologically compatible. It was lucky that there were six girls and six guys. This would make the partnering a lot easier. It also complimented the Wall quite nicely. The Wall was a theory Danni had come up with years before that separated the twelve signs. On one side of the Wall were Gemini, Aries, Leo, Libra, Aquarius and Sagittarius. These were the fiery and active signs all of which were extremely compatible together. On the other side were Virgo, Cancer, Taurus, Capricorn, Scorpio and Pisces. These were the more emotional and down to earth signs who all understood one another. Danni had always felt that for a relationship to work one should date within their own Wall but Drew and Reilly had protested a lot about this over the years and Danni was starting to see it didn't really matter. However, when it came to the upcoming dance, she hoped her group would make the right 'Wall' choices and bring a compatible member. Each member would also have to research their sign's assigned colour and wear that to the dance. That meant the girl would wear the colour on a dress and the guy would wear a suit with the appropriate coloured bow-tie. It would be fun but self-educational as well. Bouquet Reserve would be moderately decorated and there would be music and food. It was their luck that the Reserve was seen as abandoned and creepy to most J-Corner residents. This held a higher chance of keeping it a private function.

Danni felt a shiver run up her spine, thinking that Charlotte might intervene. Luckily it was twelve against one and Danni liked those odds!

Pulling out Ambrite's details from her bag, she scanned for the number 14 and found it was the next house from where she was standing. As she walked up the drive and admired the front lawn with its pretty azaleas and cornrows, she saw a familiar figure sitting on the front step. This figure had a shaggy head and a dark look on his face. Danni was startled to see it was Hunter and right next to him was Ambrite, looking forlorn and leaning on his shoulder. Scrunching her eyebrows together, Danni stood there for a moment unable to believe what she was seeing. Since when did those two know each other well, let alone be friendly enough to have physical contact?

At that moment, Ambrite looked up with a startled 'oh!' Hunter followed her gaze and sat up straight.

'Hi guys?' Danni said, walking casually over to them. 'I just came over to chat to you Ambrite but if you're busy…'

'No, not at all!' Ambrite said, getting up and blushing. 'Hunter was just consoling me over some problems I was having.'

Danni nodded. 'Ummm…did you guys know each other before the meetings started?'

Hunter stood up and to Danni's further amazement, put his arm around Ambrite.

'Nah, we started chatting after the first meeting. She wanted to know what was wrong and why I was late. We kinda clicked and have been hanging out every day ever since.'

'Every day!' Danni exclaimed. 'I had no idea! I mean…that is great and everything but are you guys a couple? If so, I think the whole group should know. Just out of loyalty of course…nothing intrusive or anything. Or you can just say what you want really; it isn't my place to interfere with a relationship.'

Ambrite let out a great laugh and Hunter chuckled which freaked Danni out as it wasn't often that he produced positive noises.

'Relationship? Oh Danni, I think you better come inside and we can have a talk. I'll make mint tea; it is quite refreshing.'

'Errgh, what is with your mint tea A? I am getting really sick of it!' Hunter groaned.

'Well, stop coming over then!' Ambrite retorted.

Danni watched the two of them glare simultaneously, then crack a smile and clasp hands. She couldn't believe how unexpected this day had become.

Walking into her home that looked like a garden, Ambrite told Danni to make herself at home and informed her that her parents were away on a business trip. Sitting on Ambrite's plush, green couch, Danni accepted a cool mint tea and watched the two sit extremely close to one another on the opposite side. Raising her eyebrows, she hinted at a fast explanation.

'Okay,' Ambrite began. 'I want to tell you what my life was like before the group got together and how it changed completely because of one Mr. Hunter McGowan...'

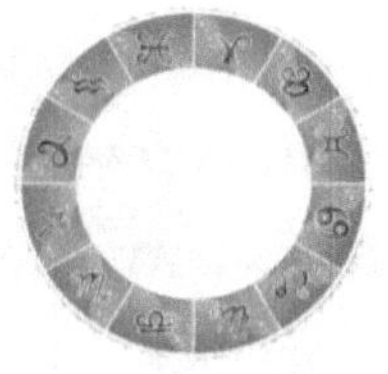

Chapter 22

A LONG, AWAITED CONFESSION

Danni felt as though she had been holding her breath for an hour. When she finally allowed herself to breathe, she found her stomach ached a little. This was the confession she had been dying to hear and it looked as if Ambrite had her own story to tell as well. She relaxed on the couch and appeared casual as Ambrite fidgeted and stared off into space. Hunter merely sat next to her looking solemn; as though he knew exactly what was coming would take a toll on all of them.

After a couple of seconds, Ambrite snapped back to reality and nodded to Danni.

'First of all, you should know I'm into girls. In case you thought Hunter and I were the new "it" couple, we're not; just incredibly close because we have had similar life journeys.'

Danni nodded back. Ambrite being a lesbian wasn't at all a big shock or in any way a big deal. However, she had thought for a second that she and Hunter were a pair after seeing their physical friendship out in the garden.

'I know that my appearance is quite extroverted

and that I am the most opinionated person there is but I wasn't always like that. A few years back…I decided to do whatever possible to get my parents' attention. They are both workaholics…for lack of a better term…and I was always second on their list. If I was to tell them this, there would be constant attacks of denial…but I know it's true.'

Ambrite looked away for a second and it warmed Danni's heart to see Hunter rub her back. Whatever her story entailed…it must have touched something in Hunter and made him open up to her. Danni wasn't hurt that he had told Ambrite before her; she knew there would be a perfectly good reason for it. Concerned, she leaned her arm over to touch Ambrite but before she could Ambrite turned around and shook her head. She didn't want or need sympathy and was clearly having as hard a time opening up as Hunter had had.

'I'm sorry,' Ambrite started. 'This is just a little bit difficult…but I really want you to know… as our leader.'

'Take your time…I would never rush you,' Danni comforted.

'Thankyou…well anyway, as I was saying…they were never home. Both my mother and father work for investors and are constantly on the road to meetings or business conferences. It keeps them so busy! This wouldn't be so awful if they just acknowledged it from time to time but they never do! All I ever wanted was for them to understand how their work took a lot of time away from me. I remember having piano recitals and, believe it or not, dance performances that they missed when I was a child and looking into the crowd to see no familiar faces. All the other girls had proud parents cheering them on in the audience but I only had my grandfather. I don't know where I would have been without him. After my grandmother had passed, he moved in with us so that he wasn't lonely. I know my parents saw this as a golden opportunity to dump me in his lap and have him pay me the attention I needed. He certainly was there for everything but I only wanted my parents to really see me shine and grow into a young adult. This went on for years and as I became a teenager, I worked my hardest to get them to notice. Instead of doing things that I thought would make them proud of me, I did the exact opposite! Nearly every week I was in the principal's office for rude behaviour or smoking on the school grounds. They were summoned for parent-teacher meetings but they could only make one or two. And when they did make it, they appeared bored or rushed and every five seconds their damn phones would ring! I still hate that sound!'

Ambrite stopped for the second time and leaned into Hunter who enclosed his arms around her. Danni got up and sat next to her, rubbing her arm. Her heart broke as she watched the tears roll down Ambrite's cheeks. It made her feel all the more grateful to her parents for loving her and being so invested in her life. She couldn't imagine how awful it must have been for her friend when her parents missed out on all the things that shaped her today.

Sighing deeply, Ambrite wiped her tears and shook her head. It was time to continue.

'I was practically close to expulsion but after seeing how my parents acted in those school meetings, the teachers and the principal understood the meaning behind my acting out. They sent me to the school's guidance counsellor and she helped me in some ways but I didn't take her advice. Every suggestion she gave me was to sit my parents down and let them know how I was feeling but I just couldn't face their answers and lame excuses, so I began to change my appearance. I shaved my hair and got multiple piercings and tats. Danni, you'll be happy to know that the first tat I got was the Taurus one. I have always loved my star sign.'

Danni smiled warmly at her and felt her own ankle tingle.

'My biggest change was making everybody call me Ambrite instead of Amber. I was tired of the piano and dance recital girl. I wanted to be noticed and this was how! I became a vegan and began cooking special meals for myself and my grandfather. He never questioned my looks or behaviour; I'm sure he knew it was because his daughter and son-in-law were guilty of negligence. I never once sat them down and told them how I felt…I just kept changing and reforming with the hope that they would take notice. I realise now that it was my own fault to expect them to be mind-readers but when you are parents you should just not ignore your child!

My counsellor started to get tired of my refusal to speak to them, or allow anyone else to speak to them for that matter, and referred me to a psychologist at the J-Corner Health Centre. I think you would know her, Danni, as Dr. Yates?'

Danni nodded in astonishment and Hunter held up his hand in apology.

'I just told her that was how we met...I didn't tell her anything personal.'

Danni patted Hunter's arm. 'It's fine...I love Dr. Yates. Was she very helpful Ambrite?'

'She was incredibly helpful,' Ambrite nodded. 'Straight away she could tell I had feelings of abandonment and understood why I couldn't bear to talk to my parents about how I felt. She asked why I would want more after years of rejection. She was absolutely right! Of course, she said talking to them was a definite step forward but she understood my hesitation. In the meantime she explained that acting out would only harm me and that I should make my life as wonderful as possible. That way if they ever acknowledged me...it was them who had missed out. I took all of that into account but when it was time to change my hair or name back to Amber I realised I enjoyed who I had become. The hair and name stayed and I was still happy with my vegan lifestyle. I got my job at the Funky Fries and continued going to school, which is the one out of Juggler's Corner but still a good one that has plenty of alternative students. My grandfather noticed the change in my attitude and took an even bigger interest in my life. He would stay up for hours helping me with my homework and was such a wonderful man.'

'Was?' Danni uttered in concern.

'He died six months ago…' Ambrite stared at Danni and then burst into tears. Hunter and Danni drew her closer. She sobbed into both of them and they comforted her in silence for a good ten minutes. After she began to quiet down, Hunter jumped up and rushed to the kitchen to get her a glass of water and tissues. Danni grasped her hand and searched her eyes for sadness. She could see the pain and grief in the Taurean's eyes and how the one man who had basically raised her left her without anyone. Hunter returned with supplies and Ambrite got herself cleaned up.

'I still haven't gotten to the worst part,' she choked out and produced a small grin.

Hunter gave a small chuckle and squeezed her hand. 'It's okay now…'

'If you can't continue I understand,' Danni said.

'No no, you have to know it all.' Ambrite urged. 'I'm alright now.'

She took a deep breath and finished her story. 'My grandfather meant everything to me. I hope he knows in heaven what his love and support did for my childhood. I would have been a lost cause without him. I'm so grateful to have Hunter now and of course our group Danni.

At the news of his death I plunged back into the depths of depression and watched my parents grieve for a week and then get right back into the business. It made me sick how quickly they moved on! I still haven't moved on and will never get over his death. Despite Dr. Yates's advice, I took one last attempt at trying to get their attention and make them feel guilty for what they had done…I attempted suicide with a drug overdose.'

Ambrite hung her head in shame and disgust while Danni watched the pain spread all over Hunter's face and he had to look away.

'I went into my mother's medicine cabinet and took a handful of sleeping tablets. Luckily for me I had gotten a random stomach bug and ended up vomiting all I had taken. I saw this as a sign from my grandfather not to go through with it. I knew he was looking after me from above. I went to see Dr. Yates the next day and told her all about it. She could see that I wouldn't try such a thing again and recommended that I should talk to one of her patients who would understand my situation. However, he constantly refused to speak about it and I kept my dark secret to myself. My parents still don't know it at all till this day. On the first meeting for the A.A. Team, I couldn't pick who Hunter was because he looked incredibly familiar. It was only until he stated his name at the meeting that I realised he was the patient Dr. Yates wanted me to talk to! I had seen him storm out before my own session and she had mentioned his name in our talks. I took him aside and told him who I was and we got a drink after the meeting and talked till 2 am about our lives. He completely changed my world and made me feel so much better about my whole situation. I know I had helped him too and Dr. Yates knows about our friendship now and how we met at your meetings Danni. She is so happy and proud of you. She is proud of all of us really.'

Danni couldn't believe that Ambrite was also a patient of Dr. Yates. Her psychologist had three members of the A.A. Team to counsel and their lives were all connected in a wonderful and mystical way.

'Wow Ambrite, what a story! I am so sorry for what you had to go through but at least you have us now and your grandfather would be so proud of you!' Danni exclaimed.

Hunter nodded in agreement and the three of them sat contented for a few minutes.

'Wait a minute!' Danni said. 'What does Hunter's story have to do with yours?'

Her mind quickly flashed back to the book Hunter was holding which explained how to deal with unfit parents.

Hunter looked at Danni with a steady gaze. 'Well, my story is neither better or worse than A's, it is just hard and every day I am getting through it. I know that Dr. Yates has certainly helped me although I would've denied it in the past and she says how much happier I have been since I met Ambrite and opened up to her.'

Danni thought about the Hunter who was so gentle and nice with her at Bouquet Reserve when he had nearly told his story. This was all because of Ambrite. She felt a surge of happiness when she realised the group had bought them together and made their lives a little easier.

'I want you now to finally hear my story…you deserve to hear it Danni.'

It was now Ambrite's turn to comfort Hunter and make sure he knew she was there for him every step of the way. It warmed Danni to see them two and she made a mental note to give Reilly and Drew the biggest hugs they would ever receive.

'That time I nearly confessed at Bouquet Reserve; I told you that it was something I had witnessed several years ago and in turn it affected my schooling. It caused my mum to send me to Dr. Yates so that I could talk about it. The thing is that although the problem is no longer a physical issue, it made me so angry inside and bitter to everyone around me. Yates did her best to channel my anger and talk about the best ways of dealing with it.'

Danni nodded, shifting in her chair. She wanted him to know he had her full attention.

'My childhood was similar to Ambrite's where I didn't receive much attention from my parents. My father was such a dropkick that my mother spent all of her time trying to fix him and meet his needs so that she never met mine. I didn't act out or anything like A; I just watched my mum try and fail every single time. He was mum's jealous and alcoholic boyfriend from High school who knocked her up, so everyone knew she belonged to him and yet resented both of us. He reminded me nearly every day of my childhood that my only purpose in life was to mark mum's territory for him and I felt like nothing but a useless prop!'

Ambrite and Danni watched the heat of anger rise in his face. There were years of emotional destruction in the boy and he was only just learning how to deal with it. Danni could now completely understand his storming out and screaming at the Centre. Ambrite ran to get Hunter a glass of water now which actually saw his face break into a momentary grin at the irony. Then his stony gaze returned and so did his story.

'The only good thing about my father was he worked to keep the family supported and he never hit my mother or me. He was more of an aggressive, verbal coward who threatened with words but never acted on them. He is what Yates calls a sociopath and reading up on them I can see now his ways were nothing personal to me; he would be that way with anyone he could control but I still hate him for it. One day, after my mother warned me to leave my father alone in his room because he was still hung over from his usual drinking binges; I stupidly walked in to take a peek. I still don't know to this day why I walked in. I hated my father but for some reason I enjoyed seeing him drunk and depressed. I got satisfaction out of his weak limbs hanging off the bed and his head in a bucket. This time in particular, I saw more than the usual after effects of alcohol.'

Hunter took a deep breath and Danni noticed how white his knuckles had become from his clenched up fists. She rubbed his arms and Ambrite smoothed his hair in a calming, motherly manner.

'I saw him injecting himself with heroin. Before that moment I had never understood my father's need to wear long sleeve shirts even in summer, but that day I saw his ugly and bright red veins sticking out of his arms and a needle suspended in his flesh. He could barely murmur two words as he was drugged out and hung over but I ran outside…vomiting in the garden for a good hour. The worst part about it is I will never get that image out of my head. I will always hold it in my mind and it makes me so goddamn angry!'

He slumped back on the couch in defeat. Ambrite widened her eyes at Danni as if to say *'that's pretty big isn't it?'* Danni nodded back with a deep sadness. Two members of her group were so damaged and she could only speculate about some of the others' stories. She wondered what was behind Ronan's sexism and knew one day she would hear that story as well.

'I don't want to focus on this part,' Hunter began again. 'I want to skip to the part where things began to get better. After my mother had found me outside being sick she knew what had happened and called the police. She just couldn't take the abuse and drugs anymore. It didn't matter that we would struggle financially; he had to go. He was immediately taken in and jailed for drug possession and alcoholic abuse. He is still in there and from what I have heard…he prefers it in there. Says there is no responsibility or stupid kids to take care of…anyway…my mother and I packed up and moved to Juggler's Corner where I began acting out at school. I went to your school Danni but Principal Mason ended up expelling me for starting fights with every kid who looked at me in a funny way and I was referred to Doctor Yates. You probably didn't know me…I wasn't there for very long and I am one year older than you all, so I wasn't even in your area.'

Danni shook her head; she didn't ever remember Hunter being at J-Corner High but then again Danni lived in her head so much of the time that she wouldn't notice even if Hunter had started a fight with *her*!

'Danni, do you know why Ambrite and I were both referred to Dr. Yates?'

Danni once again shook her head.

'Do you remember that unfit parents' book I was reading at the clinic? She wrote that...she is an expert in dealing with parental issues where children are concerned. Both Ambrite and I were referred because we had experienced similar stories. When Dr. Yates had found out that Ambrite had attempted a drug overdose she knew that I would understand how wrong that was and try to talk her out of it happening again.'

'And now I feel horrible for ever considering it after what Hunter went through!' Ambrite groaned in disgust.

Hunter gave her a quick hug which let her know it was alright.

'For such a long time I wanted to live in my anger...it was safe and I was comfortable there. I stormed out of every session and yelled at anyone who tried to help me. When you came to me Danni and proposed this group...I just knew that maybe I would meet people who understood me and I could start to forget the past. When Ambrite came up to me and told me who she was...I began to get my life back. We help each other deal with our problems and even though I am still scarred from my past and Ambrite's parents are still workaholics...we get better every day. I have now agreed to attend Anger Management sessions and Ambrite has promised to talk to her parents' about everything when they return in two weeks' time from a business trip.'

Ambrite nodded happily and squeezed Hunter's hand.

'We are so happy to have found each other and to have found you Danni. You have completely changed our lives.'

Danni felt a tear slide down her cheek. She had heard two incredibly tragic stories in one day and was so touched at how they both had managed to rebuild their lives together. She also couldn't help the swelling of pride in her chest at Ambrite's kind words.

'Thank you both so much for sharing and confiding in me. I will keep your stories safe and never tell a soul,' Danni promised. 'From now on things will only get better for you two and I know that it has been rough but rough time is over! The A.A. Team will keep us strong and united.'

The three of them stood up from the couch and stretched their tensed limbs. They all smiled at one another and broke into an emotional laugh. A bond had been formed that could surely never be broken. Not even Reilly or Drew would know of this moment. It would be theirs to keep and only the stars would know what was hidden in their hearts.

Chapter 23

THE STORIES BEHIND THE SIGNS

Danni could tell that her group were waiting impatiently, so she wrapped up her 'secret' conversation with the Leo and walked back over to the pond.

'Sorry about that guys; Crawford and I were just discussing a special event that we want to announce at the end of the meeting.'

She laughed as the entire group, including Ronan all groaned in exasperation. Drew just shook his head in disappointment and Parry was huffing and puffing, throwing her hands in the air.

'Don't worry, you won't have to wait that long,' chuckled Danni. 'Crawford and I will tell you everything once the meeting is adjourned. But for now… we are taking a trip back in time. I want all of you to go around the circle and explain the origin of your Zodiac sign. I am happy to go first to give you an example. When I was about seven years old, I first learned what Astrology was and I was absolutely fascinated. I immediately ran to the library, picked out books and read up on the history of Gemini. It is quite a long tale but I will keep it short so that there is enough time for everyone and….here is the kicker…if you do a good job of detailing your stars' background, I will give you a prize that relates to your story!'

The group cheered and clapped. Drew was screaming 'I want a fish, a real live fish!' and Ronan just grunted, feigning disinterest. Danni locked eyes with Ambrite and Hunter who were smiling at her and leaning on each other. The group kept glancing at them weirdly but Danni knew their secret and nodded warmly in their direction.

'This exercise is basically to ensure that you are all passionate and willing to understand how each sign came into existence. Of course one could say it was all myth and let's be honest, it might be but that doesn't mean we can't enjoy it, right?'

'Right' chorused the group.

Danni felt her knees wobble as she caught Crawford giving her a little wink. It had been fun discussing the details of the dance together without anyone knowing. It had certainly brought them closer together. She couldn't wait to see the reaction of the group after their exercise. There was no doubt in her mind that every member of the Astro A Team would want to be involved in this dance.

Clearing her throat she began to tell the back story of the Gemini.

'For those of you who don't know, the names of the Gemini twins are Castor and Pollux and they were brothers in arms…the closest pair the mythical world had ever seen. It was said that Zeus had disguised himself as a swan and seduced the mortal Leda who laid two eggs that produced the twins. They grew up together as friends and family and one day Castor was killed in a mythical battle. Pollux was so inconsolable and lost that Zeus, moved by their brotherly love, made Castor an immortal and placed the two together as a seven star constellation in the sky to shine down on us for eternity.'

Danni sighed deeply from the romantic tale and looked at the eleven faces staring in awe at her. She could almost swear Graham had tears in his eyes and Hannah was blushing furiously.

'Did you like that guys?' she grinned.

The team didn't speak but just nodded in agreement. Danni let out a little laugh.

'It is a beautiful story even if it's a myth. I have researched all the other signs' back stories, even those which are not the most romantic ones. I won't tell you which one is. We can have a vote at the end. Okay…who is next?'

Without surprise Parry shot her hand in the air.

'Oh oh oh, this story is so beautiful. It makes me so thankful I was born a Virgo…not that your signs are bad.'

The group groaned but Danni nodded for her to

continue.

'Well, in Egyptian mythology, the Virgo maiden was seen as carrying the tail of the Leo but in the Greek tales she was known as Erigone who lamented the death of her father who was murdered by shepherds. Zeus placed her in the sky as a 13 starred constellation with her faithful dog Maera the Dog Star. Romantic, right?'

The group just stared at her in disbelief and Hannah muttered 'how awful' under her breath.

Danni chuckled nervously. 'Yes it is a little strange but nice at the same time. Not the most romantic one yet but your story was well researched and I like that you mentioned the Egyptian side as well. For you Parry I give …this.'

Danni reached into her big library bag and pulled out a sculpted glass dog. Parry squealed and pulled it to her chest lovingly.

'Maera was very important to the Virgo myth and began the cliché of a dog being the perfect companion to a human. Keep this close and you will never be lonely.'

She could see the rest of the group beginning to get excited and eager to tell their own stories and see what gifts they would receive.

Watching Parry's success, Graham rose up and nearly bowled Danni over.

'My turn!' he sang. 'Okay Scorpio's guys, that sexy stinging beast!'

Danni couldn't help but giggle at Graham's flamboyancy. He looked so chic in a pink vest, white shirt and tight blue jeans with crocodile loafers. Hardly fit for tumble down Bouquet Reserve but that was his style and he wore it proudly.

'The legendary hunter Orion who is another famous constellation in the sky kept bragging about his meticulous hunting skills to the point he drove Apollo crazy. To shut Orion up he sent a giant scorpion down to Earth to sting him to death. Artemis who was in love with Orion tried to intervene by shooting the scorpion with her famous arrows and ended up killing Orion instead. She honoured Orion's memory by placing him as a constellation in the sky and put the Scorpion next to Libra to remind her of his death.'

Danni clapped excitedly. 'Well done Graham, oh I do love that myth because it is so tragic and epic. This shows how persistent and sneaky but amazingly loyal a Scorpio can be. For that wonderful story I present you with this statue I found in an op shop.'

She placed in Graham's palm a small figure of Artemis with a bow and arrow in hand. He grinned at it and, to Danni's surprise, gave her a quick hug. He sauntered back over to Parry who was eyeing his gift greedily.

Danni knew that Drew couldn't take the anticipation of his awaited gift any longer, so she signalled for him to stand next to her. She and Reilly chuckled as she saw him shiver in excitement.

'Alright folks, I have researched this to the point of having no life because I want that damn fish okay!' Drew yelled, scaring the group a little.

'My tale is romantic because it involves Aphrodite and her son Eros. Wow, that is like a wicked love combination! Okay…so they were walking along the banks of a river one day when they encountered a fearsome monster named Typhon. The mother and son called out to Zeus for help and he turned both of them into fish. They leapt into the river and swam away to safety. In commemoration of the event, Zeus placed the two fishes as an eleven starred constellation in the sky. This is why Pisces are such romantic creatures…born and bred from Eros and Aphrodite themselves ladies!'

The girls chuckled and the boys groaned, except Graham who was eyeing Drew with a newfound respect. Drew wiggled his eyebrows playfully at the ladies and then turned to Danni with a look of desperation.

Danni giggled and pulled out of her cooler, a bag with a goldfish in it. It swam happily around in circles and Drew let out a very feminine squeal which made Hunter jump.

Reilly stood up and placed her arm around Drew who was too entranced by his fish to notice.

'Now boyo, you should call this fish Pisces okay? It

makes sense and honours the group.'

Drew slid his finger under the fish's belly and stroked it through the plastic.

'Hey I will call it Mr. Puffer Snuggles. I just want to keep it and love it.'

Danni rubbed her hand down his back. 'Glad you like it, you deserve it after the dedicated research you did. The pet store owner said to feed her twice a day and with not too many pellets.'

Drew kissed the bag and sat down. Danni couldn't help but notice the gang shooting him deranged looks. She gestured for Reilly to have her turn.

Reilly tossed her black hair her over her shoulder and pulled out a colourful cue card decorated with arrows. Danni used to love watching her best friend doodle the Sagittarian symbol all over her school books. It was important to Danni to value and love the sign one was born under.

'Sagittarius is no normal man or beast,' Reilly began. 'It is a centaur...half man, half horse, and rides with a bow and arrow, hence the symbol. In Greek mythology, one centaur named Chiron was revered among many. He was greatly admired for his kindness and great knowledge and taught great figures like Hercules and Achilles some valuable lessons. One day he was severely poisoned by Hercules's arrows but because he was a god, he couldn't die. He gave away his immortality to Prometheus (a man chosen to suffer eternal torture) and he got to die in peace. So Chiron could be remembered for his sacrifice. Zeus placed him in the sky with the arrow that poisoned him…'

Reilly sighed and gave Danni a warm look.

'I just want you all to know that Danni told me that story once when my boyfriend of eight months left me and it has comforted me ever since. It made me feel strong and empowered. It is a really special myth that I hold dear to my heart.'

Danni pulled out of her bag a framed photo of her and Reilly in sleeping bags, holding hands. Her mother had taken it when they were thirteen and she had always kept it in a drawer. The knowledge that Reilly would tell the story that was a benchmark in their friendship, made her pull it out and frame it. Reilly looked at it in amazement and threw her arms around her best friend.

'I love you Dan.'

'I love you too Rye.'

It seemed to her that the pond was glowing brighter than usual but she couldn't figure out why. Shaking off her hallucination, she nodded in Hunter's direction. Although he had definitely showed a softer side of late, she knew the Aries was still prone to quick tempers and was curious to see if he had done his homework. He trudged to the front of the pond and she saw Ambrite give him an encouraging thumbs up.

'Ah yeah,' he began. 'I couldn't get the best information for the Aries back story so I will just quickly summarise what A and I found on a website.'

Danni could see that the group still didn't understand the friendship between the pair but seemed happy to see Hunter in a much more placid state.

'In Greek mythology, the Aries ram was golden and his fleece was removed by two gods that were siblings. The legendary Golden Fleece was retrieved by Jason and his famous Argonauts and Zeus honoured the sacrificed ram by placing him as a six starred constellation in the sky.'

Ambrite and the rest of the group began to clap and Hunter's face glowed red in pleasure. Danni pulled out a statue of a golden ram that she had bought at an Arts and Crafts Fair years before for the very same story he had told.

'You have earned this Hunter…well done.'

Hunter seemed genuinely pleased with his gift and gave her a nod of thanks. Danni noticed Ambrite snuggle into his chest as he sat down and he patted her head. They looked like an actual couple but the truth was they were the best of friends.

Ambrite proceeded to stand and walked next to Danni with a dreamy look on her face. This was not a normal expression worn by Ambrite, so Danni knew that she had found love in her back story.

'Well…Danni said that there was one story that was the most romantic and we all had to guess which one it was. I am pretty sure it is the story of the Bull.'

She looked at Danni to get a reading but the Gemini turned her head away to disguise her smile.

'In Greek mythology, Zeus fell in love with the beautiful Europa, so to get her attention he turned himself into a handsome bull and grazed in her father's herd. When Europa saw him she became immediately seduced by his charm, climbed on his back and they flew across the sea to Crete. He changed back to a human and they made love; creating three children. Grateful for the Bull's help, Zeus made Taurus into a 14 starred constellation in the sky.'

From the looks on the faces of the group, Danni could tell they considered it the most romantic tale yet and she agreed. Turning to Ambrite, she placed her hand on her shoulder.

'That was beautiful and yes that is the most romantic myth. I love that one dearly and it was great hearing you tell it with such conviction. I think you have earned this gift.'

Ambrite's eyes grew wide as Danni pulled out a beautiful heart shaped necklace. She clasped it around Ambrite's neck and watched the Taurus clutch it close.

'Keep this on you and you will find great love just as Zeus did.'

Ambrite just nodded without speaking. She was clearly touched by the present.

Nervously, Danni turned to Ronan who looked bored but slightly impressed by the whole thing.

'Ronan, do you want to share with us what you learnt about the myth behind the Capricorn?'

He shrugged his shoulders and didn't move from his spot. It was evident that he wanted to remain put while he told his story. Danni didn't push the issue; she just waited patiently for him to begin speaking. Eventually he rose but didn't move to the front where Danni stood.

'Ummm…yeah…I did some research on the topic and here is what I found. In Ancient Greece, the Capricorn was called Pan. During one of the wars between the gods and the Titans, Typhon, the fiercest of the group, drove the gods into Egypt. The only way to escape his wrath was to change their shapes. Pan turned his upper body into a goat and his lower body into a fish, then jumped into the River Nile and swam away. Zeus was so impressed by this concoction that he immortalized it forever in the sky as an eight starred constellation…Capricorn.'

Danni was surprised to see the entire group applaud Ronan and she could swear she saw a small smile as he sat back down. Feeling completely silly, she reached into the bag and brought out the fluffy goat toy. She heard Reilly and Drew snort behind her back but she still extended it to him with a blush. Once again to her surprise, he looked at it blankly, then reached out and put it into his pocket. He probably wasn't used to receiving gifts, even if they were a bit silly.

'Good job Ronan,' Danni smiled. 'I thoroughly enjoyed that story and it was well researched.'

He nodded without any apparent emotion and Danni turned to Brodie hoping she could begin and take the focus away from him.

Brodie happily skipped to the front of the queue. Danni stared enviously at her silvery blonde hair and sapphire eyes. She was such a beautiful girl and it at the beautiful girl. Parry simply sniffed in disdain and cuddled into Graham.

'Well guys,' Brodie began. 'There actually isn't a story behind the Libran sign, right Danni?'

'That's correct, I'm glad you picked up on that.'

'Basically, it is the only zodiac sign not to be associated with an animal or a figure. It is the scales which symbolises balance and justice. That is why we Librans are lovers, not fighters,' Brodie grinned.

'What I found in my research was that Libra is linked to the philosophical idea of Judgement Day, first heard of in the Ancient Egyptian text *The Book of the Dead*. In the book, the merit of a man's soul is measured by his heart on one side and a feather representing truth on the other. It is a four starred constellation that overlaps Virgo and Scorpio in the skies.'

She turned to Danni who clapped loudly and quickly reached into the bag for her gift. Danni pulled out a miniature wooden model of the scales which held a wooden heart on one side and a wooden star on the other.

'I actually made this in workshop three years ago,' Danni confessed. 'Drew had helped me out at the time because I wasn't very good at practical work but I think it is cute.'

Brodie gave Danni a kiss on the cheek and accepted it warmly. Danni gave Drew a wink but he was too busy talking in a baby voice to his fish. She couldn't believe how well this meeting was progressing and how much research they had done on their back stories. There was more than a healthy level of commitment to the group.

Turning back to the group she beckoned for Slade to tell his story. She couldn't help the blush that came into her cheeks as his steady gaze did not leave hers. He walked right next to her, their close proximity not unnoticed by Danni.

'Well the story behind the Aquarian is one I hold dear to my heart,' Slade began. 'It is about a handsome boy named Ganymede who became the most beautiful of all human men...clearly I can relate to this story...'

The group laughed. Slade was confident but not arrogant.

'He was so beautiful that Zeus, the almighty god, fell in love with Ganymede and swore that nobody else could have him. Transforming himself into an eagle, Zeus carried Ganymede to the skies where he made him an immortal cup-bearer in the 12 starred constellation of Aquarius. Since then, Ganymede is responsible for pouring wine for the gods and making it rain on earth. Two things his cup is useful for doing.'

The team applauded and Slade fixed his dazzling azure eyes on Danni's. She shivered despite herself, and handed him a beautiful blue jug she had found in the op shop. She realised it was a bit girly but it represented his story perfectly. Slade thanked her and sat down but not before he touched her hand warmly.

Shaking her head quickly she motioned for Hannah to tell her story. Typically, Hannah looked as though she would rather be a crab than tell a story about one but Reilly rubbed her shoulders and whispered something in her ear. Whatever it was, Hannah immediately stood up and walked to the front, her reddish hair bouncing. Danni noticed Drew pull away from his fish and focus all his attention on Hannah.

She wondered what that was all about. He barely looked at Parry anymore.

Reilly's meek cousin refused to look at the group and just focused on her bit of paper.

'In Ancient Greece, Hercules was undergoing his twelve trials of atonement. In one of his tasks, he had to fight a Hydra…a serpent with nine heads!'

Hannah shivered slightly and looked to Reilly who just raised her eyebrows. She quickly resumed her talk, her voice going up an octave.

'Hercules was having trouble slaying the Hydra as every time he cut off one head, two more grew back. The goddess Hera sent a giant crab to attack him as well as the Hydra but Hercules crushed the crab under his foot. Grateful for the crab's help, Hera placed it in the sky as a six starred constellation of Cancer.'

Her face tomato red, Hannah leapt back down on the grass and let out an exaggerated sigh. Reilly gave her a hug and saw Hannah let out a small grin. Hopefully, Danni thought, this would improve her confidence levels.

'Well done Han; for that story of courage and bravery, I award you this.' Danni pulled out a necklace with a small silver crab on it. She wasn't surprised to see a tear slide down Hannah's cheek as she put it around her neck.

'Remember sweetie,' Reilly said. 'Whenever you feel a little scared, think of that brave crab who Hera trusted enough to help her out. You are my brave little crab.'

The group laughed at that last remark and even Hannah giggled at her cousin.

With only one story left to tell, Crawford came forward and placed his hand on Danni's shoulder as though they were old friends. She knew Slade was watching with a glare and it still confused her. How could two gorgeous boys be so interested in her? This was such a new development! There could have been males that had liked her in the past but she just never noticed up until now…

'Lucky last,' Crawford declared. 'I shall tell you the fearsome and courageous story of the Leo, king of the Jungle of course! Much like Hannah's story of Hercules's trials, his first task was to slay and skin the much-feared lion of Nemea. This lion was no normal beast! He was immortal and grotesquely monstrous which made it difficult to defeat. When Hercules was unsuccessful in shooting the lion with his arrow, he tried a sword and a club but the lion merely yawned at his efforts!'

Danni couldn't help but grin at Crawford's storytelling skills. Like a true Leo he used grand gestures and loud expressions. There was nothing Danni loved more than seeing a person act true to their sign. It was priceless in her eyes.

'Hercules then decided to choke the lion to death…and finally succeeded! He removed the lion's head and skin with the beast's own claws, which he wore as armour and a helmet during the rest of his tasks. The Nemean Lion was forever immortalised as the fourteen starred constellation of Leo.'

The group broke into applause and Crawford did a comical bow with a flourish of his hands. Danni laughed and pulled out of her bag a statue of a lion with a crown on its head.

'Here you go King of the Jungle,' she teased. 'Fantastic story and excellent delivery.'

'Thank you my lady,' Crawford bowed. Danni noticed the group exchange glances over their obvious pleasantries. She didn't care; he would hopefully be hers one day.

Gesturing for everybody to face her, Danni put her bag down and smiled warmly at her team.

'I just want to thank you all so much for doing your research and making this meeting so special. Your stories were all fantastic and I enjoyed hearing them immensely. As an extra special treat for your efforts, Crawford and I have something we want to share with you.'

'Oh my God, you're engaged!' Drew squealed.

Reilly pushed him over and Danni blushed like never before.

'No, no, of course not guys,' Crawford laughed. 'We've been planning a special event for the Astro A Team that we want to share with you tonight.'

'Why has she been planning it with you?' Ronan sneered.

'Because it involves Bouquet Reserve and we all know my father trusts me to look after it,' Crawford explained.

Danni looked at him with much appreciation and

then turned back to the group.

'What Crawford means when he says special event is that we want to put on…a dance!'

There was a moment of pure silence and then all of a sudden Parry and Graham let out a huge whoop of joy!

'Oh my God! What do I wear; how should I do my nails? Graham, I am coming to Maltin's tomorrow!' Parry squealed.

'We can get highlights together!' Graham shrieked.

'Okay glad; you are excited guys,' Danni chuckled. 'But let me finish off explaining the rest of the details.'

She could see now that the group were getting excited. Reilly and Drew were glaring at her with 'why didn't you tell us' looks but still seemed happy. Hunter and Ambrite seemed pleased as well as Brodie and Slade. Ronan couldn't have cared less and Hannah looked scared as usual but overall there seemed to be positive feedback. Danni put her hands up to get their attention and Crawford began to explain the details.

'Okay guys, so remember that in keeping with the theme of our group, this will be an Astrological dance. This means that you are required to pick a partner from the team that suits your sign perfectly. You should go home and research about your most compatible partner and form a connection. It will test what you have learnt but will also be fun.'

'Yes,' Danni added. 'And to make it more

interesting you will have to come dressed in your sign's colour. Unfortunately for me, a Gemini's colour is yellow, so I will have to buy a bright yellow dress. For a guy you can come dressed in a suit with a tie or bow in the colour of your sign.'

The girls seemed pleased with the opportunity to buy a new dress but the guys apart from Crawford and Graham looked less thrilled.

'The dance will be held next month on a Saturday night, so during the coming weeks I am hoping to get all of your help in assisting with the decorating of the Reserve and any food, drinks or music we can bring to the night. Crawford's father doesn't know about this, so we are going to do a clean-up on the Sunday so that it will be spick and span on the Monday. Oh, and please don't tell anybody about this…it is our secret and we don't want unnecessary guests.'

Danni couldn't help think of Charlotte in that last part. It would be just her luck for that spoilt brat to come and ruin her dance. Hopefully, the night would be a success and the entire group could bond in a more social way. It was nice to see her group talking animatedly with one another. Drew and Reilly came rushing over to her with a shriek and she clasped their hands excitedly.

'Best night ever you guys!' Reilly said, hugging them both.

Danni nodded. 'I seriously can't wait!'

Chapter 24

THE MYSTERIOUS MEDALLION

When Danni had asked her group to assist in planning and preparing the dance, she meant to organise food, decorations, etc. She did not mean to drag her to every fashion boutique in the state and make her try on dresses! When it came to fashion and outfit preparation, Danni was not the most skilled. She was quite comfortable in jeans, hoodies and the occasional blue sparkly dress. Parry, however, was quite literally born to dress, design and coordinate colours and patterns.

'Let's try this one in at least four different sizes!' she squealed, holding up yet another dress that wasn't so much for a dance at the park but rather at a beach party in Malibu.

Danni groaned and wished for the millionth time that day that she hadn't asked Parry for help with what to wear. She also regretted making the rule that each girl had to buy a dress of the colour that matches their sign. Yellow was not exactly popular in fashionable attire and when it did appear, it didn't exactly look sexy or bring out any feature in Danni that Crawford would find appealing. She was also hoping that the girls: Reilly, Parry and Brodie would focus on *their* dresses but it seemed the highlight of the day was watching Danni squirm as they overwhelmed her with fashion.

'Guys, can we please take a break?' Danni moaned and slumped against the change room mirror.

"NO!" chorused the grinning girls, clearly getting pleasure from the Gemini's pain.

Danni was not used to this. She had never spent more than an hour looking for clothes. Usually it was walk in, see an item of clothing that suited her slim figure and walk out. After nearly four hours of trailing store after store, she was exhausted.

'Okay, maybe I should just give up on finding a yellow dress,' Danni said. 'If worse comes to worse, I will just paint a white dress the colour I need.'

'What about this one Dan?' Brodie beckoned.

Danni looked up to see her friend pull out a breathtaking mustard dress. It was strapless and dark yellow but decorated with black lace frills at the bottom and patterns of black across the bust. For once in Danni's life, she actually cared about fashion and practically snatched it out of Brodie's hand to try it on. While the girls oohed and aahed over the style, Danni wriggled out of her jeans and T-shirt for the umpteenth time and pulled the dress carefully over her head. Without warning, Parry walked in and zipped up the back for her. She watched Danni's smile in the mirror, squealed and yelled for the other girls to come in. Straight away they all looked at each other and shrieked. Danni couldn't stop eyeing her slightly tanned form in the dress. It looked so beautiful on her and fit her figure perfectly. She knew this was the dress for her. Not only would it grab Crawford's attention but it would finally make her feel less like an awkward teenager and more like a woman. Her parents would be so shocked to see her like this. She laughed a little at the thought.

She turned to the chatty girls poking and prodding her.

'I'm buying it guys!'

The girls whooped in victory and began helping her out of it.

'Ah,' Danni sighed. 'Now we can finally go home and rest.'

'Nah uh, Danni my dear,' Parry crooned. 'It's time for shoes!'

The girls laughed at Danni's horrified expression.

*****

Hanging up the gorgeous dress in a plastic covering, Danni sat on her bed and took a moment to gaze at it and think about what it represented. It didn't just symbolise the colour of the Gemini. It was a step toward her future as an individual and a girl. She had expressed before that she wasn't interested in just being cute anymore. She wanted to be sexy and to be noticed and it had been happening a lot lately. The hostility that seemed to burn between Crawford and Slade excited her more than concerned her. She should've been more upset by this notion but it was the first time any male had ever paid attention to her; she was going to enjoy it. But what if it ever came to the crunch and she had to choose between the two? She raced to her drawer, opened it up and took out a sheet of paper. With a pen in hand she divided the paper into two columns, wrote Slade on one side and Crawford on the other. Smiling, she knew it was more of a Virgo trait to make lists and plan things but it honestly seemed like the only logical way to make a decision. She was just about to write 'has accent' under Slade's column when she heard a chuckle. Danni jumped and dropped her pencil before she noticed the dark shadow sitting on her window sill.

'What are you doing here? And how did you get in my window?'

Danni stared at the leather clad Garth who was grinning from ear to ear. He continued to snigger and picked up her pencil, handing it to her mischievously.

'Well, hello to you too Danni.'

Reluctantly she took her pencil back from his outstretched hand and narrowed her eyes.

'You didn't answer my question.'

Without a care, he seated himself down on her bed. She noticed he smiled warmly at her Wheel of the Zodiac poster and clicked his tongue at the photo of Danni, Drew and Reilly in front of the Funky Fries leaning on each other. She took a moment to once again take in his long black cloak, charcoal detective type hat and dark skin. This time, she noticed he wore a silver medallion around his neck which resembled a whiskery dragon with flames for a tail. It intrigued her and she was certain it was significant to him in some way. This figure was so mysterious and elusive that she was almost convinced he was a figment of her imagination.

'So, did you get a good look there Gemini?'

Garth raised his eyebrows from his sitting position on the bed.

Shaking her head, Danni glared.

'Look, you are the one who came into my room unannounced and don't even have the decency to explain who you are and why you insist on tormenting me.'

Garth didn't appear one bit troubled by her outburst. He just smiled.

'I told you my name...'

Danni sighed heavily. 'Okay let me take a different tack; you obviously aren't in my room to hang and discuss the latest gossip so... why are you here?'

Garth chuckled again and walked around her room examining each object with great interest. He stopped near the Wheel of the Zodiac poster, traced a finger over the signs and then turned to Danni.

'Name the three categories the signs can belong to and what is yours?'

Danni eyed him suspiciously.

'Mutable, Cardinal and Fixed. A Gemini belongs under the category of Mutable because they are so adaptable. Why?'

Garth let out a hoot of laughter and clapped his hands so loudly that she was certain her family could hear it.

'Ye Gods I love you! You're perfect!'

Danni widened her eyes. 'Okay… well I can't say I feel the same; sorry but thank you.'

He started towards the window and Danni was certain he was going to take off again without an explanation but then he turned to her.

'Not to eavesdrop, but maybe there are more important things in your life right now than focusing on which boy is your Prince Charming? The Aquarian and the Leo aren't going anywhere if I have anything to say about it. The main thing you should focus on right now is getting your group together, work out your differences and make sure no one strays.'

Garth tipped his hat in a gentlemanly fashion and

stood on the open window, the wind blowing his cloak, the night enveloping his frame.

'Garth wait!' Danni yelled before he jumped or vanished into thin air. He stopped any movement but didn't turn to face her.

'I don't know how you know any of that but tell me one thing. Are you responsible for my dreams?'

'I am your dreams Gemini…' she heard him say before he leapt into the night sky. She knew once she looked out the window that he wouldn't be there but it didn't stop her shiver when she thought she heard a dragon roar in the wind.

***

Over the years Danni had confided her deep thoughts and feelings to Reilly and Drew. They knew when she had put blue marker in her hair to make it look edgy. They knew when she tripped over two chairs in front of Mr. Bentley in the ninth grade because she found him cute and they knew that she ate her vegetables before any other food on her plate so that she could enjoy the best parts last. But what happened the night before was different. And what happened the time before that also remained a secret. It was bad enough that her friends found her strange on account of her weird obsessions and nutty dreams. What would they think if she had mentioned a tall dark stranger hung out in her room last night and just happened to know all her innermost thoughts and plans for some weird reason? She just couldn't take the concerned stares and worried glances between her two best friends. Apart from that, she had noticed Drew had been really preoccupied at school, strumming his guitar and staring off into space, while Reilly had been incredibly moody and flustered around the Drayman twins. Every time she felt herself lapse into a daydream about hot Crawford or cool Slade she annoyingly heard Garth's voice in her head telling her to focus more on the group. Was she being an incompetent leader already by trying to work out which two members she should date? Wasn't she supposed to spread her attention to the whole team and not just to the most attractive ones? It disgusted her that she had become so teen sappy and hopeless. It was time to pull down her sock for an inky reminder of why she began the group in the first place. The mark was branded in her flesh and would forever serve as a symbol of her undying loyalty to the stars. It was a Monday and as usual school was running incredibly slowly. School had barely interested her before but now she had the dance, the group, the boys (reluctantly) and Garth on her mind. How was she supposed to spend two hours tonight on her *The Taming of the Shrew* essay and make it sound convincing in argument? She turned to Reilly for a familiar grin and squeeze on the arm but all she saw was a sour glare at her desk. On the other side of her Drew held his face on his hands, his elbows on the table, grinning stupidly at nothing. She sighed and tried to write some more plot points in her book. Her next appointment with Dr. Yates wasn't until Friday and she felt squeamish at the thought of waiting that long.

What is with those two? Danni wondered, gazing at her two very distracted best friends.

During lunch she couldn't get more than a grunt out of them, so she walked over to the usual shady fence surrounded by the fruit trees where Parry was combing her long red hair and basking in the glow of her male admirers. She waved to Parry and sat near her while the Virgo smiled and ushered her boys away to give them space. Danni couldn't believe these airheads obeyed Parry's every command but she was grateful for the privacy. As usual, the Principal's daughter wore her skirt two inches shorter than Danni's and kept her buttons open at the top. It wasn't a surprise that she attracted so much male attention, however, the minute the boys were out of sight she pulled her skirt lower and buttoned the top.

'I know what you're thinking…but trust me; it's the only way I can get waited on hand and foot.' She winked at the amused Danni.

Danni grinned and smoothed the grass out under her. 'What's it like being the Principal's daughter?'

For an instant, she thought Parry's face flashed with pain but it was quickly replaced with a smile.

'Well, it's incredible. We live in the biggest place in Juggler's Corner; I have a wardrobe bigger than my backyard and am basically the sexiest girl on the planet!'

Danni stood up and turned to leave. 'Sounds like quite a life Par.'

'Wait...' Parry called out.

Danni spun back around to find Parry standing quite close. She reached out and brushed a lock of Danni's hair out of her face.

'That was annoying me. But seriously...it's actually pretty lonely...Do you think my dad has much time for me being the Principal? Why do you think I cherish our meetings so much?'

Danni tilted her head in concern. 'I didn't realise it was like that...'

Parry walked back to the shade and sat down.

'You make me feel special just for being born in September and part of a team. It's basically all I've ever needed...'

Danni found herself being strongly reminded of Ambrite's story. It was tempting to share as they could have found common ground but as a Gemini she had to remember that her mouth could get her into trouble.

Parry let out a sudden laugh. 'But enough of that! How about we go and get another spray tan after school?'

Danni chuckled warmly. 'Oh, there is no way in hell...'

Chapter 25
KISS ME...

The other reason why a tan wasn't on the cards again anytime soon was that it would seriously clash with Danni's yellow dress. As out of character as it sounded, Danni wanted to look her finest for Crawford. She wanted her first kiss to be with him. Yes, it was embarrassing, but she had never been kissed. It sounded absolutely crazy but she almost wished she had a person to practice with so that she wouldn't be perfectly awful when it came to the real thing. Then again, practicing on another person would defeat the whole first proper kiss with Crawford, wouldn't it? She was as confused and as spacey as her friends. To her dismay, they had even stopped hanging out regularly at The Funky Fries. There used to be a time, not so long before when she could talk to Riley and Drew about anything. She wasn't even sure which one of them had changed the most but it certainly had to do with the new group. Some members had hit it off amazingly like Ambrite and Hunter while others like Slade and Crawford looked ready to duel every time they were in the same location. How was she supposed to bring them all together when their personalities ignited supreme electricity? Each weekly meeting bought new dramas. Last week's saw an argument break out over who would supply the snacks for the dance. Parry said her family knew a fantastic caterer and all of a sudden Ambrite and Hunter were complaining about how Parry was so controlling and took every opportunity to flaunt her wealth. Parry stalked off crying with Graham running after her and throwing greasy glances back at the 'haters' as he had called them. Danni had to spend her weekend helping shop for Parry's shoes and dress and she hated Ambrite and Hunter for it. Reilly was pouty at Danni when she arrived at school that morning because she had flaked on lunch with her to shop with Parry. She tried to explain to her best friend that it was for the group but Reilly just groaned.

'You know, I am starting to think that you care more about the group than your two best friends!'

Danni felt her heart sink as she watched Reilly walk off towards Drew. She didn't dare sit with them and was worried that hanging out with Parry might lead to other unwanted favours. She ran to Bouquet Reserve for her lunch hour and read her English novel by the pond. A little while before she loved her alone time and found it hard to constantly be surrounded by Reilly and Drew but since the formation of the group she found an intimacy with others that she never knew existed. She felt so lonely at the Reserve that she almost wished Garth would join her. She laughed out loud at the notion and shook her head.

'Care to share the joke Gemini?' A playful voice called out.

Danni looked up to find Crawford walking toward her in green cargos and a fitting black T-shirt. Needless to say, he looked stunning. She walked over to him, slinging her bag over her shoulder and tucking the book in one of its pockets. She smiled at him in the flirty way like Parry had taught her.

'*Remember tilt your head and raise your eyelids up with a sly smile, he will be putty in your hands.*' She heard the Virgo saying it in her head.

He responded with a cute grin. 'So why are you skipping school naughty girl?'

'Oh...this is just how I'm spending my lunch break...'

Crawford raised his eyebrows in confusion. 'Are Reilly and Drew homesick or something?'

'No, just...hanging somewhere else.'

'So I don't get it. I mean, if you three aren't together then something is definitely up.'

Danni felt tears well up and turned away quickly in humiliation. She never cried and she wasn't about to let Crawford see it. But he couldn't be fooled. She felt sparks fly up her arm as he touched her gently.

'Danni, what is wrong? Did something happen between your friends?'

She turned to find him full of concern...and quite close to her face.

'Look, it's nothing Crawford. It's just that the group and its members are taking up a lot of my time. I'm trying to please everyone and I know Reilly thinks I've changed but I am really determined on making this succeed. I want to make everyone feel special but it just isn't working.'

Crawford rubbed her arm gently. 'For what it's worth...you make me feel very special.'

She smiled and looked up at his perfect eyes, cheekbones and lips. Those very lips took the opportunity to lean in and kiss her. She felt her insides gasp as he took her in his arms and stroked her hair. She realised at that moment that practice was unnecessary. Kissing was such a natural and instinctive thing. When he opened his mouth and let his tongue brush hers, she felt a sharp spark but kept going. When he finally pulled away she was so disappointed. Her first kiss had been breathtaking mainly because it was with a guy she was really into but she hated that it had to end. He was breathing heavily and she was blushing from head to foot.

'Ahhh...' Danni coughed. 'I should probably get back to school. My hour is nearly up.'

Crawford leaned in again and kissed her mouth.

'I would say this is the best hour well spent,

wouldn't you agree?'

Danni just nodded and tried to hold back from throwing herself at him again. She didn't realise how addictive kissing could be! She also didn't notice the slinky blonde figure behind the trees watching and scheming.

Without another word, but with just a smile, she ran back to her school with her heart pumping adrenaline. As the bell was ringing for lunch to be over, she saw Reilly and Drew walking from the library steps to the South building. She raced over to them, so excited with the news, but stopped when she heard Reilly tell Drew that she was going to go shopping for her dress with Hannah after school. They had planned since the dance was announced to go shopping for Reilly's dress together as soon as she had enough cash saved up. Hannah was not Danni and it was pretty clear that Reilly's plans did not involve her soon to be fading best friend. She had to put things right and soon, before she found Garth in her bedroom again lecturing her. The stars meant everything to her, but Reilly was her closest friend and nothing would tear them apart. Not even a group full of confronting and different teens...

***

Danni once again found herself lying on her bed, staring at the Wheel of the Zodiac poster hanging in her room and wondering why she felt so lonely. After being involved in a group that consisted of 12 members, Danni being the leader, you would think she felt closer to humanity; to everlasting friendships. However, her two best friends who would usually be lounging on her bed with her were elsewhere. If being closer to Crawford, her first love, meant distancing herself from the two people who had stuck by her through sun and storm, she wasn't ready to make that sacrifice. She needed to get out of her head and figure out what was going between her closest friends. She pushed herself off the comforter on her bed and traipsed into the hallway, picking up the cordless phone perched on the mahogany cabinet. Automatically, she dialled Reilly's number. After three rings, Reilly's mother Abigail picked up and greeted the silence with a cheerful 'hello?'

Danni smiled. In all the years of long friendship, she was yet to witness a negative side of Abigail. The woman was known to drive other kids from J-Corner High home when she saw them walking somewhere after school.

'Hi Mrs Chase. It's Danni.'

Her hands felt clammy on the phone and she couldn't understand why she was so nervous calling a household that she basically lived at in her spare time.

'Danni! How are you? Are you also working on that history paper Reilly was whinging about?' Abigail laughed.

'Umm getting around to it.' Danni replied. 'Is Reilly home?'

She felt a moment of hesitation and wariness in Reilly's mother's voice.

'Well actually...I'm surprised you called. I figured you would be at the movies with Drew and Reilly. They are seeing the latest action flick right now. You know...that one with all the bazookas?'

Danni felt a sharp pang in her heart. That particular movie was something Drew, Reilly and Danni had been planning to see for ages. It looked so ridiculous that they were looking forward to loading up on popcorn and ridiculing the entire thing. Why had they gone without her? What had she done? Were they jealous about her position as leader? No, that couldn't be it. They had been so supportive of it, especially during the first shaky meetings. Were Drew and Reilly really feeling neglected because she had spent time with Parry shopping? It just seemed too trivial to be the real reason.

'Ohh...okay. Well, because of that history paper I told them I couldn't go. I just thought they would be home by now...'

She felt awful lying to her second mother but felt so humiliated at not having known.

'Good girl! I wish Reilly would shirk some social activities for homework,' Abigail chuckled. 'Do you want me to tell her you called when she gets back?'

'No! I mean...no that's okay. I'll just see her at school tomorrow...'

Danni tried to calm her anxiety. 'Bye Mrs Chase.'

'Bye sweetheart! Good luck on the paper!'

Setting the phone down, Danni walked back into her room, collapsed on the comforter and buried her face in the fabric sobbing.

Chapter 26

HASHING IT OUT

Walking up to her home room the next day, Danni noticed Reilly avert her eyes the second she met her gaze. She looked undeniably guilty. Either Abigail had told Reilly that Danni had called while she was out at the movies with Drew or she felt remorseful just for having seen the film without Danni in the first place. Either way, Danni felt betrayed and incredibly hurt. If Reilly and Drew had an issue with her, she would prefer they spoke, even yelled if necessary, to Danni's face rather than continue on this way. Her head held high, Danni sat next to Drew and Reilly, managing a weak smile and just receiving uncomfortable, sad glances back. How had this happened? She bit her lip to hold back a threatening flow of tears and focused on what the homeroom coordinator Mrs. Phillips was saying. During lunch, she was making her way to Bouquet Reserve when she felt a hand on her shoulder. Turning around, she saw Reilly's face wet with tears and Drew looking as if he would rather attend school on weekends than face Danni.

'Danni...' Reilly croaked. 'I really need to talk to

you. I'm sorry it has taken me this long but I wanted to make sure what I was saying made sense before I voiced it. I even practiced on Drew...'

Drew nodded solemnly. 'It's true.'

'Did you want to talk at Bouquet Reserve? At least we will have some privacy...' Danni offered.

The pair nodded and they walked out the gate. Technically, students weren't allowed to leave school grounds during lunch or recess but since last year they had enforced a new rule that students over 16 were allowed to spend lunch outside of J-Corner High, provided they informed a teacher first. Danni had already told Mrs. Phillips she would be spending lunch break there which meant she could vouch for Reilly and Drew if need be. They walked along the familiar wet, concrete paths and entered the silent grounds of Bouquet Reserve. Danni's heart beat fast. She was torn between hoping to see Crawford raking leaves and hoping he wasn't there so that she could have a proper, much-needed conversation with her two best friends. The latter prevailed and Danni led them to the ring of grass marked by her group at weekly meetings. Danni pulled at some grass while she waited for Reilly to begin. Drew rubbed his legs, evidently trying to warm himself up. It would have been much more comfortable and efficient if they had spent their lunch hour at the Funky Fries now that Danni was shivering from the cold wind. Reilly cleared her throat and Danni looked up, finally meeting her gaze for longer than a second. She realised just how much she missed being close to Reilly.

'Danni...I want to be able to tell you how I feel without you getting offended or defensive. It's not that Drew and I aren't proud of what you have achieved. It's not that we don't recognise how difficult it was for you to organise something new and exciting. We have all been best friends for years and we wanted to take this huge step with you. It just feels like you are doing it all on your own and don't want help. Why do you need to be leader? Why can't we all lead? Since when was Gemini the superior sign?'

Danni opened her mouth in retaliation but Reilly held up her hand.

'Please let me finish. During this past month you have been so focused on the group that you have forgotten to check in and see how we are doing. We know you are keeping things from us. We just want to know what they are!'

Danni knew Reilly was right. She wasn't exactly good at hiding her feelings. Her visits from Garth had left her feeling dazed and confused the next day. She realised how frustrating it must be for her friends who didn't know what was going on. Looking back, she acknowledged the fact that she hadn't checked in with her friends' daily lives. She had noticed Drew's distracted fidgeting and Reilly's ever shifting moods and torn expressions. What was wrong with her? The group was not half as important as the wellbeing of her best friends although Garth would somewhat disagree. Instead of voicing these exact thoughts, she muttered, 'you went to see the movie without me...'

It sounded so trivial and juvenile but it had made her feel slightly betrayed.

Drew patted her shoulder. 'I'm sorry Dan. The second that travesty of a film ended we absolutely hated ourselves. It would have been so much more fun if you were there abusing the crap out of it with us.'

Danni let a small smile escape. She tilted her head to meet Drew's gaze. 'Was it really that bad?'

Reilly and Drew laughed. 'Just awful!'

Danni held out her arms and they both collapsed into her loving embrace. She hugged them so tightly; she didn't want to let them go. Releasing them after what seemed like the entire lunch break, she grasped their hands.

'There is so much I want to tell you. So much that has happened in such a short time. I want you to be involved in the Astro A Team as much as possible! Without you guys, the group certainly wouldn't exist. It needs you Sagittarius and Pisces!'

They laughed. Even though their small argument had only lasted a couple of weeks it was completely unfamiliar and new to the trio to fight or feel animosity between each other at all. Danni resolved to pay more attention and be honest with her close friends from now. Brushing themselves off, they all walked back to school, linking arms like old times.

After school, Danni and Reilly walked to the Funky Fries for a celebratory chocolate fudge shake. Drew went to the library to borrow books for the impending history paper. They settled into their usual booth, ordered their shakes and grinned stupidly at each other. Danni was adamant about fixing her friendship, so she sat up straight and arched her eyebrows at Reilly.

'So...? What is going on with you?'

Reilly blushed and sucked on her straw for a couple of minutes. Danni just kept her eyebrows raised until Reilly was ready to speak.

'Well, I was a little hesitant to tell you this but I've noticed you've been getting along with Crawford a lot more and the sparks are totally flying between you two!' Reilly's eyes shone and she flicked her long, black waves over her shoulder. Danni's cheeks reddened as she remembered her first proper kiss with Crawford. She couldn't believe Reilly still didn't know about it! After Reilly's confession she was definitely going to tell her. Reilly looked so excited that Danni was sure she was going to bubble over like her chocolate shake.

'At the upcoming dance this Saturday...I'm going to

tell Slade how I feel.'

Danni leaned her head to the side, confused. 'How you feel?'

Reilly stared at her for a second and then burst out laughing.

'Oh I forgot! We haven't discussed any of this. A couple of weeks ago, I realised I was totally and completely in love with Slade! He is so gorgeous and everything I want in a guy. He is cute, foreign, and a great dresser! Well needless to say, I was a little moody when I noticed Slade was paying a lot of attention to you but like I said, you and Crawford are getting closer and Slade seems to have backed off. Not only that, we are going to the dance together because Aquarius and Sagittarius are completely compatible!'

Danni stared at Reilly in shock. She hadn't realised that her friend had fallen for one of the cutest members of the group. While she was feeling that she and Crawford had reached a new level, she couldn't forget her vision about the two boys duelling over her. And she certainly couldn't tell Reilly that Slade had mentioned he would do anything to be near her. While Reilly seemed to believe Slade had gotten over his fascination with Danni, she knew better. The terrifying thought that this could once again cause a massive fight between Reilly and Danni filled her with dread. She just had to hope that Slade would see her and Crawford together at the dance and truly back off. Although, to be perfectly honest, she still was unsure of her feelings for Slade. What if the vision was a prophecy of the future and Crawford really did betray her? Thinking back to the amazing kiss they shared, she shook her head. They were completely compatible and the dance was going to be the start of something beautiful.

She grasped Reilly's hands. 'That's great! You too would be so perfect together and not just because you are astrologically matched.'

She wanted to show Reilly that she was supportive no matter what. Much like Danni, Reilly had never had any serious loves either. None of them had. They had always been so wrapped up in each other that they never had time for dating. It would appear that the stars were revealing their lustful, playful side. It was all new to Danni!

***

With the dance and the winter break from school fast approaching, Danni and her friends were full of energy and excitement. All the girls had now picked out their dresses and shoes. The boys were not as enthusiastic about their coloured bow ties and suits but nevertheless it was an event to look forward to. The venue was provided for and would be decorated during the day by Crawford and Parry. Crawford insisted on keeping an eye on the place while giving Parry space to run amok and transform the Reserve into an enchanted clearing. The food would be catered by Graham's family who loved to cook without needing a special occasion. Drew had been holed up in his room organising the music and lighting for the evening and Hunter even offered to bring a smoke machine he had bought online. The research had been done and each couple had been paired up according to their astrological compatibility. The pairs would be presented as thus: Danni and Crawford, Reilly and Slade, Drew and Hannah, Hunter and Brodie, Graham and Ambrite and finally Ronan and Parry. Danni was hoping these pairings would bring them all closer together and give them an opportunity to get to know one another. She was glad Graham asked Ambrite who he didn't really know rather than Parry whom he idolised. Ronan, who still hadn't revealed his indifference towards females, didn't seem bothered by his match up with the gorgeous Parry. Hunter mentioned to Danni in the last meeting he would have preferred to dance with Ambrite or herself but she explained that Aries and Libra were an excellent pair and that Brodie was incredibly sweet and friendly.

During her session on Friday with Dr. Yates, she informed her friend and counsellor about the approaching dance and Hunter's willingness to mingle with other people.

'I'm so proud of you Danni,' Dr. Yates smiled. 'You

have helped Hunter come out of his shell and begin a whole new life with people who support him. You and Ambrite should be very happy with the difference you've made in his life.'

Danni nodded warmly. 'I am. We both are. I'm just worried I'm getting blindsided by this whole first love thing and forgetting my actual mission to bring everyone together like I did at the start.'

Dr. Yates tapped her pen against her lips. She was well informed about Danni's liking for Crawford and their first kiss. She didn't know that not that long ago Danni was confused about her feelings for Slade. She was originally going to tell her but now that Reilly had confessed her infatuation for the Aquarian, Danni had to be the good friend and let it go.

'Danni darling, you are allowed to be excited about this young man, especially because you have never had a boyfriend before. Promise me you will enjoy this dance and get caught up in the romance. Then, after it's over, you can return to spreading the love equally. Agreed?'

Danni couldn't help but laugh. 'Agreed...'

***

It was the night before the dance and Danni, Reilly and Drew were eating pizza on her bed. Due to the amount of preparations everyone had put in, she had cancelled the   Friday night meeting so the A.A. Team could relax before tomorrow. Every now and then Danni would glance at her window almost expecting to see Garth standing there grinning and eating a slice. It was so great that they were all back to normal and excited about the dance. Drew looked on the verge of bursting as he played the mix CD he made for the event. Reilly and Danni swayed to the music and kept exchanging smiles. She wondered if Reilly was hoping to end the night with a kiss with Slade the way she was with Crawford. The thought made her slightly jealous but she pushed it aside. Danni let out a chuckle when she remembered telling her two best friends about her kiss with Crawford. They had leapt out of their booth at the Funky Fries and demanded every detail under the sun. Ambrite even sidled in while on her afternoon shift and clasped Danni's hands in excitement.

Now, picking at the strands of cheese hanging off her pizza slice, Danni squirmed at the thought of their next kiss. She kept imagining how the evening would go. He would see her in her dress and open his mouth in awe; then they would slow dance to one of the romantic tracks Drew had provided and at the end of the song they would lean in and experience the most amazing kiss in history. He would walk her home in the moonlight and once they reached her doorstep, he would ask her to be his girlfriend. After the following night, her life would never be the same.

It was a night of romance. A night when the stars would collide and souls would meet. What Danni didn't realise and would soon find out, was that things never go according to plan...

Chapter 27

THE ASTROLOGICAL DANCE

Her hair was straightened with the ends curled into ringlets. Her feet were covered in shiny black pumps that boasted a generous heel. Her mustard dress with black lace hugged her figure beautifully and her lips were painted with a shade of vermillion. Staring at the lovely creature in the mirror, Danni could not believe how different she looked. Her tan had officially faded but in winter her porcelain skin blended well with her bright dress. A tan would have just made her look like a banana! Twirling around and giggling in a very unlike-Danni manner, she wondered how the other girls would look in their coloured dresses. She wondered how her date would look. Crawford looked gorgeous in just work clothes but in a suit? How could she resist? She was so wrapped up in her fantasies that she didn't notice her parents come up behind her and stare in shock.

'Darling!' her mother exclaimed. 'You look amazing!'

Danni whirled around and blushed as she caught the surprised look on their faces.

'Oh, sorry guys. Didn't see you there. Do you like the dress?'

She twirled once more so that they could admire the full outfit. Her father frowned and gave his wife a knowing look.

'Well we like it but we don't like how much other guys are going to like it.'

'Huh?'

'What your father is trying to say love, is that you look a little too good and he doesn't want boys fawning all over you.'

Danni laughed and patted her father's shoulder. 'Well Dad I only want one guy to notice my dress and trust me, he is a perfect gentleman.'

Her father frowned even deeper but was silenced by a look from his wife. She hugged her daughter from behind and whispered in her ear 'go get him sweetheart.'

Danni turned and hugged both her parents, grabbed her long black coat and ran down the stairs where Reilly and Drew were waiting in the living room. Both of them were deep in conversation which gave Danni the opportunity to study the beauty that was her two best friends. Drew was decked out in a very smart and fitting pinstripe suit with a sea-green bowtie that melded well with his dark skin. His hair had been combed back and he had on a pair of shiny black loafers. Reilly looked absolutely stunning in a strapless, dark purple dress. Her silky black hair was curled and pinned at the sides with silver clips. Her shoes were strappy silver sandals and she had silver chandelier earrings that came down to her jaw. They had dressed according to their zodiac sign's colour and resembled celebrities. They both looked up at this point and equally took in her appearance, squealing over the finished product of their usually pale-faced friend.

'This is going to be the best night ever!' Reilly shrieked.

Drew clapped his hands together and began gathering up the music equipment. Reilly brought some cupcakes that she had decorated with sugary stars. Danni opened the door for them and they raced to catch the late night bus to Bouquet Reserve. Her heart was pumping a mile a minute. She remembered this feeling from the very first meeting. It was excitement mixed with fear. Fear that her night might not be as magical as she hoped. Excitement at seeing the first boy she ever loved. Danni was so certain in her heart that Crawford was her destiny. Not only did she 'dream him into life' but he was a Leo. The perfect match in her opinion. Tonight was going to mark the beginning of an amazing relationship.

As the bus pulled up near the high walls of the Reserve, Danni was super glad that everyone in town found the place creepy. She did not want any gate crashers spoiling her perfect evening. The trio stepped down from the bus and walked slowly, in particular the two girls who weren't used to high heels yet. Drew's arms were laden with equipment and music for the event which delayed his movement. Danni just wanted to run to the entrance but tried to remain cool and strode alongside Reilly. She turned to her best friend and smiled.

'You look beautiful Reilly. Slade won't be able to resist you.'

Reilly blushed and gave Danni's arm a squeeze. 'I was going to say the same about Crawford.'

Walking into Bouquet Reserve, Danni let out a loud gasp. The entire park was decorated with colourful fairly lights giving the illusion that they were at the Tea Party in *Alice in Wonderland*. A long table, stretched across the far end of the back wall, was laden with hot food, cakes and drinks. Hanging from the branches were coloured paper stars that had different zodiac signs drawn on them. The circle around the pond was lined with cellophane hearts and the rusted torches hanging on the walls were lit, illuminating the enchanted garden. It looked exactly as she had pictured it. She ran towards the pond not caring about appearing desperate anymore. At the centre was Parry all dressed up in a lace grey gown that hugged her hips and flared at the ends. Her beautiful red hair was done up in a high bun with a white diamond tiara attached to it. She even wore matching lace grey gloves that ran up her arms. In short, she looked breathtaking. Danni suddenly became very self-conscious and hoped Crawford still found her beautiful. Shaking her head, she nearly bowled Parry over with a hug.

'This place looks amazing; thank you so much! It must have taken you all day!' Parry laughed. 'Don't mention it. I loved decorating all day. Crawford didn't want to light the torches in case of a fire hazard but I convinced him that it would top off the whole look.'

'No arguments there,' agreed Danni.

Parry grabbed Danni's hand and she noted how soft her gloves felt. 'Come, have a drink and something to eat. Crawford should be here soon; he went home to get changed.'

Danni found herself at the table and, not surprisingly, Reilly too.

'Dan, this spread is delicious! Look they have pigs in blankets! I love pigs in blankets!'

Danni laughed as she watched her elegantly dressed friend stuff her face with hot dogs. She poured herself lemonade and examined the other guests who were already here. Ambrite walked over looking bohemian in a neon green halter neck dress paired with ripped stockings. Her hair was spiked and she had a neon choker around her neck. To complete the Ambrite ensemble was her famous black lace up combat boots. She gave Danni a quick hug and remarked on how amazing the place looked. Hunter walked up beside her in a smart black suit and red bowtie. His scruffy hair was brushed back and his dark eyes twinkled mischievously. He put his arm tenderly around Ambrite and she leaned into him. Danni still couldn't believe how close those two were. It warmed her heart. Looking up, she saw Graham power walking up the path ignoring all of them and rushing over to his BFF Parry. He looked fashionable in his burgundy suit and tie with matching loafers. Graham stood out and he loved it! The pair exchanged compliments and he twirled Parry around admiring her dress and shoes. Danni smiled warmly at Drew as she watched him set up the equipment. Hunter went over and asked Drew where he should set up the smoke machine. As she observed their movements she noticed Hannah walk in with a beautiful tight white dress and gold belt. Her straightened auburn hair looked gorgeous in the torchlight and she was surprised to see Drew's jaw drop and nearly fall over. Then she remembered how Drew had been distracted the last couple of months and always singing about a red-haired beauty. She had always thought it was Parry but his expression proved otherwise. Drew was in love with Reilly's cousin. She looked over to Reilly but she was too busy digging into the potato salad to notice. Hannah shyly sidled over to Drew and Danni watched in amusement as he kissed her hand.

Well, this is an interesting turn of events. I wonder what Garth would think!

As an automatic response she whipped her head

around expecting to see Garth getting himself a drink but he wasn't anywhere to be seen. Danni was starting to think he was a figment of her imagination. A figure only she could see. Maybe she should discuss this with Dr. Yates.

The party was in full swing now but there were a few important guests missing. Just as she was about to start asking around, Danni noticed the Drayman twins enter the Reserve looking absolutely gorgeous. Brodie was in a satin blue dress with thin spaghetti straps and a blue flower in her wavy hair. Slade looked equally scrummy in a grey suit with light blue bow tie. The pair got everyone's attention and Danni could feel jealousy radiating off all the other members including Parry. Reilly blushed a deep red and put down the meat pie she was about to devour. Brushing the crumbs off her chin she walked up to Slade and kissed him shyly on the cheek. He bowed in a gentlemanly manner and Danni could tell from a distance that he was complimenting her. She felt the slightest sting but ignored it as she saw Ronan approaching in a black suit and bow tie. His blond wavy hair was gelled back and he was surprisingly carrying a bunch of flowers for Parry. She squealed and threw her arms around him. He nodded, turning red and clearly uncomfortable with everyone's stares. The music was now pumping and the party was already underway. Danni looked around but still couldn't see Crawford anywhere. She checked the time on her mobile phone and saw that it was a bit after 8:00pm. She couldn't wait for him any longer. Walking over to Drew, she picked up the microphone he brought and tapped on the top to make sure it was on. Receiving a loud echo back, she bought it to her lips.

'Hello Astro A Team!'

Everyone turned to face Danni and cheered wildly.

'I want to thank everyone for coming tonight and making this a magical evening. Firstly and foremost I want to thank Crawford who is still getting ready for letting us use Bouquet Reserve for our Astrological Dance. It looks amazing tonight and that is thanks to the lovely Parry Mason.'

Parry curtseyed and giggled as everyone clapped in her direction.

'For the music and lighting I want to thank Drew and also Hunter for bringing the smoke machine. I'm sure we will all have fun with that later. For the food, I want to thank Graham's family who brought it in earlier today and lent us their table. It is a fine spread, so dig in and don't let it go to waste! Finally, I want to thank all 11 of you for making my dreams come true. You all look amazing, dressed in the correct colours and paired up with your appropriate match. You are the reason I sing in the shower, the reason I smile for no reason throughout my day and the reason I am finally happy with the person I am. I love you all. Have a wonderful night!'

The group went wild and Danni was amused to see Hunter whistle with two fingers as he was returning the microphone to Drew.

Reilly wandered over to Danni, holding a sausage roll slathered in tomato sauce. 'Where is Crawford?'

'I don't know but I'm going to call him now and make sure he is on his way.' Danni pulled out her mobile and walked towards the entrance of the Reserve so that she could hear properly. As she exited and walked to the sidewalk bench she noticed two figures pressed up against the wall kissing passionately. Embarrassed, Danni turned to leave the strangers to their canoodling when she noticed the familiar curly brown haired boy locking lips with the silvery blonde girl. In that moment Danni's heart stopped and she felt rooted to the spot. Her palms became clammy and her lip began to quiver. The two figures realised they weren't alone and broke apart breathlessly. They both stared at Danni in surprise as she let out a loud sob. She watched as Crawford and Charlotte looked at her with shock and pity. Charlotte in particular couldn't resist smirking. Finally, finding her feet, she turned to leave as Crawford shouted out her name. Ignoring it, she ran back into the Reserve with tears spilling down her cheeks. At this point she couldn't help but remember Slade's words in her vision *'he will betray you...'*

Chapter 28

HEARTBROKEN

'I tried to warn her!' Garth groaned, throwing his hands in the air and pacing the chamber room.

'Calm down Garth,' Asterion ordered. 'How could she have known this was how he would betray her? After all, he was her first love and look how it went.'

'The Leo is not to be trusted!' Garth growled. He walked over to Asterion's throne and slumped down on the seat to the right of him.

'Yes he has done an unforgivable thing but for our plan to succeed she will have to forgive him and keep him in the group. They will not be able to enter the portal without him,' Asterion noted.

Garth put his head in his hands. 'This is my fault. Maybe if I had made the vision a little clearer instead of making Slade and Crawford duel over the pond she wouldn't be so heartbroken.'

Asterion clucked his tongue. 'Garth, it would not have made a difference. She can't help who she falls for. We tried to push her in the direction of the Aquarian and she chose the Leo. She would have been heartbroken no matter how we played it.'

Garth stood up and walked over to the aquarium. He waved at the Piscean mermaids and flushed as they both winked at him seductively. Turning to the amused Asterion he scratched the back of his head.

'I know this sounds ridiculous but I'm starting to become attached to the young Gemini. It hurt to see her so sad.'

Asterion nodded solemnly. 'How do you think I feel when I see her hurt?'

Garth looked up abashed. 'Of course my Lord, but how do you feel seeing Charlotte work against Danni?'

'Devastated.'

***

Danni didn't know what she was doing exactly or how she was going to face her group at a time like this. All she wanted to do was go home and cry herself to sleep. She had never felt so miserable in all her life. How did this happen? He was her Leo; her soul mate. They had shared an amazing kiss and he had made her feel as if they were about to embark on a magical journey. He was her date. How could he do this to her? How could he do this with Charlotte? The betrayal ran so deep that in that moment Danni thought she hated him.

Running into the Reserve, she noticed the party was

in full swing. Hannah and Drew were waltzing around the pond making googly eyes at each other. Hunter and Ambrite were doing the robot to a techno song and Graham was posing in front of the smoke machine while Parry mimicked the paparazzi taking pictures of a celebrity. She needed Reilly *now*. She felt a hand on her shoulder and spun around to find Brodie looking concerned.

'Are you okay babe?'

Danni couldn't hide her mascara stained face. She shook her head and bit her lip to keep the tears from coming. Brodie took her arm and walked her over to a secluded section of the Reserve that had a painted white bench. She was surprised to see Slade sitting on it by himself and looking frazzled. The minute he saw her approaching, he ran over to them and looked deep into her watery eyes.

'Danni, what's wrong?'

At this point it was becoming impossible to hold back tears. Danni stifled a sob and looked around.

'Have you seen Reilly?' she muttered.

Slade signalled to Brodie to give them some privacy and she walked away but not before giving Danni's shoulder a sympathetic squeeze. Slade gently pulled Danni onto the bench and put his arm around her while she cried.

Tilting her chin up with his fingers, he repeated his

question. 'Danni, what's wrong?'

She wiped her eyes realising she probably looked like a drunk racoon. 'Everything,' she whispered. 'Where is Reilly? I really need her right now.'

Slade shifted uncomfortably in his seat and for a moment Danni forgot that her heart was in two pieces.

She grabbed his arm fervently. 'What happened? Is she okay?'

Not meeting her eyes, he gazed at the stars and sighed.

'I had no idea she was so much in love with me. I honestly thought this dance would be a fun night of getting to know the members of the group but she had this big idea that we were going to start a relationship.'

Danni nodded and remembered that was her plan with Crawford. She held back tears and urged him to continue.

'Well, we were dancing and she started telling me how she had a crush on me the moment we met and felt a connection between us. She explained some astrological compatible theory about 'The Wall' and said we were a perfect match. I let her talk but after a while she could see that I didn't feel the same way. Anyway, I guess it was a combination of nerves and the amount of food she had eaten before I arrived but she ran off and has been throwing up behind the trees ever since. I guess her night didn't go exactly as planned...'

Danni let out a sarcastic snort. 'That's okay Slade; mine didn't either.'

His gaze returned to her eyes and he wiped away a tear on her face.

'What happened Danni? This is your night. You were so excited about it and even when you gave your speech you couldn't stop smiling.'

Turning away so that he wouldn't see her pain, she rose from the bench.

'I better see if Reilly is alright.'

'Danni,' breathed Slade.

She turned around to find him inches from her face.

'I don't know what happened tonight but I have a feeling that if you and I had gone to this dance together there would have been a lot less heartache.'

Her heart constricted. She moved her hand to touch his cheek but stopped herself.

'I need to find Reilly,' Danni turned and walked off.

After looking along the dark clumps of bushes surrounding the walls she finally heard her best friend sobbing. Danni was in so much pain right now and really needed love and support but she had to be there for Reilly. She knelt next to the crumpled up figure on the grass and stroked her hair lovingly. Reilly looked up and when she saw Danni she let out a loud wail and snuggled into her lap.

'Oh Dan, I'm so glad you are here. I made such a

fool of myself! I thought...I really thought!'

Reilly was now crying so hard Danni couldn't make out any more words but she understood exactly what her tears meant. Reilly, much like Danni, had found love in the wrong person. The rejection and the realisation of that fact was too much to bear. Danni kept whispering, 'I know, I know,' while Reilly continued to cry and utter nonsensical words. The party raged on and the other guests were oblivious to the pain the two girls had faced that evening.

After a while, Danni helped Reilly on her feet and promised to get her home. They walked to the pond hand in hand and Danni noticed the music had stopped and the group were gathered around the pond.

'What are they doing?' Reilly muttered.

As they emerged from the trees, all the members minus Crawford rushed toward them and gently sat them down. Slade walked to the centre and asked for everyone's attention. Danni saw Reilly wince in his direction and then drop her head in humiliation.

'Astro A Team. I want to call a quick meeting because tonight has not gone exactly as planned,' Slade began. 'Something or someone has really hurt Danni tonight and Reilly...erm...is unwell.'

Reilly let out an exaggerated moan and Danni wanted the floor to swallow her up. Slade turned towards Danni and extended his hand to her. Reluctantly, she allowed him to pull her to her feet and she looked at the concerned faces of her friends. Slade rubbed her back and whispered in her ear.

'Look Dan, I don't expect you to tell us what happened if you really can't but you are our leader and we want to support you. Let your friends be there for you. Let us help you.'

She turned to meet his gaze and shook her head. 'Not here, not now.'

He nodded and stood back to give her space.

Turning back towards her friends she realised that Slade was right. Her friends needed some sort of explanation. But she knew that if she divulged that Crawford was making out with Charlotte and broke her heart in the process, they would kick him out. She recalled Garth's earlier words in her bedroom, *'The main thing you should focus on right now is getting your group together, work out your differences and make sure no one strays.'*

It was important to keep him in the group no matter how difficult it would be to face him every Friday night from then on. Only Reilly and Drew would know the real reason. She would make sure they kept it to themselves. Regaining her composure, she turned to the group and forced a smile.

'Astro A Team. Thank you so much for coming tonight and I hope you have had a fabulous time. This evening has been difficult but rest assured I am okay and Reilly will feel much better tomorrow morning. Crawford could not make the dance due to a sudden attack of the flu and I guess I just felt a little left out without a dance partner. This has still been a night to remember and if anyone has some free time tomorrow we will all be helping to clean up the venue. I wish you all a goodnight and sweet dreams.' The group didn't look entirely convinced but they clapped and everybody hugged goodnight. Danni watched Drew give Hannah a quick kiss and the pair walked over and helped Reilly to her feet.

'We'll take her home Dan,' Drew assured his best friend.

Danni nodded and she watched them both put their arms around Reilly and walk her to the entrance.

Hunter came up behind her carrying all the music equipment and smoke machine.

'Ambrite and I are going to keep this stuff at her place and return it to Drew tomorrow. I think she is going home with Hannah tonight.'

Danni thanked Hunter and was surprised when he pulled her into a quick hug. She was glad Reilly would be spending tonight with her cousin. Hopefully tomorrow they could talk about what happened. She didn't really want to clean up the Reserve if Crawford was going to be there but she had to learn to live with this. She was the leader after all.

The group slowly moved out and Danni managed to slink past Slade without being noticed. She couldn't deal with his obvious feelings for her now. She did not want her best friend to feel the betrayal she felt tonight. The Drayman twins had announced earlier they would walk home instead of catching the bus, so it gave Danni the chance to make it home first. As luck would have it, she only had to wait four minutes for the next bus to arrive and hopped on trying really hard not to bawl in front of drunken teenagers and the crazy old man who cracked his fingers and giggled. At her stop she ran to her house, relieved to see the lights were out so that she didn't have to deal with her parents' questions. Tonight she just wanted to be alone with her thoughts. As she bent down to lift the garden gnome and retrieve the spare key she noticed a figure coming up the driveway. Her heart stopped as she recognised his curly hair. She turned to put the key in the door.

'Danni!' Crawford shouted. 'Wait!'

She couldn't deal with any more pain that night but the urgency in his tone made her face him. He was the picture of guilt with his hands in his pockets. He couldn't even look her in the eye. Danni walked over to him, tempted to slap his backstabbing face. 'What do you have to say for yourself?' Danni barked.

She had skipped over grief and was onto anger.

Crawford sighed and pulled his hands from his pockets.

'Look Danni...I am so sorry. I had no idea you were

so into me. I really thought this was just a casual thing. It doesn't make it right but I honestly didn't realise that I was doing anything wrong until I saw your face tonight. I'll never forget the way you looked at me...'

Crawford looked down again and she could see his feeling was genuine but she was still angry.

'Crawford...I don't do anything casual. I am a deep girl who has never given her heart to anyone. You made me believe that I was something special. You made me think something was there...'

'Something *is* there!' Crawford insisted. He made to move toward her but she put her hands up and backed away.

'Is it? There can't be much there if you feel the need to make out with the one person who is trying to destroy our group!' Danni snapped. 'What are you even doing with her Crawford?'

He shook his head in exasperation. 'She isn't as bad as you think.'

Danni threw her hands up. 'I'm not going to discuss the character of Charlotte Orion with you. You saw the way she spoke to me last month at our meeting. You gave me the impression that I was your date to the dance. You kissed me and made me believe I was something special. You ruined my evening and broke my heart!'

Crawford's face twisted in pain. 'Dan, I am so sorry. I never meant to break your heart. I really do like you. I do! Charlotte had been coming to the Reserve after school to watch me work and we became friends. At first I told her to stay away but she said she had apologised to you and that you guys were fine. From the look on your face tonight I realised that was a lie. She wanted to come to the dance but I told her you were my date. On the way to the Reserve tonight she ambushed me out the front and started kissing me. I kissed her back – I won't lie about that – but I definitely didn't feel for her half of what I feel for you. After you ran off I told Charlotte she was never to come near me again but I went home because I didn't want to ruin your night any further. The worst part is I was really looking forward to tonight. I can't believe it went so horribly wrong.' Slumping onto the front step he placed his head in his hands. Danni noticed Slade and Brodie walking up the path to their house next door. She pulled Crawford by hand to the side of the house. Releasing him quickly, she leaned against the wall and turned to look at his surprised face.

'Sorry,' she muttered. 'Slade and Brodie just got home.'

Crawford nodded but she noticed his face change at the mention of Slade's name. The pair slumped into the grass, their backs pressed against the wall. Danni was doing her best not to burst into tears once more. She felt she had been dumped even though a relationship had never begun.

'So...is there any chance we could start over?' Crawford asked tentatively.

Danni looked into his deep brown eyes that she had grown to love over the last couple of months. Her mind was reeling with decisions and outcomes. She wanted to launch herself into his arms right then and there. She wanted to forgive and forget everything that happened that night but something inside her was broken.

'Crawford...you have every right to be a member of the Astro A Team. You are a valued part of our group and we need to stand united.'

The Leo nodded in agreement and clasped her hand with his.

She looked down at his warm hand, bit her lip and sighed. 'But...we will never be anything more than just friends. In time I'm sure I will be able to get past this but tonight I just want to be alone and not hold back the tears anymore.'

Crawford cast his eyes down in disappointment. 'I really screwed up, didn't I?'

Danni stood up and brushed off her dress.

'Kissing any girl would've been bad. Kissing Charlotte was the cherry on top. I'll be over tomorrow to help clean up...'

She turned to leave and opened the front door. The entire house was dark and silent. Taking off her high heels she sighed in relief and tiptoed up the stairs into her room.

Expecting to spend the next few hours sobbing into her pillow, she lay down on her bed and passed out from sheer exhaustion.

Chapter 29

HELL HATH NO FURY LIKE A GEMINI SCORNED

The morning after only meant one thing to Danni: the dance was over and she had to face the pain. Her parents and her friends were going to want details and the last thing she wanted to do was talk. Climbing out of bed she finally saw her face in the mirror and laughed at the pathetic sight staring back at her. Her makeup was completely smudged and her hair frizzed up as though she had just been electrocuted. Her beautiful dress was crumpled and her shoes stained with mud and wet grass. Her perfect evening had been hell on earth! Slipping into the bathroom she brushed the knots out of her hair, tied it up and removed the makeup up from her face. She took a quick shower and allowed herself a five minute cry before turning the water off and making her way back into the bedroom. Slipping on a pair of black tracksuit pants and purple hoodie, she traipsed downstairs, prepared for the Spanish Inquisition. Surprisingly, the kitchen was empty with a note left on the table next to a stack of pancakes:

Gone to the Sunday Market with Dad and Colin. Help yourself to the pancakes sweetie. Hope you had an amazing night! Mum x.

Relieved that she didn't have to explain herself right away, she looked at the pancakes and laughed as her stomach let out the loudest rumble she had ever heard. This would make sense as she hadn't eaten one bite last night. Pulling the maple syrup from the cupboard, Danni dug in and demolished the entire plate. She then ran upstairs to call Reilly but Abigail informed her that she was still at Hannah's and wouldn't be home until late afternoon. Danni was pretty sure Reilly wouldn't be attending the Reserve clean up. She was about to climb back into bed when she heard a knock at the door. Groaning, she prayed with all her might that it wasn't Crawford. She ran downstairs and opened it to reveal a figure much worse.

'Morning sunshine!' Charlotte crowed.

She was decked out in her cheerleading uniform despite the winter chill outside. Danni made to slam the door in her face but Charlotte grabbed it and shook her head. She laughed as Danni felt her anger rising.

'What do you want?' Danni snarled. 'Haven't you done enough?'

'Relax Gemini; I'm just here because Brodie and I have cheerleading practice this morning. I wanted to let you know what a good kisser your boyfriend is.'

Danni resisted the urge to slap her. 'He is not my boyfriend!'

Charlotte laughed and let go of the door. 'Well, I guess my plan worked then.'

Danni walked outside and feeling braver, she pushed herself up against Charlotte who was only slightly taller.

'I know you think you've won but the only thing you've done is made me realise just how truly pathetic you are. Crawford is still in our group and now he knows what a liar you are, so your little 'friendship' is over. Just you try and pull something like that again! It's twelve against one and I like those odds.

With that she stormed back into the house and slammed the door behind her. This time, however, the tears flowed freely and Danni made no attempt to hold them back anymore.

***

Walking up to the Reserve, Danni was not looking forward to interacting with anyone. She knew a few members weren't able to help. Brodie had cheerleading practice and Slade needed to finish his history assignment. Reilly was not up for it and that meant Hannah would be absent as well. She remembered that Ronan was going skiing with his father and Graham was only available in the evening to pick up the table with his family. Entering the Reserve she noticed Hunter and Ambrite laughing as they removed the coloured stars from the trees. The wind kept whipping them up which caused more giggles as they chased the errant stars around the place. Drew was packing his equipment in the backpack that Ambrite had bought back for him and Parry was putting excess plates, cups and food in the garbage bags provided. It looked like things were nearly done and she didn't need to be there but she walked over to Drew and handed him some CD's.

'Hey Dan,' Drew smiled, putting the discs in his backpack and then setting it down and hugging her. 'Are you feeling better today?'

Danni nodded wanting to avoid talking about it here. She wanted to wait until the three were having dinner together. 'How is Reilly?'

Drew began to unwind the cords that had gotten tangled.

'She didn't really speak much last night. We got her to Hannah's place and she fell asleep straight away. I haven't heard from either of them today, so I don't really know. Was it really just a stomach bug?'

Danni sighed. 'Look Drew...both Reilly and I had an emotional night but we would rather discuss it with you in private. We should have dinner tomorrow night at my place and then we can tell you everything.'

Drew nodded. 'I know you guys so well that I was

sure it was more than you were both letting on. Alright, let's do Thai tomorrow at around 6:30?

Danni smiled and picked up the smoke machine. 'Sounds good. Are you keeping this?'

Drew laughed. 'Yeah, Hunter said I could. Apparently it only cost him $5 online! You know that guy is actually pretty cool. It just goes to show what the love of a good woman can do.'

Danni was about to tell him that Ambrite was not interested in boys when she remembered something she learnt the previous night.

'Speaking of the love of a good woman. You and Hannah? Spill!'

Drew flushed and took the smoke machine from Danni.

'God, she is beautiful. I hadn't seen her since she was a little girl at Reilly's place but when she came to the first meeting I was smitten! I didn't want to say anything because I thought you guys wouldn't take me seriously. I'm not saying that is your fault. I've always been a flirty dude but Hannah made me want to settle down properly.'

Danni laughed at this. Drew acted as though he was a big stud but he had never had a girlfriend before. She hugged him tightly.

'I am so happy for you Drew. You guys are a perfect match...both water signs.'

'I knew you would say that Astro Queen,' Drew

joked. 'I haven't told Reilly yet but hopefully Hannah will and save me all the questioning. You don't think she will mind, do you?'

Danni knew that Reilly would be happy with the news. Hannah had always been scared of her own shadow and too terrified to talk to boys despite how gorgeous she was. The only thing Reilly might have a problem with was hearing about love when she was rejected and humiliated the night before.

'No, of course not Drew. She has wanted Hannah to find a nice boy for a long time and she trusts you as a best friend to take care of her.'

'I know this is going to sound weird but I love how frightened Hannah gets at everything. I get to be the big man and save the day all the time…I'm like a superhero!' He pumped his fist into the air.

Danni laughed and punched him playfully in the arm. She walked over to Parry and caught sight of Crawford raking the leaves. He looked up at her and smiled warily. She gave a polite nod and continued over to the Virgo. The table was now completely cleared but the tablecloth was incredibly stained. Danni and Parry folded it together and placed it in a bag for Graham to take home.

'Did you have a good time last night?' Danni asked.

Parry nodded looking a little subdued. 'I would have had a better night if you had.'

Danni sighed and pulled at some fluff on her

jumper. She could feel Crawford watching them and continued to busy herself.

The Virgo looked over at the Leo and frowned.

'I know this is about him but I won't push. Just know that you can do better.'

Danni was about to reply when Ambrite and Hunter bounded over with the bag full of stars.

'Do you want to keep these Dan?' Ambrite asked.

There were enough stars to fill a room and Danni had an idea.

***

Danni was looking forward to enjoying some Thai food with her friends and letting them all share their feelings. She had managed to cry out most of her tears, so when her parents asked how the evening went she managed a smile and said, 'it was alright but I realised Crawford isn't for me.'

Her father was very happy with this statement and her mother hugged her and left it at that. Colin called her crazy and ran away as she stepped towards him in anger. Twice Slade had knocked at her door to talk with her and Brodie once. On all three instances she asked her parents to lie to them. Thankfully, they didn't ask her why. She would tell them when it wasn't so painful. It was imperative that she didn't jeopardize her friendship with Reilly and right now she was very vulnerable. She was pretty certain one conversation with Slade would lead to something more. Brodie, on the other hand, clearly wanted to apologise for Charlotte's intrusion the other day. Danni couldn't think about that moment without getting filled with a burning rage.

Setting the table, Danni was glad her parents and Colin had decided to see a movie that evening. She really needed time with her two best friends. After making up with Reilly and Drew, she wanted to show them that they came first and the overall group second. The doorbell rang and she opened it to find Randy, the waiter from Feeling Thai in Juggler's Corner.

'Hey Dan, here is the usual and that comes to $47.50.'

Danni pulled out a $50 and a bag of gummy bears.

'There you go Randy, keep the change as usual and enjoy your sugary break.'

Tipping his hat he eagerly grasped the bag and began chewing on one as he walked to the delivery car. Reilly and Drew waved hello to Randy as they came up the drive.

'Man, Randy really loves those gummy bears,' Drew laughed.

Reilly bowled Danni over with a bear hug that nearly sent her flying.

'You are the bestest friend ever! I love my new ceiling. I said to mum that I knew it was you straight away.'

Whilst Reilly had been at Hannah's, Danni, with the help of Mrs Chase, had managed to decorate Reilly's ceiling with the stars from the party.

'I just knew you needed cheering up. Come and sit down. Food's here and it's hot!'

She divvied out their usual orders and poured them all a glass of lemonade each.

'Pad Thai with extra satay sauce for Drew. Massaman Curry for Reilly and Tom Yum soup for me with extra samosas.'

The trio began to dig in and were soon laughing and talking. They hadn't mentioned any of the dramas yet but rather focused on the hilarity that ensued before and after Danni caught Crawford.

Drew squealed with laughter. 'And then Hunter goes to explain how it works and he...he...inhales the smoke and believes he is high!'

Reilly and Danni burst out laughing and Drew was clutching his stomach. For the rest of the night he kept saying things like 'whoa dudes, the stars really are infinite.' We didn't have the heart to tell him that you can't possibly get high off glycol based fluid.'

They could barely eat after that story and settled down onto the couch. Danni brewed a pot of mint tea which she now loved after Ambrite had offered it to her. Every now and then Drew would chuckle and that set

Reilly and Danni off.

'Don't tell the poor guy. He will be so humiliated,' Drew pleaded.

'Who am I to judge about embarrassing yourself?' Reilly muttered.

She lifted her gaze and began to recount the same story Danni had heard from Slade. Drew and Danni listened patiently while she poured her heart out and offered her tissues when she began to cry.

'And so basically...' sniffed Reilly. 'I don't know how I'll be able to face him again after that night. He must be so creeped out by me.'

'He isn't Reilly,' Danni interjected. 'He told me what happened before I went to find you and said he felt awful. He honestly had no idea you felt that way.'

Reilly groaned and put her head in her hands.

'This is one of those things that every time I think about will make me cringe and want to move to Siberia or something.'

Drew slung his arm around her and Danni poured her a cup of mint tea. Settling back down on the couch she handed her the steaming mug and a chocolate biscuit to dunk. Reilly began to nibble on the biscuit and smiled at her friends.

'So R...I gotta ask...are you gonna keep trying or just move on?' Drew wondered.

Reilly shook her head and took another biscuit from

the packet.

'I am done. I can barely look him in the eye much less try to convert him into a boyfriend. He likes someone else. Probably Danni...'

Danni choked on a biscuit and Drew began thumping her back.

'Ow! Thanks Drew.'

'No problems D-Dog.' Drew grinned. 'Anyway Reills, you can do better than Slade. You were just blinded by his Yankee Doodle Dandy! The guy is going to become a celebrity or famous model and he will be dating all types of babes.'

Reilly glared at Drew. 'Thanks...that is so much better!'

Danni laughed and squeezed Reilly's arm. 'Don't listen to him; he is dating your cousin.'

It was now Reilly's turn to choke and the duo took turns thumping her back.

'Are you kidding me?' she gasped.

Drew confessed his love for Hannah and by the end of the story Reilly had tears in her eyes.

'Awww Drew! I am so glad you guys hooked up. She so needed a guy like you to bring her out of her shell, so to speak... You think she would have said something when I stayed at her place! I'm going to drill her for details tomorrow.'

The news had cheered up Reilly considerably and

Danni was certain they were never going to get around to her. She got up to clear the table and smiled as she watched Reilly plan Drew and Hannah's wedding. Drew insisted he be the DJ at his own wedding which set off a heated debate. Danni shook her head and heard her phone beep. She noticed it was from Crawford and felt her heart lurch. Taking a deep breath she opened the text. *Thinking of you. Was good to see you at the clean up yesterday even though we didn't talk. I hope you will forgive me in time and let me start over. Leo xxoo.*

Frowning, she was angry that he signed off as Leo. It was the way to soften her and make her want to forgive him. She had to stay strong for as long as she could. She decided not to reply until later lest she come off as desperate. Putting the phone down she turned towards her friends who were now staring at her in concern.

'Time to talk about it Dan,' Drew said. 'There is more to this story than Crawford just not showing up to the dance. What happened?'

Reilly looked horrified. 'Oh my God, I was so wrapped up in my own stupidity to realise you were really upset that night too. I'm so sorry Danni.'

She rushed over and hugged her. Danni stayed in her embrace for a couple of minutes. Since the moment she saw Crawford and Charlotte all she had wanted was a long hug from Reilly.

They settled back onto the couch and waited for

Danni to begin. She picked up her mug and took a long sip. The peppermint soothed her nerves.

'Before I tell you guys anything...I need you to promise me that you will not treat Crawford any differently or demand he get kicked out of the group. Despite everything, we need him. He is a valuable asset to the Astro A Team.'

The pair nodded but she could tell they were already planning on stabbing him with his own rake.

'Well...much like Reilly, I believed that the dance was going to be the start of a beautiful relationship. After our kiss I was certain he would ask me to be his girlfriend that night. I've never had a boyfriend as you guys know, so this was a huge deal for me.'

They continued to nod, urging her to pick up the pace and get to the point.

'I walked outside after the speech to call him and see where he was but...' Danni began to struggle and she took another long sip.

'I saw him making out with Charlotte against the wall...'

Reilly and Drew leapt up and began speaking over the top of each other.

'I'm going to kill him! I'm going to kill him!'

'The nerve! With her? Oh he is so out!'

'And I thought Ambrite was the worst member of the group!'

'Get a taste of my fist Craw Craw!'

'Guys, enough! Have you forgotten your promise already?'

They both stopped and sat down looking ashamed. She laughed and patted their arms. It was nice to see how much they cared about her.

'The story…it isn't over yet...'

She continued to tell them how Crawford spoke to her that evening outside her house and explained his actions.

'Although he was sorry and appeared to have genuine feelings for me, I just couldn't do it. I told him that we would never be anything more than friends.'

She looked down, hurt and dismayed. Reilly and Drew cuddled her and they were silent for a while.

'I think you made the right choice,' Reilly broke the silence.

'Me too,' Drew added.

'Me three,' Danni concurred.

'Wow, not sure what I was complaining about. Your story has way more heartache than mine,' Reilly sighed.

Danni shook her head. 'One does not outweigh the other. We both had our hearts broken and we both felt real pain. I'm just glad we could be here for each other.'

Reilly nodded but still seemed unconvinced.

'So we are just supposed to be all chummy with

him now?'

'Just act how you did before the dance. In time I will be able to move past this but right now I want my group united more than ever. No one else should know about this, okay?'

'Not even Hannah?' Drew asked.

'Well, she isn't the type to gossip, so that's fine but the rest of the group are strong personalities who will rage and insist we burn him at the stake.'

'That nasty little bitch so planned this to hurt you. You think a girl that attractive would have a life?' Reilly snarled.

'Well, you haven't heard the half of it!' Danni chuckled.

She continued to tell them about Charlotte's visit the morning after which resulted in a slammed door. Reilly and Drew whooped at how Danni handled the situation.

'Oh that was such a good call,' Drew said excitedly.

'You're right, after this incident there is no way Crawford would go back there,' Reilly mused.

Danni had lost trust in Crawford and couldn't agree with Reilly on that point. She just nodded and went back to cleaning up.

'Anyway, now I just want to return to normal and stay strong. If our group starts to fall apart then Charlotte wins. That is the last thing I want.'

Drew and Reilly agreed that Charlotte was a pest that needed exterminating. They also called her a lot of other colourful names that made Danni glad her parents weren't home.

Somehow, the conversation turned back to Hunter's antics and they spent the rest of the night in tears, rolling on the floor. It was exactly what Danni needed and as she reread Crawford's message that night, she pressed delete instead of reply.

***

Winter break was upon Juggler's Corner and Danni only had a small amount of holiday homework that she usually reserved for the last week. She wasn't going to hold another meeting until the following Friday because Ronan had gone skiing with his father and Parry had gone interstate with her family. The trio had now become a foursome with Hannah constantly tagging along to be with Drew. Needless to say, the couple were nauseating. Hannah had been the quietest, meekest member of the group since the beginning. Now…she was a tickler.

'Are you ticklish? Ticklish? Ahhh, so your feet are your weakness!' she crooned while Drew laughed helplessly and begged her to stop.

Reilly and Danni looked at one another and face-palmed. They returned to their strawberry milkshakes as Ambrite came over and glared at the noisy lovebirds.

'How many times do I have to tell you to keep your

shoes on in the Funky Fries? Three times this week I've had to separate you two!'

Instantly Hannah retreated into her Cancer crab shell and Drew quickly pulled on his socks. Danni and Reilly laughed.

The pair stood up and Hannah immediately grabbed Drew's hand for safety. Danni was sure this clinginess would drive her best friend crazy after a while but he just looked down at his girlfriend's hand and puffed up his chest like a hero.

'I must take my lady to the cinema now. Fare thee well fellow companions!'

Hannah waved timidly and they sauntered off together.

'So...still happy for your cousin?' Danni asked raising an eyebrow.

'I would be a lot happier if they weren't so lovey dovey,' Reilly groaned. 'Every time I call Hannah she talks for hours on end about all the cute little things Drew does. You think by now you and I would know the guy inside out but he is completely different in a relationship. Did you know he is really into bellybuttons? He does this thing where...'

'Okay I've heard enough!' Danni interjected. 'As much as their love makes us bitter about our own romantic situations we need to support the two. They seem really happy and well suited.'

'Yeah...I just wish we all could've had the magical night we envisioned.' Reilly coated her chip in sauce, looked at it and then put it on Danni's plate.

Danni nodded. 'I hear that. I still haven't replied to any of Crawford's texts. I just don't know what to say. I don't think I'm ever going to trust him again. It makes it ten times worse that Charlotte was the one he kissed. How can I forgive something like that?'

Reilly slurped the dregs from her milkshake rather loudly. She caught Ambrite glaring at her and glared back.

'I don't think you can Dan, but in time it will get easier. Are you sure you don't want to kick him out? Maybe kick out some other members too?'

Danni caught her looking at Ambrite with contempt.

'No Reilly, more than ever we need to stay united. I do not want Charlotte to win and Garth said...'

'Garth?' Reilly said quizzically.

Danni went bright red and cursed her Gemini mouth.

'Ummm...look...there is something else I haven't told you but the only reason I kept it to myself is because I'm pretty sure I'm imagining it and will sound totally insane.'

'Try me babe,' Reilly said, looking hungrily at Danni's milkshake.

Danni proceeded to explain the couple of instances

she had come into contact with Garth. She was certain he was responsible for her dreams and bringing the group together. She mentioned how adamant Garth was about making sure none of the group members strayed and that he would return when the time was right. It sounded more and more ludicrous as she went on but Reilly appeared enthralled in her story.

'Dan...I think this guy is real. Whenever we have meetings at Bouquet Reserve I always feel we are being watched. When I look up I sometimes see a flash of black but put it down to shadows. It sounds as though our group is a lot more important than we realised.'

Danni breathed a sigh of relief and pushed her milkshake over to Reilly. Her best friend slurped happily.

'I am so glad you don't think I'm crazy. Garth insists that we keep the group going, so I can't just kick anyone out and I don't want to. I love my group and it was silly for me to try and get involved with a member so quickly. I need to focus on keeping us united. There are still so many personality clashes and I'm worried at every meeting that a brawl is going to start.'

Reilly nodded in between mouthfuls of strawberry milk.

Danni grinned. 'This means making nice with our waitress over there.' She nodded at Ambrite who was cleaning tables.

Reilly sighed. 'So...Drew likes bellybuttons...'

Chapter 30

UNLIKELY PAIRINGS

A week and a half had passed since Crawford's last text message. She had never replied and they were becoming less frequent. Part of her was glad and the other disappointed. She almost expected him to fight a little harder for her even though she knew it wouldn't work out. Love was so confusing that Danni realised why she hadn't participated in it until now. Slade, on the other hand, had been calling and occasionally knocking on her door. She always answered his calls but kept the conversation light. As for seeing one another, she was certain that would be a recipe for disaster.

What Danni needed was professional advice and luckily for her, her good friend and confidante Dr. Yates was always up for a discussion. She felt slightly embarrassed as she recalled all the events that had occurred at the Astrological Dance. The last time they spoke Danni was gushing over Crawford and telling Dr. Yates about their future. Now, in the space of a couple of weeks, her world had been turned upside down. Her counsellor listened to the entire story and looked genuinely sad when she heard about Charlotte and Crawford. She began to frown as the tale progressed into the Danni, Slade and Reilly saga. She smiled as it ended with the blossoming of Hannah and Drew.

'Okay, you have now heard it all...and go!' Danni flicked her hands.

Dr. Yates remained silent for a while, closing her eyes and appearing to be deep in thought. Danni began to feel a little nervous.

'First things first. Danni Hamilton, I am very proud of you,' Dr. Yates declared.

'You handled this entire ordeal with grace and maturity. A lot of girls instantly blame the other woman when a man cheats. They so readily forget that he is actually more to blame. You have shown Crawford that he is the main cause of your heartbreak and that Charlotte was just being Charlotte.'

Danni nodded. She realised that the responsibility was predominately Crawford's. He did not need to indulge Charlotte but he did and just thinking about that hurt both physically and emotionally.

'Secondly, I am so terribly sorry this happened dear. I know how excited you were about this relationship but you are lucky that this happened now rather than later when you began to do more adult things together and he broke your trust. Because once you give yourself, you can't get it back, so make sure it is the right person.'

Danni flushed bright red. She understood what Dr. Yates was insinuating but Danni had only just experienced her first passionate kiss. She hadn't even had time to think about anything else. She realised now was the age when all her friends would begin losing their virginity and she began to wonder who in the Astro A Team had already experienced sex.

'Speaking of things that you can't take back,' Dr. Yates continued, 'this Slade situation sounds potentially harmful for your friendship with Reilly. If you feel anything for Slade then you must speak to Reilly about it first. If she gives you her blessing then by all means meet with Slade and discuss pursuing a relationship. But if she says it is a friendship deal-breaker then you can never be with him. As the saying goes 'boys come and go...' Don't lose the trust of your best friend Danni.'

Danni sighed deeply. 'You are absolutely right. I have been avoiding him for so long but I know how he feels about me now and I can't tell whether I feel the same or am just really vulnerable. Whatever the case, I can't do that to Reilly. She was so devastated that night. I know what it feels like to be betrayed and I can't possibly do that to her.

'Careful dear. These things have a way of just happening and before you know it, you've done something you can never take back. I am on annual leave for two weeks. When I get back hopefully everything will have picked up and things won't be so complicated for you.'

Danni stood up and nearly gave her a hug goodbye. These sessions had become so informal that she forgot this was an appointment.

As she turned to leave the room she stopped and looked at Dr. Yates.

'I just know I'm going to do something stupid. I can feel it and the worst part is I think I want it to happen.'

Dr. Yates nodded solemnly. 'Sometimes even when we know something is a mistake, we need to make it anyway. Just remember what you may lose.'

Danni just wanted to cry.

***

The Astro A Team meeting had arrived and for the first time Danni was not looking forward to it. She was going to use this session to try and bring everyone closer together. Usually the members sat with their friends, completed the weekly task Danni had set them and went home. She wanted all of them to mix no matter how hard it was to get along.

This didn't stop the thumping of her heart and the sweatiness of her palms as she entered Bouquet Reserve. The place had returned to normal and the pond continued to glow as the members sat around it. Ronan looked fresh-faced from his skiing trip and Parry was clearly showing off the new dress and boots she bought on her holiday. Graham fawned all over his best friend's winter wardrobe and Humbrite, as they were now known, were checking out a late night movie schedule. Drew and Hannah were draped all over each other much to the disgust of the other members. Crawford was raking the leaves and the minute he saw Danni he plastered a sad, almost pathetic look on his face. Slade jumped up immediately but sat down when he saw Reilly was behind her. Brodie caught Danni's gaze and mouthed 'sorry' due to Charlotte's intrusion on the morning they had cheerleading practice. Tension was in the air and Danni had to find a way to dispel it.

Shaking her head, she stood at the head of the pond and commanded attention.

'Hello Astro A Team. I hope you all had a wonderful time at our dance and please feel free to suggest anymore group activities at the end of the meeting. As you know, this group means everything to me and I want us all to be close. I don't want you to only interact with two or three people you get along with. I want all of us to be united. This is the time to get to know your fellow zodiac signs. The theme of the Astrological Dance was to bring a member you were most compatible with.'

At this, Crawford and Danni gazed at one another sadly. Reilly hung her head and Drew kissed Hannah tenderly on the cheek. Danni couldn't believe just how much had changed in such a short period of time.

'Well, this week we do the exact opposite. We have to spend time with our least compatible sign and really get to know them. I mean delve deep into their persona and see them in a whole new light by the end of the week. Are you all up for this challenge?'

Danni had to cover her ears while a deafening babble of eleven boys and girls began to protest. Hannah looked wildly terrified for some reason and Drew was comforting her while glaring at Danni. Reilly was shaking her head in the direction of Ambrite and Hunter snorted shouting 'hells no' over and over.

'Everyone shut up!' Danni yelled.

The group ceased fire immediately and stared at her, mouths open.

'Wow, it is great to see how close you all are. You can't even spend a week with one of your fellow members? What happened to teamwork? What happened to being part of a group that celebrates a tapestry of unique personalities? This hissy fit you guys have just thrown is the exact reason why we need to do this. Now quit complaining and act mature! I was going to allow you to choose your least astrologically suited partner but now I'm going to pick and you have to live with it.'

The entire group groaned in unison. She couldn't believe how divided they were. How was she supposed to keep them from straying if they didn't form enough bonds to stay?

Walking around the circle in a direct manner, she instructed the group. 'When I call out your name, move from your spot and join your partner. You will now spend a week with this person and at the next meeting reveal what you have learnt about them. I will not accept 'loves pizza' or 'favourite colour is blue.' I want deep and honest truths. I will accept nothing less.'

Danni felt slightly uncomfortable at being so authoritative with her group but if they wanted her to be leader then she would lead.

'Reilly!' Danni called.

She watched her best friend whimper as she knew what was coming.

'You will be paired with Ambrite...no arguments!'

Sulking and throwing daggers at her best friend, Reilly shuffled over next to Ambrite who smirked and threw her arm around her shoulders. Reilly nudged it off and crossed her arms. Danni knew she was going to cop it later but she didn't care. It was high time they started respecting one another.

Hannah now looked on the verge of tears at spending time with someone who wasn't Reilly, Danni or Drew. She buried her head in Drew's chest and whimpered while he stroked her hair.

'Hannah Chase!' Danni called unsympathetically. 'Your partner for the week is Brodie Drayman. Cancers have always been frustrated at the Libra's indecisiveness while the Libra cannot understand the clinginess of a Cancer. Good luck!'

Brodie smiled and sat next to Hannah who slowly detached from Drew looking red and puffy. She appeared more relaxed at the Libran's kind nature and smiled back. Danni was happy with this match. She knew Brodie's cheerfulness and zest for life might bring Hannah out of her shell. Drew was only enabling Hannah to be a quivering mess while he played the macho hero.

The rest of the group looked at one another, fearful of the pairing Danni would make next. She chuckled to herself. This experiment would either strengthen the group or tear it apart. She was willing to take the risk.

'For centuries the Aquarian and the Scorpio have found difficulty getting along. One is completely disorganised while the other plans out every movement. Slade and Graham...enjoy your week!'

Danni winked at the pair of them. Graham didn't appear to mind spending a week with the gorgeous American and he strutted over to the clearly uncomfortable Aquarian. Danni knew Graham would be so full on with Slade that hopefully it kept him from bothering her that week. She also knew their polar opposite personalities would cause friction but ultimately celebrate their differences. Danni began to walk clockwise around the pond and like a game of 'Duck, Duck, Goose'.

She stopped on an unsuspecting member and touched their head.

'Hunter...,' Danni ruffled his shaggy black hair.

He looked up at her through gritted teeth. Ambrite might have softened him but he would always be wild at heart.

'You will be paired with Parry this week. I want you to both listen to each other without taking over the conversation and do not be judgemental in any way.'

She said this mainly for Hunter's benefit knowing Parry's tendency to outshine everybody. Hunter wrinkled his nose in disgust. Parry was the complete opposite of the kind of girl he would hang out with. She loved fashion and boys while he preferred to grunt and listen to metal with Ambrite. It was the perfect combination in Danni's eyes. Parry ignored Hunter's obvious distaste towards her and sat next to him. She frowned at his shaggy locks and Danni knew she was already planning to style them. It would be interesting to see how this pair behaved by the end of the week.

The numbers were dwindling now but the Gemini had planned the matches perfectly. She sidled over to Drew and grinned at him. He merely raised his eyebrows at her with a 'what are you planning Hamilton' look.

'I want the fishes of the ocean to merge with the king of the jungle.'

She avoided Crawford's glance but saw the

confusion in Drew's eyes. She could understand his bafflement. Why would she ask Drew to spend a week with someone who had hurt his best friend? Especially since Danni had asked Reilly and Drew to treat Crawford normally despite what he had done. She wanted to match the person she trusted the most with the person she trusted the least. Hopefully, Drew could be a positive influence on Crawford and help return things to normal. She was praying for things to return to normal. Crawford merely nodded and sat next to Drew who he clapped on the back. Drew eyed him suspiciously but then smiled.

Danni nodded, happy with her choices. 'Now for the final pairing!'

She sat next to Ronan who snorted and turned his back on her slightly. His indifference towards females was exactly what she was hoping to uncover. Finally, she had the opportunity to get close to the Capricorn and discover a whole new side to him.

Standing up again, she addressed the group who looked clearly uncomfortable with their partners.

'Okay, let's run over some ground rules guys. One, there will be no putting down, swearing at or being physically violent with your partner. I shouldn't even have to say this but where some of you are concerned, I thought I'd better cover it...'

She purposely avoided the eyes of Ambrite, Hunter and Ronan.

'Two, you do not have to sleep over at your partner's house unless you want to. Spending a week does not mean attached at the hip. It does mean, however, that you will spend a maximum of two hours a day with them and engage in heartfelt conversations. Three, before you reveal what you have learnt about them you will get permission from your partner first to announce it to the group. They may reveal two or three things to you but only be comfortable with one topic being discussed. Please respect their privacy and openness to share.'

She really didn't want Parry or Reilly to blurt out the secrets Hunter and Ambrite told her unless they allowed it.

'Four, you will not give up on your partner no matter how different your personalities are. You can't expect to put the twelve signs of the zodiac together and produce harmony. This takes hard work and commitment. Try your best not to get frustrated and please give them a chance.'

This time she looked directly at Ronan who yawned purposefully. She found herself wanting to break the first rule of not engaging in physical violence.

'For the fifth and final rule, I want no grumbling and trying to swap your partner. You will stick with the person I've chosen and bring out the best in one another. You can choose to get started now although it is getting quite late, or go home and think about the ways you want to connect with them. Either way you will meet up with them tomorrow and begin your tasks. See you in a week!'

She watched as the group dispersed rather quickly and ran out without any of their partners tagging along.

'I guess this starts tomorrow then,' Danni muttered.

Reilly and Drew hung behind with the sole intention of complaining. Ronan shuffled over to Danni looking less than thrilled. His hands were deep in his pockets and he sighed deeply.

'So...what do you want to do tomorrow? It's the weekend and I was going to help dad with the car.'

Danni noticed he spent a lot of time with his father but never mentioned his mother. This seemed a good point to start. She smiled patiently at Ronan.

'Spend all day on the car if you wish and I'll come round for dinner.'

'Ummm...is it okay if I come to yours for dinner?' Ronan looked flustered. 'Our house is a mess and...'

'That's fine,' Danni interjected.

She realised there was a lot more to Ronan's home life than he was letting on and this weekly task gave her the opportunity to find out.

Ronan nodded. 'See you at 6 then. I'll bring a pizza.'

He then turned without saying goodbye to Drew and Reilly who were still glaring at Danni.

Turning back to her two best friends, Danni decided to stop their incessant ranting before it began.

'Remember rule 5 guys? No grumbling, complaining or trying to switch partners? Goodnight!'

***

Danni knew this weekly task was all about trust. Trusting that Ronan wouldn't laugh when she told him her latest secret. Trusting that the ten other members were meeting up every day and not just pretending to. Trusting that they would become closer than ever once this was over. Somehow, someway, she could picture Garth laughing and clapping his hands together in joy. This was exactly the kind of thing he would want. But why? Why did this creepy older man in a long coat care so much about her group? She hoped it was something much more mystical and exciting rather than just a sad pervert getting his kicks from a bunch of teens. Shivering at that last thought she went to close her window. She was certain she heard a deep chuckle as she clicked the window shut.

'Get outta my head Garth!' she yelled.

Her phone rang suddenly and she jumped. She almost expected it to be Garth but recognised the number as Reilly's house phone.

Sighing heavily, she pressed the green telephone button on her mobile. 'Hello there bestie...'

'How could you do this to me!' shrieked Reilly. 'Ambrite? Seriously? You do realise we are going to end up killing each other?'

Danni groaned. 'Need I remind you of rule number 5 again?'

'Oh screw rule number 5! Get out of leader mode and come into friendship mode. Just tell me why!'

Danni sat cross legged on the floor. 'I told you, this group is falling apart and the only way to strengthen it is to pair you all up with your least compatible astrological partners. Do you really think I'm thrilled to be spending the week with Ronan who hates my guts?'

Reilly let out a chuckle. 'Well, I guess my pain is a little more bearable knowing you will be just as miserable.'

'Thanks Reilly; you're a great friend…' Danni rolled her eyes. 'Look, I know this sucks, but please promise me you will make an effort. I know you don't believe me but Ambrite is a great girl and very deep. She could teach you a few things and you may grow to be close friends.'

Reilly snorted so loudly and defiantly that Danni had to hold the phone away from her ear.

'Are you kidding me? She is going to spend the week trying to convert me to veganism or whatever she is and I'll have to watch what I eat around her. This is going to be a great test of my strength and patience.'

'Well there you go. Take that challenge and own it.' Danni encouraged. 'We could all stand to mature a little bit more. Speaking of which...' She felt her cheeks redden and hid them with her blanket only to remember that

Reilly couldn't see her.

'What Hamilton?' Reilly asked curiously.

Danni took a deep breath and lay on the floor, stretching out and feeling her body quiver in excitement. 'Who do you think in our group...has had sex?'

Reilly was silent on the phone for a while and Danni could almost hear her brain ticking over. As close as the trio were, they never really spoke about the subject without getting embarrassed. They tried once to talk about it and agreed it was really weird and didn't want to look at each other differently. But now they were all becoming adults and it was a topic that could no longer be ignored.

'Ummm...I don't know really.' Reilly said quietly. 'Maybe Parry? She always has tons of boys fawning over her that I'm sure she has slept with at least one of them.'

Danni shook her head. 'I have to disagree. I think Parry is so comfortable in her own skin that she doesn't really need anyone else. It would take someone really special to make her take that next step.'

'I guess...' Reilly clicked her tongue. 'Well, as much as I don't want to think about it, from the way Hannah and Drew act when they're together it wouldn't surprise me if that happened soon.'

Both Danni and Reilly let out a nervous laugh at the same time.

'Well, I hope Drew tells us when he does because he is our best friend and we promised we would.' Danni said.

'Why are you bringing this up Dan? Are you curious about it? I'm not going to lie and say I'm not.' Reilly muttered that last part.

Danni thought about Reilly's question. She didn't have a boyfriend or a crush anymore, so it wasn't a topic she needed to think about or even prepare for. The Crawford situation had, however, sparked her interest in the physical side of boys and she had enjoyed kissing so much that she wondered if everything else was just as special.

'I'm not really sure. I guess we are surrounded by a bunch of boys and girls that may or may not have sexual experience and I want to know...what it's like.'

'Me too,' Reilly whispered. 'I wonder if it is amazing as it seems in the movies.'

Danni chuckled. 'I don't think so. For a girl I've heard it is really painful the first time.'

Reilly whistled. 'No thanks! That does not sound appealing at all!'

They burst out laughing and Danni was really glad they could talk about it with ease unlike the last time.

'Dan, can I ask you something?'

'Anything Reilly.'

'If Crawford had never kissed Charlotte would you have let him be your first?'

Danni felt the pain in her heart. 'I think... eventually I would have but he ruined everything and I could never kiss those lips again knowing they touched Charlotte's. Would you have with Slade?'

Reilly sighed. 'I can't say I actually thought about it. I just used to picture us running towards each other in a field. Slow motion style.'

Danni smiled. 'That sounds nice. It sucks that both our loves didn't work out for us. I feel closer to you now knowing we can relate to each other.'

'Me too Dan. I love you so much.' She heard the Sagittarius sniff on the other end.

Danni felt the tears prick her eyes. 'I love you too. I hope I never hurt or disappoint you in anyway.'

'Why do you think you would?' Reilly asked.

'No reason...'

Chapter 31

ONE WEEK WITH A CAPRICORN

Danni had already informed both her parents about the Astro A Team's weekly task. Surprisingly, they were looking forward to having Ronan over for dinner and had already quizzed her about a potential relationship.

'Ummm…no!

'Sorry darling, I was just curious why you picked this boy out of the other five,' Mrs. Hamilton asked.

Danni groaned. She realised her parents didn't understand the concept of astrology in the slightest but she couldn't believe how thick they were sometimes.

'Guys, I picked him because he is least compatible with a Gemini. It is about learning to get along with a star sign you aren't usually supposed to.'

'Is he cute?' Mr. Hamilton teased.

Danni was about to scream at her parents when she realised that Ronan was quite cute. It was his personality that ruined it.

'Well, he isn't ugly but I don't see him that way. Not now, not ever.'

Her parents chuckled.

'What time is he coming over?' Mrs. Hamilton inquired.

Danni turned to run upstairs and have a shower. 'Six and he is bringing a pizza. Oh and please keep Colin out of the way. He is just going to tease us about being a couple when we are most certainly not.'

Reaching the landing, she stepped into the bathroom and turned on the shower. She loved the pressure in her bathroom and waited for the glass to fog up from steam before she stepped in. The feeling of the hot water running over shoulders relaxed her instantly. She couldn't hide her excitement about spending the evening with Ronan. So far, he was the most disagreeable, negative member of her group but maybe she could change all that. She chuckled as she noticed her Geminian nature emerging once again. The need to help another person by getting them to communicate was a classic element of her zodiac sign. Rubbing shampoo in her hair she thought about the best way to interact with a Capricorn. She knew them to be very closed and private people, so an instant inquisition wouldn't work. She needed to make him comfortable with her. Something was definitely not right with his home situation and she knew in her heart it was the reason he was so reserved towards females. However, he hadn't seemed to form any tight male friendships in the group either. She couldn't understand why he actually attended when he appeared bored the entire time.

'Is it boys that are the enigmas or Capricorns?' she wondered aloud.

Stepping out of the shower and wrapping her hair in a towel turban, she noticed her pale face in the mirror looking quite gaunt. She hadn't eaten much since the Crawford situation. Her parents hadn't really noticed but she had. Shaking her hair free and watching droplets rain against the glass, she made a decision at that moment – no longer was she going to feel sorry for herself. It was time to move on. Crawford was not her soul mate. Her soul mate was still out there and he could be someone she already met. He could be Slade... She shook her head and gathered her clothes. Stepping into her cold room she pumped up the music while she danced around and chose an outfit for the day. She found a skirt and top that Parry had picked out during one of their infamous and exhausting shopping trips. The skirt was red tartan with frayed edges and the top was entirely black with lace sleeves. She looked more like Ambrite in it but it showed off her slim legs and rested nicely on her hips. She wondered what Ronan would think of her in it and then realised the ridiculousness of that thought. She had to put off being boy crazy for a while. Slade had stopped knocking on her door and messaging her but she knew he was still interested and it absolutely terrified her. She felt guilty just living next door to him and still couldn't completely say that nothing would ever happen between them. If something was to happen, however, her friendship with Reilly would be over and no boy was ever worth that. Her head beginning to ache, she raced downstairs and ignored the raised eyebrows from her parents at her outfit. There was something she needed to do and she had to do it alone.

***

Entering the library, Danni smiled at the irony that this was the place she had first met Ronan and in less than 4 hours he would be joining her for dinner. Nervously scanning the room, she hoped there was no one there she knew.

Mrs. Pearce came bustling over to where Danni stood awkwardly.

'Hello Danni dear,' she trilled. 'Are you here for more of those hoodoo voodoo books?'

Danni narrowed her eyes. 'You mean astrology? No, I'm looking for something else...'

Mrs. Pearce frowned and adjusted her glasses. 'And what is that dear?'

Danni felt herself blush and she wished for the thousandth time that she had taken a bus to the next town's library.

'Can you tell me where...the health section is?'

'Of course. Just walk straight ahead and then turn

left at the end. All the health and lifestyle books are stacked against the back wall. Is everything okay dear?'

Danni began to walk straight ahead while nodding in reassurance. She found the health section and turned to see Mrs. Pearce hovering nearby. Luckily, a man approached her asking where he could find a particular book. He looked strangely familiar but her mission was too time-sensitive for distractions. She quickly scurried over to a book that caught her eye entitled *Everything a Teenager Should Know before Losing Their Virginity* by Leila Woods. Danni wasn't sure what she was looking for or needed to read exactly but this book was perfect for answering the taboo questions she was too embarrassed to ask. Slipping the book into her bag, she scurried over to the counter where Mrs. Pearce was sorting through the magazine rack. This was one book that Mrs. Pearce shouldn't see; otherwise she would tell her mother and Danni would never be allowed out of the house again. Usually, libraries held sensor frames at their entrances but Juggler's Corner was so small and quite crime free that they were never installed. Mrs. Pearce was about to turn around when the same man approached her and asked for directions to another section. As Danni was about to flee, the man turned around and winked. Danni couldn't believe how different he looked without his long coat and hat. She scowled at Garth, held her finger up to her lips and ran.

***

Ronan was due in ten minutes and Danni was still sitting in the same position on her bed that she had occupied for the last hour. She couldn't believe she had stolen a book. Well, she hadn't exactly stolen it. She had borrowed it like someone would from a library but had skipped the formality of getting it scanned. There was no way Mrs. Pearce would casually scan that particular book and not question why Danni wanted it. Danni wasn't even sure why she wanted it. She was just curious about sex all of a sudden and wanted to be educated as much as possible without having to awkwardly ask people she knew. It wasn't that she didn't know about the birds and the bees. Reilly, Drew and Danni all underwent sex education in Primary School about which they giggled for hours afterwards. She was now curious about what to expect her first time and what the best methods of protection were. What would it be like? Who would it be with? Not that long ago it was going to be Crawford but now that was history, she couldn't help but be curious. What would their star sign be? Obviously someone on her side of 'The Wall'. Would she regret it or would he be her boyfriend for many years to come? All these questions filled her with dread and excitement.

Recalling her earlier stealth mission she couldn't

help but wonder what Garth was doing in the library and why he was helping her. Did this guy even have a job? And why was he encouraging her to steal this book? She remembered his desire to keep the group united but did he want her to sleep with all the members too? She chuckled at the thought and felt her heart jump as the doorbell sounded. Ronan had arrived.

Shoving the book under her bed, she raced down the stairs and saw her parents waiting awkwardly in the hallway.

'What are you guys doing?' she hissed. 'I told you this is not a date!'

They held up their hands in defeat and shuffled into the living room. Groaning inwardly, she opened the door to reveal Ronan looking less than thrilled and holding a pizza box. She couldn't help but notice how cute he looked in his black jeans and long sleeve maroon shirt. His sandy hair flopped lazily to the side and his icy blue eyes searched hers in confusion.

'Ummm...can I come in?' he asked.

Blushing, she stepped aside and let him enter her house. In that moment she realised this was going to be a lot more difficult than she anticipated and felt a twinge of sympathy for her best friend. Reilly and Ambrite were supposed to hang at the Funky Fries that night. Drew had said in a text message that he had arranged to play basketball with Crawford which was apparently an excellent way for two males to bond. It was nice to know that he was making an effort with someone he really wanted to punch for hurting his best friend. She tried to put her sudden attraction to Ronan as a way to make up for not being able to be with another blonde member of the group. Even though Ronan was a Capricorn and her least compatible mate, she would rather find him cute than go traipsing after Slade and commit an unforgivable act. Danni called for her parents and they stepped out nervously together.

'Mum, Dad, this is Ronan. He is a member of our group and a Capricorn.'

She watched with interest as Ronan shook hands with her father but barely grunted at her mother and refused to look her in the eyes. They looked on with surprise and then dismissed themselves back to the living room. Danni glanced at Ronan but he just gestured with the pizza box and she led them into the kitchen. They were completely silent as she set their placemats, plates, cups and napkins. She held up a bottle of lemonade and he nodded in agreement. What were they going to talk about over dinner? These awkward silences couldn't continue!

Sitting down, she opened the box to reveal half a pineapple pizza and half mushroom. Two of her favourite toppings. She dug in hungrily and smiled at Ronan in approval at his pizza choice. He smirked back and took a pineapple slice. For a while the silence was filled by the chewing and slurping of good food and drink. She could hear the loud movie playing in the living room and was thankful Colin was staying at a friend's house. It almost felt like a first date without the flirtation and friendliness. When there were only two slices left, Danni stood up to clear the plates.

'Do you need any help?' Ronan asked politely.

Danni jumped at the sound of his voice. He hadn't spoken one word since he asked if he could come in. She nodded and scrubbed the plates while he dried them with a dish rag. The silence was deafening and she couldn't take much more.

'Do you want to come in my room?' Danni asked.

Ronan looked at her in surprise.

'Lead the way,' he muttered, avoiding eye contact.

Damn Capricorns, Danni thought. She trudged up the stairs with Ronan closely behind. She couldn't help but laugh at his reaction when they entered her room.

'Wow, you really love Astrology, don't you?' he noted.

Posters among posters of the Wheel of the Zodiac covered her walls, Gemini stencil photographs, the leftover stars lining her ceiling and her loud Gemini bedspread. Her mini whiteboard leaning against the wall on her desk was filled with information about the weekly meetings and she saw Ronan acknowledge his name next to hers for the task.

'Mmmm,' Danni nodded. She loved the feeling she got every time she came into her room. It was her haven where she truly belonged. The only other place she felt like that was Bouquet Reserve.

Ronan sat down on her soft bed and kicked his leg against something hard. Bending down to remove it, he noticed the book Danni had 'borrowed' from the library and stared at it.

Danni felt her cheeks flame up and she wanted the ground to swallow her whole.

'Ummm...that is nothing...just you know...education?' she stammered.

She prepared herself for the worst because she was hanging out with one of the most judgemental and icy members of the group. Instead Ronan merely nodded and placed it back under bed, out of sight.

He turned to her and grinned. 'So I guess we can start by talking about that?'

Danni slumped next to him still feeling the heat on her face.

'I was just...curious. Reilly, Drew and myself have never...and now that we are older and hanging around in a group where romances seemed to have blossomed...it is time to learn I guess...'

Ronan nodded appearing to understand. 'I...have...you know?'

Danni turned to gaze at him with curiosity. Finally

she had found a person who had experienced sex and could discuss it with her.

'How old were you?'

'15...it was only once and with my brother's best friend. He held a party one night when my parents were out of town and everybody was really drunk. I was in my room minding my own business when she barged in and started kissing me. Hell I was 15, how could I say no?'

Danni smiled. 'Do you regret it because it wasn't with someone special?'

Ronan tilted his head to the side. 'Danni...boys and girls are very different in this area. In my experience a first time for boys is almost like a 'take what you can get' situation. For girls it is much more special and they need to feel loved. Even though I felt like a complete stud the next day I can honestly say I wish it was with a girl I cared about. She just walked out afterwards without so much as a goodbye. Something I'm used to...'

Danni noticed the emotion in his voice at the last part. 'What, what is it Ronan? You can tell me?'

He shook his head and looked away. 'I will tell you eventually but tonight I want to talk about you. What happened at the dance?'

She couldn't believe Ronan was discussing serious issues with her and appeared to be interested in her story. She prefaced the conversation the same way she did with Reilly and Drew. She warned him not to act any differently towards Crawford or try to remove him from the group. He nodded that he wouldn't before adding he was never a huge fan of the guy in the first place. This bought a smile to Danni's lips and she explained the entire story in great detail. She left out the Slade and Reilly saga to spare her best friend's embarrassment but told him about Charlotte's visit the next day, the texts from Crawford and how she felt about love now.

'I just feel as though there is no point giving my heart again because it got stomped on so quickly,' Danni confessed.

Ronan shifted on her bed and picked at the rubber on his shoes.

'I know what it feels like not to want to get close to another human being for fear of being hurt...but let me tell you something Dan...that isn't realistic. You need to trust again and love again or life isn't worth living. I'm just starting to realise that. It has taken me a long time and a lot of angry nights in the garage with the punching bag but I can slowly see the light now.'

Danni was so grateful for these words. It filled her with such joy to be getting closer to a member of the group who was even more reserved than Hunter.

'Thanks...I didn't mean to be weird or anything; it's just that I haven't had a proper chat about this since it happened. I love Reilly and Drew dearly but they were so angry at Crawford and then talked about their stuff. It is nice to get an outsider perspective. Well... kind of outsider.'

Ronan nodded. 'I get that. It is hard when there are 12 different personalities in one group and not everyone can be heard. Look Danni, when you start thinking about taking that next step with a guy just think of my story and make sure it is special. I can't go back but I can help someone from making the same mistake...'

Danni nodded, trying not to think of her and Slade taking that next step. How could that be special if it ruined a friendship? She just wanted to cry and scream. It was so unfair that the first guy she liked decided to hook up with her enemy and the second one was a love interest for her best friend. When would it ever work out for her? Who would be the first and could she make it special?

Ronan checked his watch and stood up. Danni felt a slight twinge of disappointment. The Capricorn had been a great source of comfort and value for her. Hopefully, from this day forward they could be close friends. She walked him to the front door and was glad her parents were in their bedroom now.

'Ronan, can I ask you something...?' Danni paused. The cold wind blew around her doorstep and she pulled her sleeves down.

He nodded despite looking hesitant.

'Why do you come to the meetings? I think it is great you are there but you don't seem to like anyone or make friends. What do you get out of it?'

He was silent for a moment and all Danni could hear from the distance was a siren.

'I...don't know why I keep coming back. I don't hate the meetings. I actually enjoy this stuff even if it doesn't seem that way. I guess the main reason I come is because I feel I'm supposed to. That sounded weird, didn't it?'

Danni shook her head. 'Not at all...this group is happening for a reason. I just don't know what it is yet...'

He nodded and waved goodbye. They would be meeting up again the following day for an afternoon walk. She found herself looking forward to it, which was a big surprise considering it was Ronan. Closing the door behind her she ran up to her room and slumped on the bed. Her mind was reeling with the conversation they just had. Ronan had provided her with a lot of good advice and insight into life, love and sex. The time was coming to make a pivotal decision that could either make or break her. She picked her phone up and called Reilly. Danni knew they had to discuss this first as Dr. Yates had suggested. Reilly answered her mobile on the third ring. She was giggling and out of breath.

'Hey Dan!' Reilly laughed.

Danni smiled into the phone. 'So hanging out with Ambrite isn't as horrible as you anticipated, I take it?'

'Oh my God! She is hilarious Dan! I don't know what you were worried about!'

'I wasn't worried about anything! It was you that...'

'Haha, sorry, what was that? Amby Bambii is mocking another of the waitresses that works at The Funky Fries. You know the one that speaks and spits at the same time?! Oh she does it so well!'

'Amby Bambii?' Danni muttered.

'Hey Danni can I call you tomorrow? We are going to grab some frozen Cokes and watch a movie.'

'Sure Reilly. I'm glad you're getting along so well. Say hi to her for me!'

Reilly hung up still killing herself laughing and Danni stared at the phone in despair. Time was running out and she didn't know how much longer she could be a good friend...

***

The following day Danni resolved to start digging at Ronan's core and uncover some deep wounds she knew were hidden. They decided to go for a walk around the town of Juggler's Corner. Danni was feeling very confident in a pretty spring dress that Parry had forced her to buy. It was cornflower blue with white spots and frilly straps. She paired it with her white flats and a headband that complimented her long, brunette locks. The weather was now fining up and despite all the drama life was pretty good. She couldn't stop thinking about Slade which would then spark the vicious circle that led to her thinking about Reilly's reaction to them hooking up. Would Reilly really stop being her friend? It was the first time in her life that she truly understood the saying about having your cake and eating it too. For the zillionth time that morning she raked her fingers through her hair, pulling on the tendrils and screwing up her face in frustration.

'Something wrong Hamilton?' Ronan inquired.

Danni jumped and blushed when she noticed the Capricorn holding two orange sorbets and raising his eyebrows in concern.

Adjusting her headband and gingerly accepting the sorbet, she shook her head. 'Just...itchy...'

'Uh huh,' Ronan muttered, clearly disbelieving.

'Shall we go for a walk?' Danni squeaked, embarrassed and desperate to change the subject.

Ronan tried to stifle a laugh and nodded. He licked his sorbet and gestured for her to lead the way.

Danni and Ronan strode in silence for the better part of their session. She became lost in her own thoughts as she passed Maltin's and the Juggler's Corner Library. The familiar and weathered old buildings that she knew and loved now held special memories associated with meeting various members of her group. As the pair strode past the Juggler's Corner Health Centre Danni broke the ice by revealing a bit more of herself.

'I see a psych there you know?' Danni pointed behind her at the clinic. Ronan looked up in surprise and threw his sorbet cup in the bin. Licking his sticky fingers he turned to face her.

'Oh...why?'

'I guess I never told the group, apart from Reilly and Drew, why I decided to start up the Astro A Team in the first place. I've always been a little psychic and intuitive but a couple of months ago my premonitions and dreams were becoming more and more vivid. Something or someone was urging me to form this group and even in my dreams I was able to decipher the clues and hidden meanings within them in order to locate certain members...'

Danni didn't want to reveal to Ronan the truth about Garth even though she still wasn't entirely sure of his role in all of this. It was bad enough that Reilly knew having witnessed his shadowy presence at the weekly meetings. Ronan remained silent and nodded, so she knew he was listening. She wanted her story to lead into his own secretive past but she had to word it the correct way. They were now passing the Juggler's Corner Aquatic Centre and she was surprised to see Hannah's car parked out the front. Clearly swimming a few laps was Brodie's idea as she couldn't imagine Hannah initiating anything with someone she wasn't entirely comfortable with. She was tempted to go inside and see what the two girls were up to but she remembered her own mission and continued.

'The first two people I dreamt of was Reilly and Drew which wasn't surprising as they are my two best friends and have different zodiac signs. The third person I dreamt of was...Crawford...'

Danni felt her heart sink as she remembered the wonderful warm feeling of seeing this brunette beauty in her dreams and flashing forward to the present where they barely spoke to each other. Ronan could sense this was difficult for her and lightly touched her shoulder. She smiled wanly at him and shook her head to indicate that everything was alright.

'So did Crawford go to your school? Is that how you knew where to find him?' Ronan asked.

'Ummm...well, that's the weirdest part...I had never met him until I dreamt of him...I saw his face in the dream and then went to Bouquet Reserve where I found him raking the leaves.'

Ronan widened his eyes. She knew the practical and logical Capricorn was trying to discern how this could have really happened.

'You must have seen him around town and it stuck in your subconscious?'

Danni shook her head. 'That's what Reilly and Drew said but trust me, if I had seen *him* around town I would've remembered!'

She said it with such conviction that her cheeks reddened and she realised just how much of an impact Crawford's physical form had on her. Crawford had all the perfect traits of a Leo – charming, generous, proud and strong. He was beautiful inside and out but failed to meet one of the strongest characteristics a Leo presented – loyalty. Much like the Lion, a person born within the months of late July and the majority of August was supposed to remain faithful to those he or she held dear. Crawford had failed to remain loyal to her, and inadvertently the group too, by fraternising with their enemy. It made her wonder if she could ever get past this and unite her group properly as Garth had urged.

They had now reached the centre of town and Danni could spot the corner of Bouquet Reserve where she had caught Crawford and Charlotte in the act. Shaking her head and sighing deeply, she turned to Ronan and smiled. They continued down the path a couple of blocks from their school which reminded her of how she had introduced herself to Parry. Ronan chuckled as she explained how the only way to gain Parry's membership was to get a fake tan which led to meeting Graham.

'Wow, I guess it really was fate then?' Ronan reluctantly remarked.

'It really was...ooh let me tell you the long and tiring saga of getting Hunter to join.'

By the time they reached the school Ronan and Danni were laughing at how many times Hunter had hung up on, yelled and stormed past her before he had shown up at Bouquet Reserve on the first meeting.

'You know Danni...a lot of people would've given up on someone like Hunter but you persisted and look at him now! The guy is actually hilarious and he is in love with Ambrite. Those two do seem like a great pair. She brings out the best in him it appears.'

Danni chuckled. 'I shouldn't tell you this but I'm a Gemini and we can't keep our mouths shut...Ambrite prefers the company of girls...Hunter is just her best friend and they are really close. But don't tell anyone what I told you!'

Ronan was so surprised that he could barely speak. 'Well, that's a piece of news! I guess what I said still stands though...she does bring out the best in him and they are a great pair.'

Danni nodded warmly. 'You have no idea how thankful I am that those two found each other. This group has had the ability to unite and destroy at the same time. It baffles the mind. That is why I am doing this task to begin with.'

Ronan and Danni entered Juggler's Corner High and she couldn't help but notice just how eerie the empty school looked. She strode over to the shady tree area where Parry usually braided her hair and enjoyed her circle of male followers fawning at her feet. Ronan leant against the tree while Danni sat on the bench nearby. She stretched out on the termite-infested plank and allowed the warm spring rays touch her face. She was enjoying reminiscing about the remarkable twists of fate that led her to form the Astro A Team. Twirling her hair in her fingers, she smiled as she knew what was coming next. Right on cue Ronan cleared his throat.

'So...how did you know where to find me? Did your dreams involve the library or books?'

Danni sat up, preparing for the session to get deep and real.

'Actually...meeting you at the library was pure coincidence even though I don't believe in such things. In my dreams I saw that you had sandy blonde hair and that you were frowning in the direction of the girls of the group. Unfortunately, our first impression of you was that you were quite sexist...I'm sorry.'

Ronan looked as though somebody had punched him in the stomach. He staggered over to the bench and sat next to Danni. She immediately looked concerned but he held up a hand in defence.

'I consider myself to be a practical and reasonable guy. I mean I am an Earth sign after all! But there is no way in the world that you could've known how I felt about females without the use of some black magic!'

Danni laughed. 'Ronan, this isn't black magic...it is fate. When we bumped into each other at the J-Corner Library and you seemed repulsed by the fact that I was even talking to you I knew, in that very moment, that I had found the boy in my dreams. I wanted to kick you in the groin but at the same time help you get over whatever hang-ups you were holding onto.'

Ronan grinned at Danni's bluntness. She could tell he was struggling much like Hunter did that day in Bouquet Reserve before he nearly told her the truth about his past.

'I guess you have shared a lot of your story and as the theme of the week is unity, it is only fair that I reciprocate...'

'I don't want you to feel pressured though!' Danni jumped in.

She felt slightly guilty at the fact that a couple of members had spilt their deepest and darkest secrets because of her curiosity and willingness to help.

'No, it's fine,' Ronan assured her gently. 'My brother and I have been living with just my dad for about three years now and that is also the amount of time I haven't seen or heard from my mum...'

Danni noticed the clenching of his fists and the tightening of his jaw as he expressed a hurt stronger than any force. As much as Danni wanted the Astro A Team to be able to fill the void in Ronan that his mother had left, she was well aware that nobody could ever repair that pain. Even his mother could not heal him because the damage had already been done. Instantly, she thought of Dr. Yates's book on how to deal with unfit parents and noticed that a lot of the members had carried hurtful baggage passed down from their mothers/fathers. Perhaps in time Ronan would agree to a session with her psychologist and dear friend but right now it was a big enough step for him to confess it to her. Danni didn't react; she just lightly rubbed his back and allowed the silence to prompt him to continue.

'My dad has never gotten over it...' Ronan muttered. 'Most of the time I have to cook dinner, clean the house and help Brandon out with other chores because dad just doesn't leave his garage. That is why I didn't want you to come over...it isn't exactly the happiest place on earth. I let dad know I'm there for him by working on the cars together but most of the time it is done in silence and he barely looks up from what he is doing. I keep him informed of my school work, my friends and even the group, which he doesn't really understand but nods from time to time. The skiing trip we just went on was mine and Brandon's idea. He came, but once again barely seemed interested and by the time we returned it felt pointless. Danni, you have to understand that every time I see my dad's sad face or really take in how lonely he is, I can't help but hate my mum and that leaves me with a lot of distrust for women in general. I know it's silly because I can't group every single female into the same category as my mother but she was supposed to be the most important person in my life and if I can't trust her, then who can I trust?'

Danni had guessed that Ronan's hesitance towards her coming to visit could be traced back to his unhappy family home. Still, she was amazed at how mature Ronan was for his age. When she had first met him, he had seemed so angry and disagreeable but a couple of months with her group had made her see his ingrained wisdom from having to grow up earlier than expected. She couldn't imagine how painful it must be for Ronan to watch his father so sad and empty day in and day out. Danni adored her father, even if his super friendliness got him into trouble sometimes.

'I'm so sorry Ronan...I could say the usual crap about how it is nothing personal and you are better off but I know it doesn't help. All I can say is that I hope I never give you a reason to not trust me...I and certainly the group won't ever abandon you.'

Ronan clearly looked touched but didn't say anything.

'So...do you know why she left? I mean did she ever give your father a reason?'

The Capricorn's face changed from calm to catatonic in a millisecond.

'No! She seriously just got up and left! Not a word...not even a note! My mother has always been materialistic and superficial, so I assume when dad was made redundant from his job at the firm two towns over she didn't feel as secure or important anymore. When dad does talk about it he says it was his fault for not paying enough attention to her but I know it has nothing to do with him. What kind of woman just leaves her husband after twelve years of marriage and doesn't even tell her two sons? Last we heard, she married another lawyer and is living in another state. Brandon and I always seemed like a nuisance to her anyway...more of an accessory to show off to her friends but not worth putting in the actual hard yards for. I do realise that we are better off but it doesn't erase the fact that I will never have a mother who cares about me or my brother and that my dad may never get over the hole she left in his heart. There is nothing I can do and I feel so helpless sometimes...'

Danni rubbed his back gently again. 'Ronan, even if you don't realise it...everything you do and say is helping your father bit by bit. Just being with him when he works on his cars or suggesting the skiing trip is healing for him. I'm sure he secretly enjoys hearing about the group and your school life because it makes him feel you are getting on with your life and not pining for your mother the way he is. I know with one hundred per cent clarity that he does not want you to become like him. All I can suggest is that you keep doing what you're doing...keep suggesting trips and involving him in your life. Who knows...one day he may meet someone else and she will show him what true love really is. It isn't materialistic or about social status...it is about looking at the person in front of you and having no doubt that they are what you want for the rest of your lives.'

He looked up at her and she knew he was softened by her words.

'Thanks Danni...maybe you would like to meet him sometime?'

Danni's heart leapt for joy. This was a definite breakthrough.

'I would love to. How about in a couple of days we cook dinner for him and Brandon?'

Ronan patted her hand. 'I think dad would love that. He loves a good veal scaloppini.'

Danni laughed. 'Veal scaloppini it is!'

Chapter 32

THE STARS ALIGN...

The spring air was crisp and Danni felt light and free as she and Ronan parted ways at the corner of Blossom and Anderson Street. The second she got home she was going to research the best recipe for veal scaloppini there was and make sure that Ronan's father started the healing process with good food and a loving family. This was what the weekly task was all about – sharing stories and helping one another come to terms with the past. She hoped that all the other pairings were just as successful. At the meeting on Friday night Danni would discover whether her group was doomed for failure or destined for greatness. She was hoping the latter would prevail and there wouldn't be too great a mess to clean up should they all rip each other apart. At least Ambrite and Reilly were now bosom buddies...she never saw that one coming! It made Danni happy to know that after the terrible month Reilly had had after the Slade fiasco, someone she perceived to be her greatest enemy was now making her laugh.

As if he had read her mind, Danni's heart sank as she saw the Aquarian leaning against her mailbox waiting for her to come home. The second he saw her, his face lit up and he raced over, nearly bowling her over. She noticed his hair was without product today and lay flat on his head which somehow made him look even more gorgeous. His stonewashed jeans and tight white shirt looked impeccable on his toned figure and his piercing blue eyes gazed at her with slight caution but obvious adoration. Danni couldn't deny how glad she was to see him but at the same time wished he wasn't there. It was a very confusing situation and made her head hurt on a daily basis.

'I...ummm...have things to do Slade, so I should probably get...'

'No!' Slade interrupted and caused Danni to jump. 'I am tired of you avoiding me and getting your parents to tell me you aren't home when you clearly are. I just spent a gruelling day getting a facial with Graham and the last thing I need is someone I care about blowing me off for the umpteenth time! You are going to hear me out and by the end of this discussion we will have returned back to normal because this distance and awkwardness is killing me!'

Danni was speechless but nodded in understanding. Her parents and Colin were out, so she let him in and they sat on the couch. She was well aware of how close they were sitting...their arms slightly pressed together and the smell of his heady aftershave intoxicating her.

She jumped up. 'Would you like a drink? Peppermint tea perhaps?'

'No!' Slade repeated in the same frustrated tone. 'Sit back down and talk about this weirdness with me!'

Everything sounded better in an American accent, Danni realised, and she didn't even mind how demanding he was getting. She knew deep down that his frustration was justified. If only he knew that the main reason she was avoiding him was due to physical temptation.

Sitting back down, she looked him in the eyes and held his gaze for as long as possible.

'Danni...tell me what I did wrong...' Slade uttered mournfully. 'I like you so much and if I can't have you as my girlfriend then I at least need you to be my friend again the way we used to be.'

Danni's heart melted a little when he mentioned having her as his girlfriend. She pictured them holding hands down the street and seeing movies together as a regular couple. It all looked so perfect in her mind but was completely unrealistic where her best friend was concerned. Reilly would never give them her blessing.

'You know...you warned me about Crawford...'

'Huh?' Slade asked, clearly confused.

'One day in class I zoned out and had a vision that you and Crawford were duelling to the death over me in Bouquet Reserve. You were fighting over the pond with actual swords and as the vision ended you looked at me and said, 'he will betray you.' I didn't realise it then, but after the Astrological Dance I realised that you were right. You warned me and I didn't listen...'

Slade grabbed her hand and Danni didn't pull away. She didn't want to...his hand was soft and warm and her skin tingled as his fingers lightly caressed her palm.

'So something did happen with Crawford? I knew he did something...'

Danni chuckled. 'I know you never liked him to begin with but please don't treat him any differently, as I asked Reilly and Drew, or else the group will disband and I need you all to stay united...hence the weekly task.'

Slade nodded. 'You don't have to tell me what happened but he obviously hurt you in a way that changed your feelings toward him. It would make sense that you need some healing time before giving your heart again.'

Danni let go of his hand reluctantly and lay back against the couch. She sighed deeply and felt so incredibly vulnerable.

'Slade, this has nothing to do with Crawford...don't you realise that Reilly is in love with you? She is my best friend and to pursue something with you could ruin one of the most important friendships I have. Can't you see that I am trying desperately to be a good friend? We spending time together like this, holding hands, is enough to lose everything.'

The Aquarian appeared to have heard nothing of what she just said; he was mesmerised by the passion in her voice.

'You are such a good friend Danni, but answer me this honestly...if Reilly was never in the picture...would we be together?'

'It doesn't work like that,' Danni protested.

'Answer the question!' Slade demanded.

'Yes! We would be together!'

That was enough for Slade. Leaning forward he grasped Danni's face in his hands and pressed his lips hungrily onto her mouth. She let out a small moan and wrapped her arms around his neck. For what seemed like hours the two remained intertwined on the couch touching and kissing one another without taking a breath. Danni forgot about the world outside and the consequences to come of her actions. All that mattered was the here and now. There was no time for guilt...she couldn't deny how long she had wanted and needed this. The two Air signs combined made her feel she was floating. She let out all of her frustrations from the past month. Not being able to kiss Crawford properly like this, feeling rejected by him, feeling as though she had to be a good friend to everybody, struggling to keep the group united and resisting the urge to smother Charlotte in her sleep. After what seemed like a year, Slade pulled away from Danni's lips looking flushed and adorable. Danni's mouth felt numb and her head was swimming. She was going to need a good rest after he left. Turning her side on, he draped his arms over her body and cuddled her close, his breath on her neck. It was one of those moments that felt so incredibly right and wrong at the same time.

'I'm not going to lie...that was very nice for me,' Slade crooned into her ear.

'Mmmm,' Danni replied, still unable to speak properly.

'Do you regret this?' He whispered so softly that she almost didn't hear him.

Danni opened her eyes and suddenly the cold reality slammed into her stomach like an icy punch. Sitting up in alarm she turned to face Slade who was looking at her with concern.

'Oh my God, what have I done?' Danni moaned. 'Slade, we can't let anyone know about this. Reilly will never forgive me!'

Slade sat up and rubbed her shoulders. 'Danni, don't worry...I'm sure if we explain it to her and tell her how serious we are about each other, she will understand.'

Danni let out a non-humorous chuckle. 'Slade, that is incredible, wishful thinking...you don't understand just how much she liked you. That night at the dance she was hoping you two would become boyfriend and girlfriend! When you rejected her she couldn't stop crying and even till this day she is still so hurt from it. I supported and even encouraged her to make a move at the dance because at that time I was certain that Crawford would end up with me but it didn't work out that way.'

Slade looked so surprised and hurt that Danni wasn't sure whether it would be appropriate to kiss him again and hope that he forgot what she just said.

'So...because it didn't work out with Crawford I was second choice?'

'No!' Danni replied. 'I tried to keep you at bay because I liked you and didn't trust myself to be alone with you. Obviously I was right not to trust myself after what just happened but Slade, I couldn't deny that there was always something there between us. It's just that I met Crawford before you and he was my first proper crush. He broke my heart! You could possibly heal it and make it whole again but unfortunately you come with a price! The price of my friendship with Reilly...'

Slade appeared thoughtful and subdued. 'I didn't realise she felt so strongly about me...I guess I have been kind of a jerk...'

Danni leaned on his shoulder and was happy when he began stroking her hair.

'You can't help how you feel Slade, and you were actually quite kind to her at the dance but now what we are doing...what we just did...as amazing as it was...was incredibly selfish.'

'Don't you think it's more selfish of her not to allow a great relationship to unfold? Shouldn't she be happy for her best friend?'

'Slade, how do you think I would've felt if Crawford and Reilly hooked up, knowing exactly how I felt about him and then being with him anyway...I know it is a cliché but boys really do come and go. I have picked a boy whom I only met a couple of months ago over my best friend of twelve plus years! What does that say about my loyalty and strength of character?'

Slade nodded and appeared to have finally understood.

'So...where does that leave us? Do we just go back to being friends?'

Danni's heart throbbed and she wanted nothing more than to find a way where everybody could be happy but she knew it was impossible. Trying desperately not to burst into tears, she took his hand one last time.

'I think so...I'm sorry Slade...I wasn't lying when I said that if Reilly had never been in the picture then we would have been together, but this isn't a perfect world and we need to do what's right. Thank you for understanding.'

'As much as this sucks and as much as I'm hoping Reilly meets the love of her life tomorrow so that she forgets about me, I want you to know that I admire how good a friend you are Danni. You really do have all the best qualities in a leader and there is no one I would rather have as my neighbour too.'

Danni nodded and smiled. 'Thank you...that means a lot. Despite what has happened today I'm really glad it did because after what happened with Crawford I just needed a little affection from someone who actually cares about me. I have been vulnerable ever since it happened but you put me right again and I don't feel quite as murderous towards the Leo anymore.'

Slade laughed and stood up. 'Well, I'm happy to help especially when it comes to getting back at a jerky guy like him!'

'Slade! Don't forget the theme of this week!' Danni protested half laughing, half serious.

'Trust me...after enduring a facial and a salt scrub this afternoon how could I possibly forget?' he groaned.

He walked towards the front door and turned to face her before he stepped out into the sunshine. Then he said, 'Danni...I'll always be here no matter what. If you ever change your mind and want to be in a relationship...I'm all in.'

She watched him leave and lay down on the couch with her hands over her eyes. Life was not fair and love had certainly not been very kind to Danni. She was starting to understand why Ronan's father didn't participate in life anymore. What was the point if you could only experience true happiness for a little while before it was ripped from you? Standing up, she walked over to the family computer and switched it on. The CD Rom started to whirr and the desktop flickered into view. She clicked the tab for the Internet and searched for the best veal scaloppine recipe the worldwide web could provide. Just because her life sucked at the moment didn't mean she shouldn't try to improve the lives of others. Now, more than ever, she couldn't wait for dinner at the Tate's!

***

For the first time in Danni's life, she was happy to be cooking. Her usual culinary skills involved burnt toast and honey jumbles (a childish treat consisting of cornflakes and honey stuck together in a patty pan). To transition from this type of 'cooking' to veal scaloppini required all her mental attention and a thorough reading and re-reading of the recipe. This distraction was providing some relief from the fact that only a few days before she had committed the ultimate betrayal towards her best friend. Her unforgivable secret felt remarkably like a game of *Jenga*, wobbly and prone to fall apart at any second. She had moments where she managed to convince herself that Reilly would never find out and even concocted visions of them laughing about it in years to come. She pictured Reilly reassuring her she was never that into Slade in the first place and was baffled why Danni was so worried. Almost in an instant, she saw Reilly's crushed face at finding out and vowing never to forgive her. Danni had been happy for so long when the group had initially begun. Eleven fresh faces and friends ready to unite and discover the hidden secrets of the stars. Connections formed and romance was blooming for the first time in her life. Now, it felt as though the honeymoon period was over, the novelty had worn off, and reality kept prodding her in the back.

'Hurry up Dan, my dad's gonna be home in half an hour,' Ronan interrupted her negativity.

She looked up to see his familiar blonde mop covering his sky blue left eye and fidgety hands adjusting the velcro strap of his watch one too many times. Clearly, this dinner meant a lot to him.

'Calm down Capricorn, I'm almost done stirring the mushroom sauce. 'Mmmm that smells amazing,' she sniffed the saucepan and held it out to Ronan.

He leaned in with a glint in his eye and inhaled. She could tell he didn't want to admit that her recipe following skills were up to scratch, so he just smiled and began setting the table.

'Where is Brandon by the way?' Danni asked, looking around the kitchen that opened up into the living room.

Ronan's house was quaint but immaculately furnished. Everything was matching, colour-coordinated and cleverly placed. She guessed the design and layout of the place was all Ronan's mother's doing and his father didn't have the heart to change it nor move anything out of place. She hadn't received a proper tour of the place; she had literally arrived in the afternoon and became immediately acquainted with his kitchen. She found herself wondering what his room looked like. Whether he was a minimalist like a typical Capricorn or ordered his video games in alphabetical order. Was his bed messy…?

'Drums…' she caught the end of Ronan's sentence.

'What?' Danni shook her head in confusion.

Ronan frowned. 'Were you spacing out again Gemini? I said he is in his room probably practicing the drums.'

Danni concentrated and for the first time she heard the tingle of the cymbals and then some deep booms.

'How didn't I hear that before?'

'Brandon is pretty shy,' Ronan stated, carrying some green and gold etched dinner plates.

'Sign?' Danni opened up the steamer full of broccoli and carrots.

'Ummm, I know he is born early July...'

'You don't even know your brother's birthday?' Danni shook her head in mock disgust.

Ronan opened up the china hutch and retrieved a glass jug for the lemon water.

'Why would I? One, we are guys so birthdays and dates aren't really our main focus and two, I don't care for astrology the way you do.'

'Hmmm, well, for your information, your brother is a Cancer like Hannah. They are deeply sensitive and take a long time to warm up to people; hence his need to stay behind closed doors and only emerge when the dinner is on his plate.'

Ronan widened his eyes in surprise and Danni felt the familiar thrill of being on the money once again.

'Wow, I guess knowing so much about astrology means you can read people pretty well.'

Danni picked up the fancy plates from the bench and served the steaks that looked juicy and succulent in her opinion.

'You would think so but not everybody acts like their sign, so sometimes it's hard to tell. It's those that couldn't be more like their sign that are the easiest to understand. I have to say that everyone in the group pretty much acts in tune with their zodiac sign.'

Ronan nodded seriously. Then he waved some pink napkins with a goofy grin and laid them on the dining table. She didn't get him sometimes; that was for sure. He usually produced the serious Capricorn demeanour – very logical and practical – but then this silly side would sometimes shine through and his laugh, however rarely she heard it, was infectious.

'So Graham really has a scorpion sting then?'

Danni found herself frowning and then was struck with a pang of guilt.

'Ahhh…to be honest…Graham is the only member of the group I haven't really gotten to know yet…'

Ronan shrugged. 'Don't feel too bad; the guy isn't very forthcoming with any of us either besides Parry. Those two are stuck together like Humbrite but at least the other two make an effort with the rest of the group.'

Danni shook her head. 'Not good enough Ronan. I'm the leader of the Astro A Team. Graham not only got a tattoo for our group but provided us all with discounts for them and supplied a lot of stuff for the party. The least I could do is get to know the most mysterious and secretive member of our gang. Ironically, those two traits describe a Scorpio perfectly.'

'I guess it's a shame you weren't paired with him then for the weekly task…'

Danni was surprised to feel her heart sink a little. 'Do you really mean that?'

'No, of course not,' Ronan added, looking a little flushed. 'What I meant was, if he had been paired with you, you wouldn't have to feel guilty right now.'

'I guess...but then maybe I would've felt guilty with him right now for not making any effort with you.'

Ronan laughed and threw his hands up. 'And the guilt cycle continues! I'm glad you picked me...otherwise my dad would've had a pretty crappy dinner tonight.'

Danni could tell this was his way of complimenting her and letting her know he appreciated the time they had spent together. Capricorns had a funny way of saying so much without saying anything.

'Thanks...I'm glad I picked you too. Or rather I'm glad both our signs are the least compatible.'

'They seem pretty compatible to me...' Ronan said. He edged closer and picked up the first plate full of food from her hands and she nearly dropped it when their hands brushed.

'Ummm...looks good, don't you think?' Danni blushed. She turned and busied herself loading up the next plate.

'I'm sure Dad will love it,' Ronan agreed.

She heard the door click and the sound of a heavy step hit the hardwood floors.

'Speak of the devil,' Ronan grinned.

Chapter 33

THE SECRETIVE SCORPION

It was the day before the next meeting and Danni was set to visit Graham at Maltin's in the afternoon. She wanted to make sure he felt included and as important as all the other members. So far, she had had personal moments with all of them except him. How could she call herself a true leader if she didn't connect with each member of her team? Plus she was pretty sure this was what Garth would've wanted, though why she even cared for what an eccentric stranger in a trench coat thought was beyond her. Graham wasn't expecting her and she was disappointed to find out from the receptionist that he was on his lunch break. It was a pretty late lunch he was having as she had come there straight from school.

Seating herself on the plush white chairs in the waiting room, she took the time to reflect on the dinner with Ronan's father.

She felt her smile widen as she remembered the look on his face when he took that first bite of the veal scaloppini. If her goal had ever been to win him over, the meal had done just that. Brandon had skulked out of his room and Danni noticed how withdrawn he was at the table until his father began to laugh and tell stories of his childhood. Ronan's brother began to chuckle himself with a small look of disbelief. It was true what others said: food certainly brings people together.

Ronan was beaming and throwing grateful looks Danni's way which reinforced the fact that this wasn't the usual dinner-time setting they were used to. She also noticed that his father was treating her a lot like he would if she were Ronan's girlfriend. He kept asking her questions about her friends, family and school all the while glancing at his son with what seemed to be approval.

The thought made her cheeks flush. Stupidly, she glanced around Maltin's to check if anyone could see her bright red face.

The dinner was a great success and seemed to help Ronan's father forget for a night what his ex-wife had done to him. She could tell he was pleased that Ronan had brought a friend over and that Brandon had managed to come out of his room. They shook hands and as she turned to leave, Ronan looked so happy that she wanted to fling her arms around his neck. It almost seemed as though he wanted to do the same to her. There were no words in that moment, just a nod and an expression that spoke volumes. The weekly task for the Gemini and the Capricorn had been a huge success and she couldn't wait to share it with the group. Perhaps they would be the shining example for all the others.

Hearing the door squeak open, she saw Parry and Graham walk into Maltin's arm in arm and chattering away. They stopped short when they saw Danni and rushed over to her.

'Hello darling,' Graham purred. 'What are you doing in my little neck of the woods?'

Parry's eyes widened. 'Are you here for another spray tan? Yours *is* starting to fade.'

'God no!' Danni laughed. 'Sorry to disappoint Par but one was enough for my lifetime. It just isn't me. I'm actually here to chat with Graham but you might as well hang around as you're both bosom buddies.'

Graham looked at her with surprise. She was certain he was wearing foundation. No skin was that flawless!

'Am I in trouble?'

'No, of course not. Sit down. I just want to have a chat with you.'

They snuggled into the same couch and Danni envied Parry, her perfect red locks draped over the white leather.

Danni suddenly felt nervous and guilty once more. How could she have let him go by the wayside when she had put so much effort into getting to know all the others?

How excluded he must feel? She reached out and tapped his hand gently.

'Oh dear, someone's died,' Graham groaned.

Parry pressed her hand against her mouth.

'No,' Danni reassured. 'I just wanted to apologise to you…'

His curled lashes flicked up in wonder.

'Why honey? You haven't done anything to me.'

'I know. It's more what I haven't done.'

'Well…what haven't you done?'

She looked at Parry who was now engrossed in a bridal magazine. No doubt she was picturing how she would look in a wedding gown.

'I feel out of all the members of the Astro A Team, you're the only one I haven't taken the time to get to know and for that I am so sorry. I want you to know you are just as important as everyone else and if you'd like to share a story of your life with me I'm more than happy to hear it.'

Graham looked truly uncomfortable now and Danni was certain it was too late to make amends. Surely he had noticed that she had been neglecting him, even if it was unintentional.

'Danni, I was going to bring this up at the meeting tomorrow but I might as well tell you now as we're on the subject.'

She had never seen him look so serious and even Parry pushed the magazine aside and smoothed the creases on the arms of his shirt.

'Tomorrow I'm going to announce to the group that I want to leave. I'm so sorry Danni; I know you've put so much into this group and you'll need to find another Scorpio but it's obvious I don't belong and it's making me uncomfortable.'

Danni felt a physical pain in her chest. This was worse than being dumped. This was like being told that everything you believed in was a lie. Graham was one of the chosen twelve. How could another Scorpio possibly take his place?

'Please Graham; can we please just talk about this before you make any rash decisions? What makes you think you don't fit in? Ambrite is a vegan, Goth lesbian for Pete's sake! Hunter is a ball of fire who has been expelled from school! Hannah literally cries when milk is spilt and Drew calls his pet fish Mr Puffer Snuggles!'

She noticed how loud her voice was getting and took a moment to catch her breath. She was so desperate to keep him, not to lose him that she would tattoo the whole Wheel of the Zodiac on her back just to prove her loyalty.

Graham pressed his hand on Danni's face. She couldn't believe how close to tears she was. This was all her fault.

'Darling, it's nothing you've done,' Graham reassured her, almost reading her thoughts.

'Then what is it? What is making you want to leave? Are people not treating you well or are you finding it boring? We can make it more fun; just tell me what you want to change.'

Parry's lower lip was sticking out and she looked ready to burst into the waterworks as well.

The Scorpio unbuttoned the top of his shirt in a fluster.

'I know who I am. I'm comfortable with who I am but after this weekly task you set us I realised that others aren't ready for it. They're still teenagers dealing with the pressures of school. *I'm* still a teenager even though I feel like a grown man with a swimmer's body.'

He laughed lightly and Parry looked him up and down in admiration.

Danni couldn't understand what he was trying to say. Did Slade say something homophobic? She would rip his head off if he had.

'Look, the point I'm trying to make is, I tried to be myself with Slade and whilst he is very nice and beautiful, he clearly wasn't comfortable with the things I wanted to do and the secrets I wanted to share. I'm not saying he is against gays; I'm just saying he isn't ready for the realities of this world and maybe none of the others are, apart from you and Par.'

Danni felt she was losing this battle. Scorpios are very determined and once their mind is made up, there is no stopping them. What was she going to tell the group? There had to be a way to convince him to stay.

'Just tell me,' she croaked. 'Did Slade say anything homophobic or mean?'

Graham shook his head rapidly. 'No, he is a lovely guy. He just withdrew a little when I told him my coming out story. Maybe it was too full on for the weekly task but I couldn't think of anything personal I wanted to share and I'm not ashamed of it. It was his reaction that made me think the group might not be ready for me.'

'Is there anything we can do to change your mind? Maybe the fact that you have a tattoo binding yourself to the group?'

Danni realised she was clearly grasping at straws and Parry was still mute with glassy eyes.

Graham chuckled and lifted his chinos to reveal the Scorpion symbol.

'I love this tattoo and what it represents. I will never regret getting it. Trust me when I say I'm doing this group a favour. Don't worry; I will tell them all tomorrow; you don't have to do it. I'm sure they will understand dear.'

Parry finally spoke although she didn't make much sense.

'No, I won't let you; you need to stay and be beautiful with me!'

He turned to his Virgo best friend and brushed the hair out of her face.

'My love, just like diamonds, you and I are forever.'

Danni was surprised to see Parry burst into tears at this statement and throw her arms around him.

Even though Graham wasn't leaving Juggler's Corner, it seemed he was moving on. It hurt her to think he didn't want to stay because he felt like an outcast. Was her group too immature for somebody like Graham?

She didn't want to think about what this meant now. Would Garth come down on her like a ton of bricks when he found out? Would she dream of another Scorpio the following night that could replace him? How would they all react and would this potentially lead to other members dropping out? She couldn't bear to focus on that last question.

Nodding solemnly, she took his hand and squeezed it. Parry had let go now and the girls in the salon were offering her tissues and tea.

'Okay, I can see you've made up your mind and I would never want to make you stay in a group that didn't feel right anymore. After we've discussed how the weekly task has gone, we can announce your leaving the group.'

'Thanks Danni,' he squeezed her hand in return. 'I've really had a great time and you've taught me so much. I'll never forget the Friday nights we've shared together.'

Danni felt a tear slide down her cheek. 'I just wish I had gotten to know you more…'

'Well, don't be a stranger sweetpea. Please come visit anytime for a gossip session and treatments will always be on the house.'

She got up and hugged both of them. Parry grasped her tightly and whispered in her ear, 'I'll never leave the group.'

Danni smiled, her eyes full, and walked outside.

***

The Gemini felt that day would be forever known as Judgement Day for a multitude of reasons.

The first was that Dr. Yates was back from her holiday and would be able to tell that Danni had betrayed her best friend. She just hoped her psychologist wasn't as disappointed in her as she was. The second and most depressing reason was that it was Graham's last meeting and essentially the entire club's. She figured that once he dropped out, others would follow and that would be the end of that. The end of fulfilling her vague destiny, the end of her close friendships, the end of even Garth tailing her, which she couldn't help enjoying despite appearing annoyed every time he showed up.

As usual, Danni was procrastinating, thinking all of these negative thoughts instead of rising from her bed and getting ready for school. Sheer will and hunger forced her from her astrological sheets and she trudged downstairs to see her family eating around the table.

'Morning darling,' Danni's mother greeted, holding up her cereal packet.

Danni nodded and sat down while her mother poured her a bowl of fruit muesli.

'Do you still have your appointment after school sweetheart?'

Her mother set the milk next to Danni and raised her eyebrows with a 'don't expect me to pour it too' expression.

Danni picked up the carton and filled her bowl with soy milk. She was still getting used to the taste but Ambrite had begged her to try it, so she had complied.

'Yep, then I've got a meeting with the Astro A Team tonight…'

Colin jumped up and ran into the lounge room without clearing his plate. She heard the TV turn on and grinned, waiting for her mother to scream at him to turn it off. Instead she looked at Danni's father with concern. He didn't appear to notice, his nose deep in his morning paper.

'You don't seem too thrilled about this meeting darling, am I wrong?'

Danni picked up her bowl, held it to her mouth and drank the remaining milk. She cleared her mouth, stood up and took both her and Colin's dishes to the sink.

'Not overly, I think it may be over…'

Her father looked up from his paper and widened his eyes at his wife.

'Over? You love that club! Why would it be over? Didn't it just start?'

Danni felt the tears well up. She really didn't want to get into it.

'It's okay darling, you don't have to tell us.'

She turned to go up the stairs and take a shower but stopped when she saw her parents' worried expressions.

'I love you both; you're great parents. I hope you know that.'

They smiled at one another and as she walked upstairs to the landing, she realised she had no idea what had compelled her to say that.

Chapter 34

THE PORTAL TO DESTINY

It was extremely difficult hiding Graham's plans from Reilly and Drew at school all day but she managed by focusing on mundane topics like homework, plans for the weekend and how Mr Puffer Snuggles liked to entertain himself. She found herself avoiding Parry's sad stares at lunchtime because all they did was make her lip quiver in despair. There were so many moments in the day where she wanted to call Graham and just beg and cry for him to stay. Tonight was going to change everything and she wasn't ready to say goodbye yet.

After school, she hugged her two best friends and walked into Juggler's Health Care Centre for her most difficult session with Dr. Yates yet. Sitting in the waiting room, she smiled fondly at the memories of Hunter originally hating her and yelling every time he walked out of the building. Now they were the best of friends...but would they remain...after tonight? She shook her head and looked up to see a familiar face smiling and beckoning her.

Danni walked into the quaint green room she had grown to recognise as her safe haven. Dr. Yates settled into her usual chair and beamed at her patient. She wanted to believe that, despite the fact that Dr. Yates saw so many different people, she had a soft spot for Danni. It had always been important for Danni to feel important to other people and be unique in their eyes although she wasn't sure where this insecurity stemmed from.

'So, did you have a nice break?'

Dr. Yates chuckled and waved her pen at Danni.

'I'm meant to be the one asking you questions but yes, it was very relaxing dear. I stayed with my sister on the coast and did nothing but read and take walks on the beach. It was a much needed getaway.'

'That's nice. Not a lot going on since you've been away…'

She felt her face droop and it was instantly noted by her counsellor.

'What's wrong dear? Did something happen since our last session?'

Danni was horrified to feel herself burst into tears and sob uncontrollably in her chair. She buried her face into her hands so that Dr. Yates couldn't see how messed up she looked.

The doctor immediately jumped up and handed Danni the tissues. She reached out a hand to accept a tissue while the other hand clasped her nose and eyes.

'Just let it out lovey, and we can discuss when you're ready.'

Calming down after a few minutes, Danni wiped her red eyes and nose. She put her massive wad of tissues in the bin next to her and was touched to see the depth of concern on Dr. Yates's face. Maybe she did have a soft spot for her.

She managed to gurgle out her fear.

'I'm…so worried you're going to be disappointed in me…'

Dr. Yates smiled and handed Danni a glass of water that she must've poured whilst she had been hysterically crying. She accepted gratefully and gulped it down.

'Love, first of all it isn't part of my job to get disappointed or even give a patient advice although I can't help myself sometimes.'

They both grinned at her admission.

'Secondly, I couldn't be disappointed in you even if I tried. I never felt that way about Hunter and he called me some choice names in some of our sessions. What would a lovely girl like you do to inspire that?'

'I kissed Slade!' Danni blurted out.

Dr. Yates didn't seem surprised by Danni's outburst but gestured for her to continue.

'I kissed him…even when I said I wouldn't and I knew it would hurt Reilly. I've absolutely betrayed my best friend and even though she doesn't know about it, it's killing me and I know it's going to come out sooner or later. Not only that, after it happened I felt so guilty that Slade and I have promised to just stay friends, so it wasn't worth it anyway! I didn't even get love out of it! And tonight, one of my members is dropping out because he is gay and feels the other male members in the group are uncomfortable around him. Once he leaves, why should anyone else stay? The greatest months of my life are about to be over and I just can't stand it. Why give me something so amazing and then take it away from me? It's cruel!'

Dr. Yates said nothing but took Danni's glass and refilled it. Once again, the thirsty girl gulped it down quite quickly. She smiled and set the glass down.

'Sorry for the rant…'

'I'm going to stress what I said before Danni. I'm not disappointed in you at all. In fact I'm proud of you.'

Danni raised her eyebrows in confusion.

'Proud? How could you be after I just admitted to hurting Reilly?'

'Because the way you cried today shows you are a person with a big heart. You feel such strong remorse for what you did and not a lot of people do, believe it or not. I know you don't see it now, but one day all of this won't matter. The issues formed as a teenager are seldom remembered as an adult. This is one of those things you and Reilly could laugh about one day. I think, if you did this with Reilly's husband once you were adults…well that's more cause to feel disappointment in yourself…but what happened in the last two weeks is okay and will be okay with enough time.'

Danni nodded but felt unconvinced.

'I know it will play on your mind,' Dr. Yates said.

It was as though she had read Danni's thoughts.

'As for the group tonight, you are making the assumption that with one person leaving, all the rest will disband. That isn't true. I've never seen Hunter happier or more settled since he's been a part of your team. Ambrite has flourished immensely. That was because of you Danni. These friendships are for life and you know it. Please just wait and see. He might even change his mind.'

She wanted to believe that with all of her heart but the true test would be what happened once Graham walked out of Bouquet Reserve for the last time. In her positive fantasy, the group remained stronger than ever and helped Danni locate the new Scorpio. In another, they formed a circle around Graham and wouldn't let him leave until he felt truly accepted. And of course, there was always the ridiculous fantasy of him turning around and saying it was a practical joke that they were all in on at Danni's expense. It was well known that whenever you planned something in your head, it almost always turned out completely different, so Danni wasn't banking on any of those fantasies becoming realities. Most likely, they wouldn't make a fuss, he would leave and in the coming weeks more and more would drop out until it was her, Drew, Reilly, Hannah and Parry left. Not exactly the Astro A Team she had started out with!

Noticing their time was up, Dr. Yates closed her notebook and set it on the table with her pen.

'Before you leave, just remember what I said. If Reilly does ever find out or you wish to tell her yourself, I'm sure that the friendship you have built since infants is strong enough to withstand anything. And the same goes for the friends you've made this year. If they truly love you and are loyal, they won't leave. If they do, it was never meant to be and you will make better friendships in the future.'

Danni knew it wasn't proper counsellor/patient protocol but she reached out and hugged Dr. Yates around her middle. The old woman hesitated for a second, rubbed her back and gently led her to the door. The first part of Judgement Day had passed quite smoothly. The second and most intense part was about to begin.

***

The Astro A Team would be arriving in twenty minutes. Danni had purposely arrived earlier so that she could be alone and collect her thoughts. Trailing her fingers in the cool water of the pond, she wondered whether this would be the last time she sat there and conducted a meeting. Leaning over, she peered into the ripples and saw a beautiful yet scared face staring back at her. As usual, the pond was illuminated and shining green. This sacred body of water that had haunted her dreams shone so bright. It was almost trying to comfort her, its reeds and damp blades of grass swaying in the evening breeze. She usually dressed up for her meetings and put extra effort into her hair, makeup and clothes but tonight she was decked out in a comfortable pair of jeans and black hoodie. There were no more boys to impress; there were no events like the Astrological Dance to look forward to and certainly no more Graham to ooh and ahh over every little outfit Parry picked out for Danni before a meeting. Stretching out on the cold ground, Danni stared up at the stars and felt comforted. Her destiny was already written and so if her group disbanded after that night, it was meant to happen. It didn't mean she had to give up pondering the universe and the zodiac.

Hearing the familiar creak of the entrance gate, Danni turned around and felt her nerves race as she saw Crawford coming up the path. Standing up quickly and brushing the grass of her jeans, she walked over to him.

'You're here early,' Danni pushed her hands into her denim pockets.

Crawford looked perfect as usual in a pair of beige chinos and black shirt. His chocolate curls lopped to the side and his eyes gleamed in the night.

'I wanted to make sure it was clean enough before we began.'

Maybe it was the fact that tonight could be their last meeting or that time had healed her wounds, but Danni saw herself reach out and clasp his hand. He looked down at it and smiled, squeezing her palm. It felt just like that first dream she had had of him all those months before.

'I forgive you,' Danni whispered.

She couldn't tell in the dark but his eyes seemed shinier than usual. He gripped her hand one last time and dropped it.

'Thank you, I'm so glad you're okay with me now.'

She nodded and sat down next to the pond again. He followed suit and she found that even with him sitting so close, she no longer had feelings for him and it was the biggest relief.

Crawford cleared his throat nervously and Danni raised her eyebrows in question.

'I think…Charlotte is actually in love with me…'

That name made her blood boil but Charlotte was really the least of her problems at the moment.

'What makes you say that?'

'She is still visiting me when I'm working here and asking me all about my life. She seems genuinely interested in what I have to say. Sometimes we don't say anything and she picks up excess litter while I rake.'

Danni couldn't imagine how helping Crawford clean Bouquet Reserve could possibly hurt or harm her group. Maybe she did love him. She could have him. Danni didn't want Crawford anymore. She didn't want anyone anymore.

'Do you love her?'

Crawford began pulling out grass and tossing the blades in the pond.

'I wouldn't say love, but I find I'm really enjoying her company and might ask her on a date soon…if that's okay with you?'

Danni sighed heavily.

'Crawford, it's your life, do what you want with it. You know I don't like her but I want you to be happy and as long as she doesn't have any ulterior motives then I don't see any harm.'

Crawford nodded and was about to say something when they noticed the rest of the Astro A Team slowly trickle in. Danni's heart began to thump and her palms were sticky with sweat. The moment had finally arrived.

Reilly, Drew and Hannah, all had their arms linked like a scene in *The Wizard of Oz* and Danni couldn't help but laugh as they skipped down the path. At least she would always have them.

Humbrite strolled in laughing and playing air guitar. They didn't appear fazed by the weekly task, so she assumed it had gone swimmingly. Brodie and Slade were in a deep conversation and stood out as only they could. Danni couldn't make eye contact with him. She was too scared it would give the game away. She turned and saw Ronan wander in and wave at her with a cheesy grin on his face. She waved back and couldn't believe how much she cared about him. He was another person she couldn't bear to lose now despite the fact that just a few months before he couldn't stand anyone or anything. She was pretty sure they had completely owned the weekly task. The last to enter was Parry and Graham who were easily the most sullen and obviously nervous. For some reason they were wearing matching outfits, like some sort of act of solidarity. Graham was dressed in a burgundy pinstripe suit and Parry in a dress of the same shade. Danni didn't understand why they were so dolled up if they were just going to leave before the meeting ended. They walked over to her and embraced in a three way hug.

'You guys look amazing…what's the occasion?'

'After I make my announcement I don't want to dwell on the sadness, so I'm taking this little fox dancing.'

Graham kissed Parry's hand and she twirled in her burgundy shift dress.

'Isn't it amazing? Would you believe I found it at a thrift shop?'

'You look beautiful as usual Par…so you're still doing this,' Danni stated without asking the question.

Graham nodded and led Parry to the pond. She had hoped one of her fantasies would've kicked in about now but the reality was that the Scorpio had made up his mind and nothing could alter it.

Danni called everyone's attention to the pond. She knew it was time to rip off the metaphorical bandage. She wanted to hold onto the image of all of them sitting around her forever. It was so perfect in and out of her dreams. It was where they belonged.

'Okay, thank you as always for coming and being present under the stars. You are the closest people in my life and I hope that…no matter what happens, you will always be in my life.'

She was happy to see them all nod with loving smiles. Graham in particular blew her a kiss. Reilly and Drew faked boredom and then cracked up and drew hearts with their fingers to indicate they were joking. She laughed at their idiocy.

'Love you too guys! Let's discuss the weekly task. How did we all go? Let's start with Reilly and Ambrite?'

The Sagittarian and Taurean looked at one another with mutual respect. It was a look she never thought those two would exchange. They stood up and huddled together. Ambrite patted Reilly on the back, encouraging her to deliver the verdict.

'Well, we spent a lot of time together this week. Mainly I hung out at The Funky Fries and pigged out while Ambrite worked but it was still quality time! We went to see movies and made the effort to discuss it afterwards. Even though our opinions were the complete opposite, we tried to see each other's point of view.'

Reilly looked at the nodding Goth girl and smiled warmly.

'I like her; she's a real individual who isn't afraid to speak her mind. I envy how comfortable she is in her own skin and how passionate she is about animals and the environment.'

Hunter looked at Ambrite adoringly. She could tell that if Ambrite didn't prefer girls, he would love to have been her boyfriend. He basically was without the physical. There was something different about him but she couldn't put her finger on it.

'I love how big Reilly's heart is. She is so loyal to her friends and would never betray any of them. She really listens when I speak and attempted my tofu scramble.'

'It was disgusting by the way,' Reilly laughed.

'But the important thing was you tried it!' Ambrite chuckled.

Danni was so touched that Ambrite saw her best friend the way she did but at the same time the guilt was pouring off her when Reilly's loyalty to her friends had been mentioned. The reality was that Reilly would never do that to Danni and it was killing her that she had the capacity to do so. For the first time that evening Slade and

Danni met eyes and looked away quickly. They were both feeling it.

'I'm so glad that the two people I thought would end up killing each other have managed to become so close. What did you learn about each other? Just give me one thing…something personal.'

Reilly put her hand on Ambrite's shoulder and Danni wondered whether the Taurean had shared her biggest secret.

'When Ambrite first learnt what the Holocaust was in Year 8, she cried for an hour straight. That really touched me.'

The whole group appeared to feel the same and Danni thought that was the perfect example of something personal and valuable.

'Well, when Reilly was five…'

Danni and Drew immediately looked at one another and grinned.

'She chased her Uncle's chicken around his farm and tried to bite into it because she was hungry and didn't realise the chicken had to be dead and cooked before you can eat it.'

The whole group burst into laughter including her two best friends who knew that story all too well. It was classic Reilly to chase her food. Reilly curtseyed and giggled with good nature.

Ronan and Danni stood up next and announced to the group how they cooked dinner for his father in order to bring the family closer together.

'It was such a great success thanks to Danni and I can tell my dad is slowly opening up more and spending less time in his garage. Even my little brother hung around the dinner table for a bit longer last night.'

Danni's heart swelled. She was so happy for the Tates and loved that she had been a part of uniting them once more.

'I learned that Ronan has been hurt in the past by his mother. I won't get into details but it explains why he has trouble trusting females. Once you get to know him...he is actually one of the kindest and most considerate people I have ever met.'

They turned to look at one another and Danni could swear she saw more than friendship in his gaze. Her face felt hot. She couldn't fall for a Capricorn! They were the least suited astrologically. How could it possibly work?

'After spending some quality time with Danni, I realised that she really underestimates herself in a lot of areas. She has a lot of insecurities but all of them are extremely pointless because they only exist in her head. I hope one day she sees just how amazing she is.'

The group made immature 'oohing' noises and Danni noticed Slade looked less than impressed. Ronan and Danni both blushed but before they sat down she mouthed 'thank you' and put her hand to her heart. He nodded and gave her an encouraging thumbs up.

Hannah and Brodie confirmed that they went swimming as part of their weekly task which was surprisingly the Cancerian's idea. She admitted to Danni's delight that as a water sign, she felt most comfortable in her element. Hannah felt supported by the Libran and mentioned her patience and understanding when she confessed she suffered from a form of social anxiety. Brodie put her arm around Hannah who only came up to her neck and hugged her tight. While this display of affection made Danni happy, it also saddened her that now with everyone getting so close, a member was going to leave and create an irreplaceable hole. Brodie explained how non-judgemental Hannah was, especially when she informed the group that she shoplifted a pair of designer sunglasses when she lived in the States.

'She just listened and told me not to feel ashamed. Hannah made me realise that just because we do bad things sometimes it doesn't make us bad people. If we feel bad, then we are one step closer to growing as a person.'

If Dr. Yates was here right now, Danni knew she would point at Brodie and say 'see, that's exactly what I was telling you...'

Crawford and Drew had taken a similar path and played basketball while they bonded. The pair didn't appear to be best buddies but Danni could tell an understanding had formed between them.

'Crawford is a good dude,' Drew admitted.

He looked at Danni, unaware that she had already forgiven Crawford before the meeting had begun.

'He wants to be a fire-fighter when he's older and sometimes trains at Bouquet Reserve to keep fit.'

'I like that you want to fight fire Crawford,' Danni smiled. 'You're a fire sign and like Hannah, feel most comfortable in your element. It's the right decision for you.'

'Thanks Danni...I hope I'm worthy when it becomes time to take the tests. Well, the main thing I learned about Drew is that he is a mean basketball player and a surprisingly good rapper.'

The group laughed and Drew struck a pose.

'The stars in your eyes do not tell lies and my sweet rhymes keep you feeling sublime.'

Danni and Reilly rolled their eyes but Hannah looked ready to jump on her boyfriend and be arrested for public indecency.

'Hey, my modern day poetry is a personal thing. It was a big deal to share that with Crawford.'

Danni laughed and ushered for him to sit down.

'Parry and Hunter? What did you two get up to?'

In true Parry fashion, she squealed and ran next to him with excitement.

'I took Hunter to Maltin's and we trimmed his shaggy black head!'

The whole group suddenly took in Hunter's new look and Danni realised what was so different about him. He certainly looked cleaner and more handsome. She thought he would be grumpy with her grooming but he just shrugged with a grin.

'I like it and so does Ambrite which is all that matters...'

'It looks fab,' Graham agreed. 'More man and less wolf-man.'

Ambrite ruffled Hunter's clean cut and high-fived Parry.

'Fantastic. A makeover is a great way to bond. But what did you learn about one another?'

Parry looked at Danni with sadness.

'Hunter doesn't have a relationship with his father and goes to counselling. He is working on anger issues and trying to accept that the dysfunction in his family isn't his fault.'

Danni was pleased that Hunter had shared such intimate secrets with the Virgo. It was a testament to how far he had come as a person.

'On the subject of fathers,' Hunter began. 'Parry feels hers doesn't pay her enough attention and wishes they could spend more quality time together. She finds she spends money on clothes when she's upset and this is her way of dealing with the neglect.'

This didn't surprise Danni as Parry had mentioned this before. She couldn't believe how many members of her group had abandonment issues with their parents. Dr. Yates might as well do a big group counselling session at Bouquet Reserve.

Ambrite snuggled into Parry and Graham stroked her hair. She smiled and patted them on the back to signify everything was alright.

Danni looked at Graham and nodded gravely. He stood up and so did Slade with a slight hesitancy. Parry nearly stood up too but instead continued to groom Hunter in a motherly fashion.

'Before I talk about what I've learnt and how I went with this week's task...I want to make an announcement that Danni and Parry already know.'

The group immediately looked at the two girls with confusion. Drew and Reilly appeared annoyed as usual that Danni had left them out. Danni just shrugged sadly in their direction.

Graham pulled Danni and Parry to their feet and they stood on either side of him.

'Tonight is my last meeting. I am no longer going to be a part of the Astro A Team and I apologise to anyone who feels I am bailing on them, especially Danni.'

Danni expected the group to be surprised but not to this extreme. Hunter, Ambrite and Ronan stood up and started talking over the top of each other. Drew and Reilly rushed over to Graham begging for answers and Hannah, Slade and Brodie just stared open-mouthed.

'Please everyone sit down!' Danni urged. 'Let Graham explain for himself.'

Reluctantly, the group found their way back to the grass and waited, but not so patiently, for his explanation.

Slade remained standing and walked over to the Scorpio.

'Is it something I said or did? I am so sorry…'

Graham appeared touched by Slade's concern.

'No, it's just…well, let me explain.'

Slade walked back over to his spot.

'It's no secret that I'm gay and I act a lot older than I am. It's not that I feel you're all too immature for me or anything but I can just tell that some of you are uncomfortable. In this fragile state of my life, I need to feel supported and that I belong. I think it's best for everyone if I find a gay community that can help me grow into who I am more. Please understand.'

The group began talking all at once again and Danni couldn't make out one word they were saying. Parry, Hannah and Ambrite were crying. Hunter appeared furious at no one and Ronan was pulling so much grass out that they would soon be sitting on dirt.

'Quiet!' Slade yelled.

It was instant silence as the usually cool, calm and collected Aquarian strode back over to Graham's side.

'I spent a week with Graham and yes I participated in things that weren't super manly but I still enjoyed his company and getting to know him. After my sea-salt scrub, facial and pedicure I realised just how genuine he was and how much I liked that he was so different to me...it was refreshing.'

Graham nodded seriously. 'He had pores you could see from space...'

'And I thank you for healing them,' Slade admitted. 'I learnt that Graham or anybody should never feel the need to apologise for who they are. That's the beauty of this group. We are all special and unique.'

He turned to Graham with determination and Danni felt a tear run down her cheek.

'Graham...if you leave then that part you play will no longer be there. We don't want a straight, boring Scorpio. We want you and everything that makes up who you are. I'm sorry I came across as uncomfortable this week; I was a little out of my comfort zone but that didn't mean I was disgusted by you or unhappy to be paired with you. If you're feeling that we are put off by your presence, that's your own insecurities but don't put that on us. We love you and wouldn't have you any other way...'

Danni was surprised to hear her group break into applause and Graham reached out to embrace Slade. The boys hugged and when they broke apart, Danni knew they hadn't lost him.

'Okay…I'll stay.'

Tears streamed down Graham's face. It was a significant moment in his life. Slade had helped him realise that he was subconsciously pushing people away because he was afraid of their judgement. The group jumped up and began hugging one another. Danni danced around the pond with her arms and legs flailing. It was the perfect moment and nothing could take it away from her.

'Awww what a lovely moment, if only I had a camera…'

Danni froze at the familiar, sickly sweet tone. Looking up, she saw Charlotte dressed once again in silver and walking towards the group in heels.

The celebration was over and Crawford ran over to her. Danni noticed Charlotte soften when she saw the Leo.

'What are you doing here?'

'Nothing to do on a Friday night…did you want to go see a movie once this crap is over?'

'It's not crap!' Reilly yelled. 'Get lost bimbo!'

Charlotte looked up at the Sagittarian and giggled.

'Oh I don't think you will be so defensive of your group when you watch this little clip.'

With that she pulled out her mobile phone and pressed the screen up to Reilly's face.

Danni couldn't hear or see what was happening but Reilly's expression spoke volumes.

'What?' Reilly gasped.

She looked up at her best friend and Danni knew in that moment exactly what was playing on the phone.

She marched over and grabbed it off the smirking Charlotte. The video was playing what she had feared. Somehow her evil Gemini twin had managed to film through Danni's curtains – she and Slade tangled together on her couch, kissing.

The rest of the group appeared confused. They crowded over the phone and Danni wanted to die with humiliation. Slade was the first to speak.

'Reilly, please don't blame Danni for this. It's not her fault. I kissed *her* okay?'

Danni couldn't bear to see the hurt, anger and disappointment in her best friend's eyes and handed the phone back to Charlotte in defeat.

Reilly immediately snatched it back out of Charlotte's hands and threw it on the ground. With a scream of pure pain, she stamped it to pieces and threw the remains into the pond.

'Hey! That's my phone you little bitch, you better buy me a new one!'

The fiery archer spun around and slapped Charlotte so hard in the face that she fell back into Crawford.

'I hope you're happy now! You've ruined everything! Do you know how much happier I would've been if I didn't know that?'

Charlotte began whimpering into Crawford's arms.

The Astro A Team had forgotten all about Graham staying and were now just staring from Reilly to Danni, wondering what would happen next.

Danni walked over to her best friend.

'Reilly…I am so sor…'

'Save it!' Reilly cut her off. 'You knew I liked him, you knew and you did this behind my back! I'm not even that upset that you did it. I'm more hurt that you kept it from me. Just because you're the leader of this group doesn't mean that you rule everything. You can't have everything Danni. You can't have Crawford, Slade or Ronan. You can only have one, so make your choice!'

Danni was completely taken aback. She couldn't believe how much hate Reilly felt for her right now.

'I don't want any of them! I want my best friend! I know it's no excuse but after Crawford I felt so vulnerable…'

'Are you seriously going to play that card?' Reilly snapped. 'If you feel vulnerable then have some Thai food with your friends, cry, and write a bloody country song but don't kiss the one guy that you knew I liked. I can't believe you betrayed me this way…I quit.'

Danni burst into sobs and Drew ran over to Reilly.

'Reilly, I know you're upset but we've all been best friends since day one. Please don't quit. Danni's sorry, aren't you?'

'Yes…I'm so sorry Reilly…please forgive me.'

'Sorry doesn't take back what she did Drew! If you're really loyal to me then you'll quit too and so will you Hannah.'

Hannah looked ready to pass out from emotion and Drew went back to his girlfriend to steady her.

Danni couldn't believe this was happening. How could they go from a team united to complete destruction? She noticed Ambrite pick up her bag.

'Where are you going?'

Ambrite shook her head in disgust and Hunter looked furious.

'How could you do that Dan? You talk about loyalty to the group all the time and this is how you show it to your best friend? There wouldn't be the Astro A Team without Reilly. I'm quitting too and so is Hunter.'

'No…please…it was a stupid mistake but I swear it will never happen again.'

Danni's head was throbbing. This night couldn't possibly get any worse.

'NOBODY'S GOING ANYWHERE!'

Everybody stopped dead in their tracks as a dark figure strode up the path. He was cloaked in black leather and furious beyond belief.

'Who the hell are you?' Ronan asked the obvious.

Garth positioned himself in the middle of the teenagers but not before wiping a tear from Danni's miserable face.

'Tell them who I am Danni…' he whispered.

Shaking, she walked over to Garth and rested her hand on his shoulder.

'This is Garth,' she muttered. 'I don't know much else about him except that he knows about our group and wants us to lead it for some reason.'

She realised how ridiculous that sounded but didn't care anymore. What did she have to lose? She had already lost everything else; why not add her sanity to the mix?

Reilly walked over to him, purposely ignoring Danni.

'It's you…I know I've seen your shadow before.'

Garth nodded and tipped his hat.

'As Danni poorly introduced…I am Garth. I am the Chief Advisor to Asterion…keeper of the stars.'

Danni let out a yell of frustration.

'Poorly introduced? You never mentioned being a Chief Advisor or Asterion…whoever the hell he is!'

Garth appeared amused at her outburst. He wasn't exactly the most sensitive guy on the planet.

'Danni…you've known for a long time that this thing you've formed has a much deeper meaning than just some after school hormonal group. All twelve of you were handpicked by Asterion himself to serve a greater purpose.'

'I repeat…who the hell are you?' Ronan demanded.

'Go on…' Danni urged.

This may have been the worst night of her life but she was about to get some much needed answers.

'In an alternate universe, one unbeknownst to mere mortals, lies the keeper of the stars, Asterion. He's a dapper old gentleman, looks great for his age if I do say so myself.'

Garth sat down next to the pond and motioned for everyone to sit around him. Despite the intense feud, they all, including Charlotte, followed his orders. He pushed his fingers into the pond and smiled as it began to glow so brightly that the others shielded their eyes.

'This can't be real,' Parry whispered.

'I've worked here my whole life and the pond has never done that before,' Crawford gasped.

Garth chuckled and looked at Danni.

'Do you remember a dream you had when I was pointing at the pond and then pointing to the sky? That one gave me such a headache.'

'Me too…and yes I do…what did it mean?' Danni inched closer to Garth, almost afraid she would miss the answer.

'This pond is a portal to the alternate universe I mentioned. It will take you to a place called Bastion where Asterion and I reside. I need you and your group to come with me to Bastion and save the universe from the stars themselves.'

Ambrite snorted. 'Assuming I believe in alternate universes…which I don't…what is wrong with the stars?'

'Ahhh a true Taurean…I cannot wait for you to face your counterpart.' Garth rubbed his hands together with glee.

'What counterpart? Start making some sense!' Hunter demanded.

'Such a fiery Ram…yes, you will do nicely.'

'Should we drown him in his own portal?' Slade looked to the males of the group.

'Okay, okay!' Garth stood up and pulled Danni to her feet.

'Danni, I know I should've given you more of an explanation when I first came to visit you here but I needed to make sure you were committed and driven enough to face what you're about to do.'

'Garth, most of my group hate me. If you wanted a united team then you've lost…'

She began to walk away when she felt a hand grip her shoulder. Parry stared at her with wide eyes.

'I'm not going anywhere, I told you that Danni. Graham isn't going anywhere and I know the rest of the team will stick by you as they should.'

She turned to the rest of the group.

'Whatever Danni did, she is sorry and we are all strong enough to get through it. I have no idea who this Garth is although I must say I love the Matrix look.'

'Thank you my dear,' Garth bowed.

'And even though he could be some crazy hobo who lives in this park and just wants drugs…'

'Hey!' Garth retracted his bow.

'He is telling us that it's our destiny to unite and save the stars. So let's put our differences aside, band together and do it!'

Danni hugged Parry tightly and wandered back over to Garth.

'Okay…what's our mission? I want to save the stars. I know this is my destiny. I've known it for a long time and my two best friends have known it too.'

She looked over at them with love in her heart. Drew smiled and Reilly nodded grimly. It was good enough for her.

'I'll let Asterion explain more when we arrive. There isn't much time and we need to go right now.'

Garth stood up and turned to jump in the pond.

'Wait!' Hannah screamed.

They all jumped in surprise. Since when did Hannah yell anything?

'We're leaving now? What about our families? Don't we need clothes wherever we're going?'

Garth sighed. Danni thought he had pretty high expectations of a group that had just learned about him. She was surprised they weren't more amazed by what was happening.

'Everything you need will be provided for you and time moves differently in this universe. One second here is days over there. Nobody will even know you're gone.'

'What about me?' Charlotte muttered.

Her cheek had a big red imprint where Reilly had slapped her and her face was stained with mascara.

'You my dear are just as important and must come too.'

'What? Why?' Danni demanded.

Garth extended his hand to Charlotte and she reluctantly allowed him to lead her to Danni.

'Danni,' Garth softened. 'She is your twin sister…every Gemini has a twin, you know that.'

'Twin?' Charlotte scoffed. 'I look nothing like that dirty rat.'

'You are bound by the stars! In our universe, you are twins and will need each other to face off against your Gemini counterpart.'

'This is all so surreal,' Ronan muttered.

'It sure is Capricorn,' Garth agreed.

He turned around once more to jump into the pond that was blindingly green at this point. The water had started to bubble and churn. Danni was terrified.

'Are you ready to go? I promise all will be explained when we arrive.'

The group looked at one another for reassurance and then they stood up and grabbed each other's hands.

Parry was on Danni's left and Ronan on her right. She knew these two loved her and wouldn't abandon her in this new world.

Looking across at Reilly, she saw that she was holding onto Ambrite and Drew pretty tightly. They met eyes and in that moment no words needed to be said. It was a long road ahead of them and they knew it but Danni wasn't going to give up on her best friend. She would never stop trying to get her back.

'Are you ready?' Garth called.

The pond was now close to boiling point and it was time to take the leap of faith.

'Yes!' the Astro A Team chorused.

Garth met Danni's eyes. He winked at her petrified face.

'The stars are calling you my love…'

And then they jumped.

ABOUT THE AUTHOR

Rebecca Rossi is a 24 year old first-time author from Melbourne, Victoria who works in Executive Education.

She is passionate about reading, writing and all things Astrology.

During her teenage years, she was part of a writing group called The Inkspotters where she met devoted mentor and friend Eve Martyn, author of *Killer McKenzie* and writer of numerous plays for local theatre companies. Her and Eve worked together to bring Astrology Pond to life and in 2011 when Eve passed away, Rebecca made it her ultimate goal to finish the story and dedicate it to the woman who believed in the concept from the very beginning.

In 2007, she graduated from Sunbury College with Honours in History and Drama. In 2012, she graduated after four years of study with a Bachelor of Arts, Major in History, Minor in Philosophy and a Graduate Diploma in Museum Studies. She has volunteered at the Chinese Museum in the Melbourne CBD and the Wool Museum in Geelong to gain experience and work with the collections. Rebecca loves reflecting on the past, momentous events in time and pondering the universe. Her spiritual side has developed through a love of meditation, tarot reading, astrology and a passion for the environment.

Her inspiration comes from her favourite authors Anne Rice and Cate Tiernan who are both originally from New Orleans; a destination Rebecca is dying to travel to in the near future. Her genre of choice is classic literature and fantasy fiction for teenagers which she believes allows readers to utilise their wild imaginations and discover worlds beyond the norm. Her favourite book is *Blackwood Farm* from Anne Rice's famous *Vampire Chronicles*. Her favourite series is *Sweep* by Cate Tiernan who is famous for her novels on teenage witches. She is a self-confessed lover of Robert Frost's poetry and Shakespeare's plays. In her younger years, two of her poems 'A Trip Around The World' and 'Falling Through' were published in poetry competitions.

In her spare time she enjoys reading, writing, quality time with her partner Francis, going for walks and listening to many types of music. An active vegan, Rebecca tries to do her part for the environment and inspire others to refrain from participating in animal exploitation. She has a wide collection of headbands and depicts her style as 'bohemian' stemming from her love of her favourite movie *Moulin Rouge.*

She is, what she would call, a typical Gemini who enjoys social interaction, communicating about anything and everything and flitting from one craze to the next. Her love of Astrology developed after a lot of star-gazing and reading up on the subject. Today, she uses the zodiac to understand how others operate and interact.

With an incredibly close relationship to her mother, a breast-cancer survivor of 9+ years, Rebecca admits her love of reading and writing stemmed from her equally creative parent who taught her to be curious, open and a seeker of knowledge.

Rebecca is planning to write a sequel to Astrology Pond and will continue to develop the characters she has fallen in love with over the last seven years.

BOOK 2

'FACING THE STARS'

COMING SOON!